Sutcliffe Cove

Ariel Tachna
Madeleine Urban

Dreamspinner Press

Published by
Dreamspinner Press
4760 Preston Road
Suite 244-149
Frisco, TX 75034
http://www.dreamspinnerpress.com/

This is a work of fiction. Names, characters, places and incidents either are the product of the author's imagination or are used fictitiously, and any resemblance to actual persons, living or dead, business establishments, events or locales is entirely coincidental.

Sutcliffe Cove
Copyright © 2009 by Ariel Tachna and Madeleine Urban

Cover Art by Dan Skinner/Cerberus Inc. cerberusinc@hotmail.com
Cover Design by Mara McKennen

All rights reserved. No part of this book may be reproduced or transmitted in any form or by any means, electronic or mechanical, including photocopying, recording, or by any information storage and retrieval system without the written permission of the Publisher, except where permitted by law. To request permission and all other inquiries, contact Dreamspinner Press, 4760 Preston Road, Suite 244-149, Frisco, TX 75034
http://www.dreamspinnerpress.com/

ISBN: 978-1-935192-82-4

Printed in the United States of America
First Edition
March, 2009

eBook edition available
eBook ISBN: 978-1-935192-98-5

One

THE paved road led from the minor highway back into the trees, leaving the city behind. It was a pocket of quiet surrounded by bustling civilization, somehow untouched yet maintained. The road wound through the trees, eventually leading into the wide green spaces of the horse farm named Sutcliffe Cove.

Gerald Saunders steered his car down the lane, enjoying the difference in scenery, surprised at how nice it was here. He'd have never thought a place could remain so unspoiled here in the heart of Connecticut.

A black-painted split wood fence lined the road up to the cluster of buildings: a couple of barns, a long line of stables, a big old farmhouse, and some smaller outbuildings. He could see the road led beyond the parking area back behind the stables and figured that must be for horse trailers. He pulled up beside a sedan and parked.

Brett Sutcliffe looked up at the sound of a car pulling into the gravel parking lot. His father had resisted paving it, saying asphalt was harder to maintain, and Brett kept it gravel because he liked the warning he was about to have visitors. He leaned on the pitchfork he was using to muck out stalls and watched the long, lanky form climb out of the car. The automatic appreciation of a well-built body brought a smile to his face. The man moved with the same controlled grace as the thoroughbreds Brett loved to watch but would never have the money to own. And there was never any harm in looking. As the man drew closer, he took automatic note of the dark hair and eyes and the surprisingly light complexion. The man must spend most of his time indoors.

"Welcome to Sutcliffe Cove," he called, drawing the man's attention to him. "Can I help you?"

Gerald turned when he heard the voice and raised a hand halfway in greeting. "I found your Web site when looking for riding lessons," he said. "Am I in the right place?"

"You are indeed," Brett agreed, mentally sizing up a new client. "Have you ever ridden before?"

"Once, and I wouldn't call it riding. On a trail up at the state park," Gerald said reluctantly, looking a bit abashed. "But I loved it and thought I might try some lessons."

"I'm glad it piqued your interest," Brett replied easily. "Although trail riding in the state parks isn't quite the same as riding on your own. Those horses could do the trail rides on their own, they've done it so many times. Were you thinking group lessons or private lessons? We offer both at various times and with a variety of instructors."

Gerald shrugged one shoulder, a gesture Brett found quite endearing. "Don't know enough to have an opinion, really. What would you suggest?" Gerald studied the other man as he spoke, noting how laid-back and friendly he was. He seemed really comfortable in his own skin. His cowboy hat hid most of his hair, but the reddish scruff on the other man's face made Gerald envious of the freedom not to have to shave every day.

"It's a question of how fast you want to learn and how much you're willing to pay," Brett replied honestly. "You'll make progress much more quickly in private lessons because they'll be tailored specifically to your ability instead of to the level of the entire class, but they're also more expensive." He glanced over the obviously fit body. "You'll also get a better workout in a private lesson because you'll be actively riding the whole time instead of spending part of your time waiting for the other people in the class to do each exercise."

"Sounds like the way to go then. At least until I decide whether I want to stick with it," Gerald said agreeably. Money wasn't a problem; he was comfortable enough to indulge in something like this, and he didn't have any other plans for the time being.

Always the entrepreneur, Brett started calculating income while he looked forward to the opportunity to ogle the brunet under the guise of helping him improve his form. "So when would you like to start?"

"I don't have any other commitments besides work right now. I finish up about four most days," Gerald said, thinking about how long it would take him to get here after leaving the office. "I could be here five-ish during the week and any time on weekends."

"Then the next question is how often you want to ride," Brett said, mentally examining his schedule. "I have openings on Tuesdays and Thursdays at six, and several different times on Saturdays and Sundays. Just a warning, though. It's a lot harder workout than it looks, so you may want to start slow and build up. Beginner riders often find once a week is all their legs can handle for the first few months."

"I don't want to ruin it right off," Gerald admitted. "I'm in pretty good shape. How about Tuesdays and Thursdays?"

"Sounds good to me. We generally ask for the month's payment up front, but we'll give you the first lesson free so you can decide if it's really what you want to do before you commit to the full month."

"Thanks. That's really great," Gerald said, smiling. "I'm Gerald Saunders."

"Brett Sutcliffe," Brett replied, pulling off his glove and extending his hand. "It's Tuesday. Do you want to start tonight or wait until Thursday?"

"Now's good," Gerald said, peering at the man who must be the farm's owner. He looked to be about the same age as himself and tanned from working outside so much. "I'm here." He shook Brett's hand with a firm grip. "You look busy, though. I can go walk around awhile."

"Mucking stalls is a never-ending process," Brett admitted. "I've got some kids who volunteer on the weekends in exchange for free lessons, but during the week, I'm not as lucky." He stood the pitchfork against the manure cart. "Shah's out in the pasture. He won't care how long it takes me to finish up. He'd rather be out there than cooped up in his stall anyway. Let me give you the fifty-cent tour."

"Sure. Is Shah one of the horses for lessons?" Gerald asked as he followed Brett along the outside of the building.

"No, he's my pride and joy," Brett replied. "He's a purebred Arabian, the only stallion in the barn. I got him when he was a foal and helped train him myself. There he is, along the back fence. The one with his tail high. He's a proud old man."

Gerald looked where Brett indicated to see the obviously spirited stallion. Even with his untrained eyes, the horse was gorgeous. "I bet he's popular with the ladies," he joked.

"Very," Brett agreed. "He's sired about a dozen foals since we started breeding him. We have about fifty horses here on the property. Most of them are privately owned, but about twenty of them belong to the stable, and those are the ones we use for lessons unless the owners are taking lessons. Then they ride their own animals, of course. The farm's about a hundred acres. A chunk of it's pastureland for the horses when they aren't being used, plus the buildings you see here. The rest is forest."

"Quite a setup," Gerald commented, turning in a slow circle to look around. "And since you're pretty much inside the city, it's convenient. Although to look around, I would think we were miles and miles out of town."

"When my great-great-great-grandparents bought the land, it *was* miles out of town," Brett replied with a laugh. "It was great in high school when I still thought I wanted to pick up girls. They'd come out to see the horses, and it wasn't so far away that their parents would have a problem with it."

Gerald chuckled and grinned. "Possibility of rolling in the hay, huh?" He looked Brett up and down, and his lips twitched into a smile. He could see the appeal, though it didn't register any more than that thought. "Girls go for the rugged cowboy look."

"I don't pay much attention to what they go for these days." Brett chuckled. "I don't have time for their drama anymore. I did get a few good tumbles out of it, though."

"Women aren't the only ones who do the drama," Gerald murmured, looking back out into the pasture. "But I steer clear anyway. My work gives me enough of that as it is."

Brett laughed, glad once again to have escaped the drudgery of office life. "No, the horses are pretty damn good at it too. Come on; let me introduce you to Tiny. He'll be a good start for you, I think."

"Tiny, huh? That sounds reassuring." Gerald said, shoving a hand into a jeans pocket. "Maybe," he tacked on.

Brett snickered and led the other man to a stall at the end of the stable block. A black head poked out through the door at their approach, whickering softly. Brett stroked the velvet nose, batting it away when the horse lipped at his shirt pocket in search of a treat. "After lessons, Tiny," he scolded affectionately. "You have to earn that carrot first."

He grabbed a halter and lead rope and stepped inside the stall to fasten them and walk the animal out into the breezeway. Tiny followed docilely, perfectly content to be tied to the hitching post. "Tiny, this is Gerald. Gerald, meet Tiny."

Gerald sighed and nodded, looking up at the huge animal. "How did I know?" he said drolly. The horse's back was above the level of his shoulders, and he was just over six foot tall. "You pick him on purpose, don't you?" he accused Brett. "If a beginner can get over the scary thought of riding him, then they're good to go?"

"No," Brett disagreed with a firm pat to Tiny's flank. "I pick him because he's the gentlest animal in the stable. He'd rather fall over himself than have a rider fall off. And on the rare occasion when he can't stop someone from falling, he's more upset than they are. I swear he cries when someone falls off. His eyes get all sad and his lower lip quivers just like a baby about to start bawling."

Amused, Gerald patted Tiny's shoulder, and the horse snuffled and nudged Gerald back with his head, drawing a laugh. "I think we'll get along fine, Tiny," he said.

Brett smiled and went to get the tack. Returning with a saddle, bridle, and pads, he quickly tacked Tiny. "If you decide to stick with it, I'll teach you how to do this for yourself, but for today, let's focus on the riding itself," he proposed.

"Okay," Gerald said amiably, stepping back out of the way to give Brett room to work. He played unconsciously with the zipper on his light jacket as he looked around the inside of the stables.

When Tiny was dressed, Brett unfastened the lead rope from his halter and handed Gerald the reins. "Walk on his left side with your right hand directly under his chin. That way you have control of his head, and you're out of the way of his feet. We'll take him down to the end and around to the inside ring. It's still a little cool to ride outside."

Following his direction, Gerald started walking, and Tiny went right with him. "Like this?" he asked, holding his right hand about where Brett had said.

"Yes, just like that," Brett replied from the other side of the horse's head. With a different horse, he wouldn't have walked on that side, but

Tiny was placid enough not to be bothered by much of anything, and he knew and trusted Brett anyway. As they passed the tack room, Brett snagged a helmet. "See if this fits."

Gerald took the helmet with one hand and tipped it onto his head. It flopped over loose on his close-cut hair. "A little big, I think," he said with a chuckle.

Brett smiled and grabbed a half-size smaller. "Try this one instead."

Switching the helmets got Gerald a better fit, and when he shook his head, it stayed in place. "That'll work," he said. "Should I fasten this?" Gerald asked, brushing his fingers along the leather chin straps.

"Yes, right under your chin. You don't want to choke on it, but you also don't want to lose the helmet while you're riding."

Gerald's tapered fingers clumsily juggled the reins as he fumbled with the straps, the metal fastening jingling.

"Here, let me help," Brett said, deftly fastening the strap through the rings. "There; all set."

"Thanks," Gerald said.

Brett led the way to the ring and told them to stop. "Put his reins over his head and then go ahead and mount," he directed.

Gerald was game enough to try. He got the reins in place without any trouble; Tiny even dipped his head to help. He eyed the horse with concern. "I might not make it up the first time," Gerald admitted. "Tiny's... not tiny."

"Lower the stirrup on your side," Brett suggested, "so you can get your foot in it. Then use the saddle to pull yourself up. I'll brace it from this side so it doesn't twist. You can grab Tiny's mane too. It won't hurt him."

"I'm not going to pull on his mane! That's mean!" Gerald exclaimed as he took up the stirrup and looked at it before fiddling with the straps to extend it.

"He can't feel it," Brett assured him. To demonstrate, he reached up and tugged hard on a handful of mane. Tiny didn't even turn his head. "And it's far more secure than the saddle."

Gerald was still unsure, and it showed on his face. "All right," he said, obviously reluctant, but he slid his fingers into the thick hair and stopped for a moment to pet before awkwardly putting his foot in the stirrup. "Why do I get the feeling this is going to be embarrassing?" he muttered to himself while reaching up to grasp the saddle horn with his right hand.

"You're going to hurt yourself," Brett joked. "Grab the cantle. The back of the saddle. And don't get used to having that horn. It'll go away in a few weeks when we switch you to an English saddle."

Obediently moving his hand, Gerald took a deep breath and then shifted his weight, bouncing a little a few times to swing his weight in the stirrup. After a second of struggling for balance he threw his long leg over and thumped into the saddle with a soft grunt of surprise.

"And you thought you wouldn't be able to get up there," Brett teased, automatically running his hand along Gerald's leg to adjust the stirrup to the proper fit. He walked around to the other side and shortened the one his student had lowered to mount. Reaching up, Brett adjusted the reins in Gerald's grasp. "There you go. You're all ready to ride."

"I'm surprised I didn't fall on my ass, actually," Gerald said with a self-conscious laugh. "But hey, buddy," he said, patting Tiny's neck. "Thanks for standing still."

The horse shook his head and whickered softly.

"He says you're welcome." Brett took a step back. "Move your hands forward just a little so there's a bit of slack in the reins and tap his sides lightly with your heels," he instructed. "And no, that won't hurt him either."

Gerald did so, and when Tiny obligingly lurched into a slow walk, a huge smile broke across his face.

Brett couldn't stop his answering smile. He loved that first moment when his students realized they were really riding a horse. He let Gerald enjoy it for a few minutes, Tiny walking obediently around the outside of the ring even without direction from Gerald. Eventually he interrupted their moment of communion. "Ready to learn how to tell him what you want him to do instead of just sitting there and letting him do all the work?"

Breaking out of his little space of happiness, Gerald nodded and looked to the man on the ground. "What do I do?"

"Ask him to halt," Brett said. "Lean back just a little in the saddle, pull back lightly on the reins, and say 'whoa'."

"Whoa," Gerald repeated as he leaned back and tightened his hold on the leather straps in his hands. Tiny came to a stop with a whuff.

Brett came up to Gerald's side and adjusted the angle of his leg, pulling his heel down. "If you don't feel the stretch in your Achilles' tendon, your heels aren't down far enough," he advised. "I know it feels awkward right now, but it'll keep your feet from ever getting caught in the stirrups if you happen to fall, and it gives you better balance once you get used to the position." He stepped back to give Gerald and Tiny room again. "Have him walk to the letter B and then stop."

Gerald watched as Brett moved his foot, his hands pressing along his jeans as he shifted Gerald's Asics in the stirrup. He glanced up at Brett's direction to look around the indoor ring. The letters were several inches tall and painted in black against the light gray barrier, easy enough to see. B was halfway around. He loosened his hold on the reins and kicked his heels back.

"Keep your heels directly in line with your hips," Brett directed as Tiny began moving. "If you pull them back too far, it tips you forward and messes up your balance."

Shifting slightly in the saddle as well as moving the stirrups, Gerald tried to find the middle ground Brett was prompting him toward. Tiny kept moving, apparently oblivious to the shuffling above him. When the horse started to edge toward a different letter, Gerald pulled slightly on the rein in the direction he wanted to go without thinking.

Brett smiled when Gerald corrected Tiny's bit of willfulness. As wonderful a horse as Tiny was, he occasionally decided to wander over to Brett in the middle of a lesson in hopes of finding a treat. Gerald had had no trouble adjusting, even without instruction. While his form was still mildly awkward, the stable owner suspected the other man would be a natural given a little time to practice. When Gerald drew Tiny to a halt at the designated spot, Brett smiled. "Good. And you steered him well. Ready for something a little more complicated?"

"I don't mind trying," Gerald said, turning his chin to give Brett a pleased smile. Although this was really simple stuff, he knew, it was really, really neat, and he loved it so far.

Returning Gerald's smile, Brett grabbed a stack of cones and set them in a row down the middle of the ring. "Guide him through the cones, weaving back and forth."

A look of concentration formed on Gerald's face as he told Tiny to walk again, this time pulling the reins right and left as the horse clomped around the cones with a few snorts. Gerald stopped him at the other end, that same grin appearing as he turned his chin to find Brett.

Gerald's enthusiasm was infectious. "Enjoying yourself?" Brett asked, echoing the other man's huge smile. "Want to try a trot?"

Nodding immediately, Gerald took the initiative to get Tiny to turn around so they were facing Brett. "Not being too ambitious, am I?"

Brett shook his head. "We're not done, by any means, even with the walk, but there's no reason not to let you see what the trot feels like. Put both reins in one hand, grab Tiny's mane with the other, and push up so you're out of the saddle. Don't worry about steering, just about keeping your balance. Remember, heels down, directly beneath you. Tiny's trot is relatively smooth, but it's definitely a different feeling from the walk. When you're ready to stop, just pull back on the reins and sit back."

Standing up in the stirrups proved easier than Gerald expected, especially since Brett had already positioned his feet correctly. By holding on to both Tiny's mane and the reins, he didn't feel like he was going to fall anywhere. And before he could think anymore about it, Tiny started moving and then bouncing. He actually bounced a laugh right out of Gerald.

Brett sat back and watched, letting Gerald's joy warm him. He worked with so many spoiled kids who didn't have the patience to learn or the experience to appreciate simple pleasures. To work with an adult who wanted to learn and embraced the entire experience was a real treat.

On the second round around the ring, Gerald was feeling much more comfortable, so he sat down as directed, and Tiny came to a slow stop. Turning the horse's head, Gerald looked around for Brett again. "That was great," he said happily.

"So have I hooked you?" Brett teased, pretty sure he already knew the answer to that question.

"I'm grinning like a fool," Gerald said with a laugh. "I think it's pretty clear I'm hooked." He leaned over and patted Tiny's neck again, and the horse nickered and huffed.

"Then we should go look at a schedule and get you on it for the next month," Brett replied. "Bring Tiny over here, and let's see if you can walk after all your exercise."

Gerald raised his eyebrows, looking worried already. "I hope you're teasing," he said, getting Tiny to ride over to Brett. "As much as I like riding so far, I'm rather fond of walking."

Brett chuckled. "Mostly," he agreed. "You haven't been riding all that long or hard today anyway, but there's very little else that uses your inner thigh muscles the way riding does, and so until those get built up, you'll be stiff and sore after you ride. I've been riding all my life, and I even feel it some days if I ride harder or longer than usual."

"Great. I didn't fall on my ass getting up here, but I will getting down," Gerald said, heaving a sigh. "Oh well." He halted Tiny next to Brett. "Off now?"

"Just do the opposite of what you did to get on. Grab his mane, swing your leg back over and slide down," Brett told him. "I've got Tiny's head, so you don't have to worry about him going anywhere on you."

Gerald took a steadying breath and made sure he was holding on tight before shifting his weight slowly to his left foot and sliding over and off the saddle. He landed unevenly on his right foot, bumping against Tiny before getting the other foot out of the stirrup, and then backed away slowly, hands out to each side of himself in case he lost his balance. "Okay," Gerald said cautiously.

"How do you feel?" Brett asked, coming to stand at his side, Tiny following along behind like an overgrown puppy.

"Fine, I guess," Gerald said, straightening up to stand casually. "I guess I'll see, huh?" Without realizing it, so caught up in the new experience, he offered that pure smile to Brett again. "Thank you. Really."

"You're welcome. Let me put Tiny away, and then we can go in the office and get you on the schedule," Brett said. "You can just wait in the office if you want, although you might find it easier to keep walking."

"I think I'll be smart and take your word for it. Mind if I wander around a little outside?" Gerald asked.

"Go ahead," Brett said. "Just don't open any gates. There are a few horses out, and I don't want Shah getting in with the mares. I'd rather choose when and with whom I breed him."

"Okay." Gerald watched as Brett turned and led Tiny out of the ring. With a soft harrumph Gerald realized he was watching the man more so than the horse. Something about the way Brett moved caught his eye, but he couldn't quite figure it out. But he liked it. Wrinkling his nose, Gerald turned and started walking.

Getting Tiny settled back into his stall, Brett returned the equipment to the tack room and walked outside to find Gerald after a few minutes. The man was walking slowly back and forth along the fence line, looking out over the fields. Coming to lean on the fence, Brett just watched, smiling at the familiar stiff gait of people who'd ridden for the first time. It would get worse before it would get better, as they worked seldom-used muscles, but eventually, if he kept with it, Gerald would lose that stiffness, moving between horseback and ground with relaxed ease. Brett hoped he'd get to see it. He had a feeling it would be a sight very pleasing to the eye, what with those long legs and lean body. He wondered what Gerald did to maintain that. Run, maybe? Swim? Horseback riding would fit well with either of those.

Gerald spent the time walking and watching the horses. He could feel the muscles in his legs tightening up, just like Brett had warned. He smiled ruefully. It didn't hurt as much as his first skiing lesson—at least not yet. After some musing, he turned back and saw Brett waiting. He studied him some more as he approached him, noting idly that he really was a good-looking man. Brett had mentioned being done with women. Maybe he was divorced.

"Doing okay?" Brett asked when Gerald reached his side. At Gerald's nod, he tilted his head toward the office. "Let's go inside and look at the schedule. You can tell me what days you want to come."

"Yeah, sounds good," Gerald said. "Lead the way."

Brett showed Gerald into the office, sat down behind the desk, and pulled out a large planner. He opened it up and skimmed down the month. "Tuesdays and Thursdays at six definitely work," he told Gerald. "Private lessons are forty dollars an hour. You might want to start with half-hour lessons though, until you get used to riding. Otherwise, twice a week could be painful, and I don't want you to get burned out or turned off it. So it would be forty a week, if you want to do it that way."

Gerald turned his wandering attention from the office back to the man in front of him. "Sounds good. You're the expert, you know. What do you take? Check, credit?" he asked.

"Either," Brett replied, amazed at the ease with which Gerald accepted the price. He didn't look like he was one of the snobbish society types, but some of the other people who came at least hesitated a bit.

"How about I pay a month down, and we'll go from there?" Gerald said as he pulled his wallet out of his back pocket.

"That's how most of my customers handle it," Brett agreed, filling the lessons into his appointment calendar. "It'll make it a hundred sixty for the next four weeks."

Gerald offered a standard Visa without comment. "So is what I'm wearing okay to start?" He was pretty sure he wanted to stick with it, but he'd learned over time not to jump quickly into committing to things.

"Yeah, jeans are fine," Brett replied, taking the card and processing it. "If you've got an old pair of shoes with a heel, they're better than gym shoes, but don't buy anything fancy or expensive. The only time you'd need them is if you were showing. Otherwise, just a beat-up old pair of hiking boots is your best bet."

Gerald nodded and shifted slightly back and forth on his feet. He was feeling it on the insides of his thighs, just like Brett said he would. It reminded him sort of how he felt after a marathon session with his legs wrapped around.... "Excuse me?" Gerald asked, clearing his throat, realizing Brett had said something.

"Hiking boots," Brett repeated, a little confused at the odd look on Gerald's face. "You know, those things you wear in the woods to protect your feet."

"Yeah. Sorry, got distracted for a sec. Hiking boots. I've got an old pair around somewhere, I think," Gerald said, nodding.

"Great. I'll see you Thursday a little before six then," Brett said. "If you come early, you can help me get Tiny ready without it cutting into your riding time."

"It'll depend on work, but I'd like that," Gerald answered, signing the sales slip and putting the card back into his wallet.

Brett showed Gerald back out and leaned against the corner of the stable as this Gerald Saunders got into his car and started to drive off. If Brett stayed there, staring into space long after the car disappeared, well, that was nobody's business but his own.

GERALD jogged out of the house Thursday afternoon, dragging the door shut behind him. He'd already decided that he liked having a reason to leave the office on time or even a little early. He admitted that he worked a lot more than most anyone else, but it was mostly because he had nothing else to do. When you worked half again as much as your peers, just by sheer numbers you tended to get ahead. Today, he'd closed up his computer and left a little past four, just because he could. It took about twenty minutes to drive to the farm, and he pulled in about twenty to six.

Gerald climbed out of the car and shut the door, looking around. There was a group of horses with riders out in the pasture, and there were more cars here than the other day. Not sure where to go, he headed for the stable where Tiny was.

Brett refused to let himself stand outside and wait or even check to see if a car was coming up the road to the farm. Gerald would get here when he got here. He had more than enough work to do without waiting like a teenager with a brand-new crush on a man who probably had no interest in other men. But Brett looked up automatically when he heard a car door shut, unable to stop the smile that crossed his face at seeing Gerald arrive. He ran a hand over his sweaty, stubbly face, glad he'd decided not to make a move in Gerald's direction to see if there might be some interest there. He'd be off to a lousy start if he had, looking like a mess! Throwing a last bale of hay onto the wagon, he closed the door to the storage room and called out a greeting to Gerald.

"Hey," Gerald answered with a wave. "It's busy today."

"Yeah, I've got a group of beginners out today, older elementary kids. Horse crazy. Lisa works with the kids during the week," Brett admitted, "since I far prefer working with adults."

"So who's going to be my teacher?" Gerald asked, looking over Brett's shoulder at another couple of guys working with the horses further into the stable.

"I figured I would," Brett replied, hoping the relative dimness of the stable and his tan would hide the flush he could feel heating his face, "unless you'd rather one of the other guys."

Gerald blinked, tipped his head to one side, and paid a bit more attention to the man in front of him. Lessons from the owner? He wondered how usual that was. "I'd like you to teach me," he said before he smiled awkwardly.

"Let's get started then," Brett said, enjoying his pleasure at Gerald's agreement. "The tack is in here." He led Gerald down to the tack room. "Tiny's bridle is there with his name on it, and I'll grab a saddle. You'll need a blanket and western pad. They're right outside on the shelves along with the helmets. I leave them there so they can air out."

Tiny's bridle in hand, Gerald followed Brett and paused at the shelves to pick up the indicated items. Then he tagged along as Brett hefted the saddle. "I guess you don't lift weights in the off hours."

Brett chuckled. "No, saddles and hay bales and bags of oats are all the lifting I can handle in a day. I don't think I've ever actually lifted weights, now that you mention it."

"It's boring as hell," Gerald muttered, his nose turning up.

Brett chuckled. "If you really don't enjoy it, you can hang out here on the weekends. I'll put you to work, and you'll never know you didn't lift."

"I make myself do it at least a little to even out all the running I do in the mornings," Gerald explained as they stopped at Tiny's stall. "I just might take you up on that offer to help around here, though. If I have to watch one more minute of CNN once I leave work, I think I'll go postal."

Brett laughed again, something he just now noticed he did a lot when Gerald was around. "No CNN here," he promised. "Just horse shit and screaming kids. And I won't make you deal with the kids." He slid open the door to Tiny's stall and handed Gerald the halter.

"I honestly couldn't tell you which I think is worse," Gerald said, taking the tack automatically. "At least the crap doesn't yell."

"No, it just smells," Brett said with a grin. "You gonna put that on halter him, or you just gonna stand there?"

"Huh? Oh!" Gerald slung the blanket and pad over the stall's wall and turned the halter over. "So just up over the nose?" He looked from the leather in his hands to Tiny's bobbing head.

"Put the buckle in your left hand and the strap in your right hand. Reach under his chin like you're going to hug him, and flip the strap over his head behind his ears," Brett instructed. "Then fasten the strap."

Following Brett's instructions made it easy, and soon the halter was in place. Tiny whuffed and pushed his nose into Gerald's chest; Gerald stumbled a half-step back. "Whoa, Tiny. A little warning, huh?" Gerald righted himself and stroked along the horse's nose.

"He isn't big on warnings." Brett chuckled, "but he doesn't have a malicious bone in his body. He's just saying hi and hoping for a treat. Give him a couple more weeks, and he'll be saying 'Hi, Gerald'… and hoping for a treat."

Gerald grinned and patted Tiny's side. "I think I'm seeing a pattern there, Tiny," he said. He turned his attention to his instructor. "Now what?" Gerald bounced a little on his toes, excited to be there and happy that Tiny seemed to like him so much.

"Now we take him outside and get him dressed," Brett replied. "Unless you think you're ready for bareback."

"What do you think? Is bareback any better or easier?" Gerald asked as he grabbed the blanket from the wall to offer to Brett.

Brett had to turn away. God, the man was cute. Clueless, but cute. If he weren't so obviously straight, he'd push Gerald up against the wall of Tiny's stall and kiss him senseless right now, but he didn't have time to educate a straight man. "You'd better wait until you know Tiny a little better."

"Okay," Gerald agreed, unfazed. He looked over to Brett and held out the blanket again. "I'm guessing this goes under the saddle."

Oh boy. Clueless.

"Yes, it protects Tiny's back from the leather, but you have to make sure it's completely flat and straight or it can rub a sore," Brett explained, watching carefully as Gerald put the blanket on Tiny's back. "Scoot it forward a little."

Gerald made sure the blanket was just so, smoothing it out carefully and making sure he remembered exactly where Brett had the padding laid out. "Okay, I think I've got it," Gerald said. "What's next?" He glanced over his shoulder to see Brett's eyes focused on him intently, and he raised one brow in question.

"Saddle next," Brett directed, ignoring the questioning look on Gerald's face. If he stopped to explain, they'd be here for the next hour and completely miss Gerald's lesson.

With Brett's direction, Gerald got the saddle settled on Tiny's back and the girth strap fitted. Tiny bobbed his head and leaned forward to snuffle at Brett's pockets, and Gerald smiled. "Looks like somebody wants his reward before he performs."

"He figures he's performing by standing here and letting you fumble with the blankets and the saddle." Expertly, Brett grabbed the bridle, slipping it on with a single practiced move, bit between Tiny's teeth, headpiece over his ears. "We'll save the bridle for a little later," Brett said as he fastened the chin strap. "It's a little harder to put on, even when Tiny's being agreeable."

Gerald watched anyway, although his eyes were caught more on how deftly Brett's hands moved so easily while at the same time petting Tiny. "I think he's a ham," Gerald said of the big horse.

"You're just now figuring this out?" Brett asked with a grin. "Come on; put your helmet on and walk him to the ring so we can get started."

"So what's the lesson for today?" Gerald asked as he walked alongside Brett after putting on the headgear. Tiny clomped right behind them placidly.

"First, we'll see how much you remember from Tuesday," Brett replied, "then if you've still got that down, we'll work on trotting some more, see if you can't steer while you're trotting."

"Sounds good to me," Gerald answered with an anticipatory smile.

The lesson passed far too quickly for either man. Gerald remembered everything Brett had told him on Tuesday, even managing to keep his heels in place most of the time. They worked on trotting and on Gerald keeping his balance and his seat in the saddle instead of standing up as Tiny picked up the pace slightly. Gerald wasn't satisfied with his progress, but Brett was.

"Well, if you're sure. I still felt awfully off balance, though," Gerald said as he dismounted, gnawing a little at his bottom lip.

Brett wanted to kiss the abused flesh. He ached with it, but he knew that kind of desire was purposeless and futile. "It takes time," Brett reminded the other man. "And you were starting to get tired. Working more when your legs are about to give out isn't going to make you a better rider. Believe me, when you come back on Tuesday, it'll feel much better."

"Okay," Gerald said, letting it go with a slight shrug. "I hope I don't forget much by then." He took Tiny by the reins and starting walking back out of the ring toward the stables.

"You could come this weekend," Brett blurted out before he could stop himself. "We can always use an extra pair of hands with the kids' classes," he added, trying to cover his slip.

Gerald turned his chin. "I've got no problem with kids," he said. "Don't know that I'd be much help with riding lessons, though."

Brett nodded. "I understand. Don't worry about it. We've usually got plenty of extra hands around, with the older kids trying to earn free hours of lessons by working on the weekends. Enjoy your weekend and come back on Tuesday ready to work." He led Tiny into the stall, intending to untack him by himself.

Gerald followed him in to pet Tiny some more. "Didn't say I wouldn't come," he said mildly as he watched the other man remove all the equipment. "Just that I don't know what good I'll be," he said. "But I can't this weekend, regardless."

"Big plans?" Brett asked, shouldering the saddle in one arm as he lifted off the pads with the other.

"Work," Gerald said with a slight shrug. "An account needs to close by Sunday, so it's got to be finished up on Saturday."

"Better you than me," Brett declared, stepping out of the stall. "Spend as long as you'd like with Tiny," he offered. "Just make sure you latch the stall door behind you when you're done."

"Okay. Have a nice evening, Brett. And thanks," Gerald said, smiling at the other man.

"You're welcome," Brett replied, reluctantly heading back toward the tack room and his office and the next round of lessons in half an hour. Maybe if he were lucky, he'd have time to eat that apple that had been sitting on his desk since lunch.

Two

As the car tooled along the highway, Gerald lifted the bottle of water and took a slurp. He was still thirsty after the long run in the cool morning air. But once he'd gotten home after the run he'd known he had no desire whatsoever to go to the gym to lift weights. No, he wanted to be at the stables, to ride, to visit with Tiny, and maybe even to move grain bags if Brett needed the help he said he did. That was several weeks ago now.

Gerald had been to Sutcliffe Cove twice a week ever since, taking lessons and falling more and more in love with riding and horses. Even now that he rode other horses sometimes and left the big horse for the true beginners, he always went by to visit and sneak Tiny some carrots. And although he saw him every time for his lessons, Gerald tried to take a few minutes separate from that to visit with Brett. Though Brett was usually busy, he always had time for a short talk, and he was always friendly. Gerald liked him a lot.

Happier now with his prospects for this Sunday than he'd been in quite awhile, he figured an extra stop at the farm wouldn't hurt anything. If Brett didn't need the help, he'd just visit awhile and then go to the gym. Gerald hummed softly as he turned the car onto the lane that led into the farm. He knew the way very well by now, and it didn't take long to get to the parking area.

As soon as he climbed out into the quiet, he realized there must not be lessons this early in the morning on Sundays. He glanced at his watch. It wasn't even ten yet. He frowned a little, wondering if he should have waited until after lunch. With a shrug, he started crunching across the gravel toward the stables to see if anyone was around. If not, he'd head for the office.

As Gerald rounded the corner of the large barn, movement in the side pasture caught his eye. There were jumps set up in a circuit; he'd seen it before with some of the older students. But the rider obviously wasn't someone just learning.

Brett had decided to take advantage of the rare free morning to do a little riding of his own. It'd been weeks since he'd had time to really give Shah a good workout. So he'd raised the bars on the jumps to really stretch his stallion's limits, saddled the bay, and led him into the ring. Shah had danced in anticipation and as soon as Brett let him, the horse headed for the first fence, as excited about the exercise as Brett was. For half an hour, now, they'd moved together, man and beast working in tandem to defeat the challenging course. The air was cool on Brett's cheeks as Shah's gait sped them around the ring, an exhilarating, refreshing rush.

Line up the approach, send Shah at the fence, bunch, release, land, check the lead, across the ring, flying lead change, line up the next fence. Eyes up, heels down, drive him on, keep him balanced.

The thoughts ran through Brett's head without him even being conscious of them. They'd done this so many times he didn't even need to think. His body just did what it was trained to do, and Shah responded, letting out a long, clarion neigh as they cleared the last fence again.

Gerald watched, fascinated as the man and horse moved as one through the course. To that point he'd always thought of riding as fun. But now he could see it was also about skill and beauty. Shah was a gorgeous horse. And, he realized, Brett was quite a good-looking man. He wondered why he hadn't really noticed before.

Brett drew Shah into a finishing circle, and then let him walk on a loose rein to cool off. When Brett pulled Shah to a halt, Gerald applauded, still watching Brett speculatively.

The sound of clapping drew Brett's attention to the side of the ring. He squinted, trying to figure out who was watching him before he recognized Gerald's stance. What was the other man doing here this early, on a Sunday of all days? He guided Shah over to the fence. "I didn't expect to see you today."

"I'm playing hooky from the gym," Gerald admitted. "That was really great. You and Shah, I mean," he said, leaning against the fence as he watched them approach.

"Thanks," Brett replied, swinging down off Shah's back. "We don't get a chance to play as much as I'd like. I spend all my time in the barn or the office. One of these days, I've got to hire a secretary."

"You should ride like this for the students some time. Give us something to aspire to," Gerald said. Then he tipped his head and grinned suddenly.

"What?" Brett asked, seeing the sudden, odd smile. "Do I have something on my face?"

"You've got *nothing* on your face," Gerald said, still smiling. "You shaved. What happened? Had a hot date last night?"

Brett flushed. "Yeah, actually, I did," he admitted, not sure he wanted to go into more detail than that, but he'd finally convinced the hot, young guy he'd met at the gay bar in town to go out with him last night. He'd shown Robbie a good enough time that the man had agreed to a second date next weekend. Brett was hopeful that one would lead to more than just a scorching good-night kiss.

Gerald chuckled. "Really? I thought you swore off women." He lifted one foot to brace it on the lowest bar of the fence.

Brett raised an eyebrow. "Who said I was with a woman?" he asked, turning and leading Shah toward the gate. As much as he enjoyed talking with Gerald, and as much as he wanted to see the other man's reaction, his horse was blowing, breathing hard. Shah had to come first.

Both Gerald's brows jumped, and he just watched Brett walk away as surprise rippled through him. "Well, damn," Gerald said under his breath. He hadn't seen that one. And now Brett was apparently taken. With a sigh, Gerald straightened up and followed with a resigned shrug. Seemed like all the good ones were always taken before he figured out they were even good.

He caught up with Brett inside the stables. "So, anything I can help with?"

"Yeah," Brett replied immediately, pulling his saddle off Shah's back, "if you don't mind. Grab the hose, and make sure everybody's water bucket is full."

"Sure, that's easy enough," Gerald said. As he uncurled the long hose, he glanced up. Brett's back was to him, and he took in the other man's body as he hadn't thought to do before, and then rolled his eyes at himself. *The guy's taken,* Gerald thought. *Buzz off, Saunders.* So he dragged the hose out, turned on the water, and got to work.

Brett finished up with Shah, rubbing him down with a clean rag to dry the sweat before brushing him well. Satisfied, he led him outside to his paddock, turned him loose, and laughed when the big bay immediately rolled on his back and undid all Brett's hard work in getting him clean. "Big baby," he muttered affectionately.

With a shake of his head, he turned back into the stables. "So," he called to Gerald, "ready to do some real work?"

Gerald looked up from where he was filling up the last couple of buckets. "Real work, huh?"

"We've got hay to spread, stalls to muck, and sawdust to put down," Brett explained. "You may wish you'd stayed home."

Gerald felt mild concern, but nodded anyway. "Ahh. All right, I'm here," he said. "Guess we ought to get started?"

Brett smiled. "Come on, rookie. I'll show you the ropes." He led Gerald down the long aisle to the storage room where he kept the hay. Opening it up, he pointed to a wheelbarrow propped against the outside wall. "Wheel that in here, and we'll fill it up. Each horse gets two flakes of hay."

"I'm not real prepared. Have you got an extra pair of gloves?" Gerald asked, looking down the long line of stalls. "I think I'm going to need them."

"Look in the cabinet in the tack room," Brett suggested. "I usually have a couple of pair in there. If not, I'll find some up at the house."

Gerald gave Brett a crooked grin and headed to the cabinet. It occurred to him now that Brett had a lot of charisma, and he wasn't necessarily immune to it. He wrinkled his nose as he dug through the supplies and found an old pair of gloves and pulled them on. On his way back to Brett, he wondered what he'd missed to not even see that he might be interested in Brett as more than an acquaintance. Gerald glanced toward Brett as he walked to get the wheelbarrow. "All right, abuse me."

"Don't tempt me," Brett joked, tossing another bale of hay into the wheelbarrow, his muscles working with accustomed ease to move the heavy load. "I haven't had anyone to abuse in a long time."

"I find that hard to believe," Gerald answered. He looked at the hay bale. "Don't we need a pitchfork or something?"

"Nah," Brett replied, snapping the twine. "See, it flakes off. Two flakes in the feed trough for each stall." He separated the first two sections of hay and fed the horse on the end. "Come back when you run out, and I'll give you another one."

"Okay," Gerald agreed. He walked from stall to stall, smiling, though he didn't realize it, as he looked at each horse when they approached him to eat. He tried not to linger too much; there was obviously more work to be done.

Brett glanced down the aisle periodically to check Gerald's progress. It did his heart good to be reminded of the joy of first discovery. It'd been so long since he'd just stopped and looked at all the horses in his care. Sure, he took time with Shah, and the others got what they needed, but not a lot of his time. Maybe it would be a good thing to have Gerald hanging around more often.

With that thought in mind, Brett grabbed another bale of hay and walked it down to the wheelbarrow. "Here's another one," he offered, glancing into the stall where Gerald had paused. "That's Lucky. He was a rescue horse. They found him in a barn, starved half to death, with no sign of the owner anywhere. My dad offered him a home."

Gerald watched as the horse nosed into the feed while it was right in his hand, not waiting for it to drop into the trough. He lifted one hand and patted Lucky's neck. "Plenty of food, buddy," he said.

"He's been here six years, but to this day, he never leaves a crumb in his bucket, whether it's hay or oats," Brett explained, looking at the chestnut gelding fondly. "I have to be careful he doesn't eat too much. Obesity is as much a problem for horses as it is for people, and Lucky doesn't have the sense to stop when he's full."

"I imagine if you've been starved, you're afraid it would happen again," Gerald said. Lucky had already eaten up the biggest part of the food. "You've taken good care of him, though. He looks good."

"I can't abide a starving animal," Brett admitted sheepishly. "Stray dogs, cats, horses, the occasional raccoon... I feed them all. My father despaired of me when I was growing up, but an extra scoop of dog food isn't going to break the bank, so I just keep on feeding the ones that show up at my doorstep."

"You're a kind-hearted man," Gerald said as he fed the next horse. He was facing away from Brett as he dropped the hay into the bin. "I've never had an animal of any kind as a pet."

"Why not?" Brett exclaimed. "You obviously love animals, or you wouldn't be out here on a Sunday spending your free time with the horses. Do you travel a lot with work?"

Gerald shrugged as he turned around. "No, I don't travel. I work a lot of hours, though. Just never thought about it, I guess. My parents both worked a lot when I was growing up, and it wouldn't have been fair to have a pet just to leave it at home alone."

"You'll just have to adopt one of the strays out here then," Brett declared impulsively. "He can stay out here, but he'll be yours to take care of while you're here."

"Adopt?" Gerald said in surprise, turning to blink at Brett blankly. "Me? I don't know anything about horses."

"I actually meant one of the dogs," Brett replied with a chuckle, "but you're welcome to adopt one of the horses as well. Most of them get ridden by the kids who come in here for lessons and don't get the kind of personal attention they really deserve. So what do you say? Want your own horse?"

"Uh?" Gerald tipped his head to one side and sort of shrugged. "Okay?" He wasn't too sure about it. "As long as you don't let me do something wrong, I guess." He looked bemused.

"Don't get too enthusiastic," Brett teased. "I might think you weren't interested."

"Oh, I'm interested," Gerald quickly insisted. "I'm just surprised, is all. I tend to think about things awhile before making decisions. But this won't hurt anything, and you're right—I do love the horses."

Brett smiled. "Nothing wrong with thinking things through," he said. "But this is a no-lose situation. And it'll give you a chance to really see the other side of the equation, in case you decide at some point you want to buy a horse of your own." He grabbed the next two flakes of hay and gave them to the horse next to Lucky. "I'll introduce you to some of the ones who belong to the stable, and you can decide who you want to adopt."

A smile curved Gerald's lips as he started to warm to the idea. "Will I get to ride mine sometime? When I've learned more?" he asked.

"Sure," Brett assured him. "The stable's horses are all used for lessons on various levels. Once you've decided who you want, we'll just have to get you up to that level so you can ride him."

Gerald picked up an armload of flakes. "Let's go then. You can introduce me as we work."

"So do you want a mare or a gelding?" Brett asked, pushing the wheelbarrow down the aisle in Gerald's wake.

"Well, they both have their positives, I'm sure, but a mare, she could have babies, right? That would be an awful lot of responsibility. I'm not too sure what I think about that. I'd worry, you know, even more, since I'm a beginner with horses," Gerald rambled as he thought it over.

"She could," Brett agreed, "but I try to keep that to a minimum unless it's planned. Shah has a separate paddock and a separate stall, so he can't get to the mares except when I want him to, and he's the only stallion in the barn. I've got plenty of geldings for you to choose from."

"Okay, that would probably be best," Gerald agreed as he picked up a couple more flakes for the last stalls. Then he stopped in place and looked over his shoulder. "I probably should have asked what was involved, huh?"

Brett threw his head back and laughed uproariously. It took a minute for him to get it under control. "Mucking his stall, making sure he's got food and water, spending time spoiling him, making sure he gets enough exercise," Brett said when he could talk through his laughter. "I promise, I haven't signed you into slavery for the rest of your life."

Gerald visibly relaxed as Brett laughed. "I think I can handle that. It's more than a twice-a-week responsibility, though," he pointed out. "I'll have to be here more." He wasn't at all bothered by that thought. In fact, he thought he might be looking forward to it.

"You're welcome as often as you want to come," Brett told him honestly. "You've been spending enough hours here helping out that I owe you a few free rides anyway. You may as well take them on the days you're not taking lessons. That'll give you an extra excuse to come take care of your horse."

"I've not been here that much. A few hours a couple times a week," Gerald dismissed Brett's claim. "But I would like to ride more," he added. He finished distributing the flakes and returned to Brett's side. "So now what?"

"Now we turn them out and get started shoveling manure," Brett said with a mock scowl. "This is when I usually lose my volunteers."

Gerald sort of grimaced. "I said I'd do it. Sooner we get started, the sooner it's over. Then we can get lunch."

"Grab a lead rope. We'll take them out to the side paddock," Brett instructed. "If we can get this aisle done, I'll buy you lunch."

"You don't have to do that," Gerald objected automatically as he led a horse out of a stall, carefully mimicking the way he led Tiny around.

"I know," Brett replied, clipping halters and lead ropes on the next two horses and leading them toward the paddock, "but it's a good excuse to treat myself too."

"This is a round-the-clock, everyday operation, I'd imagine," Gerald said as they entered the ring and released the horses. "How do you manage to get out, even for a date?" He glanced to Brett and his clean-shaven face and raised an eyebrow.

"Yeah, it takes pretty much all of my time, but mostly it's nothing urgent. As long as the horses have food and water, everything else can wait a few hours. For a date or whatever."

Gerald nodded as they walked back to the stalls for a few more horses. "Who all helps out here? Surely you have staff besides the teachers."

"I have a couple of guys who work during the week, mucking stalls and stuff, and the other instructors, of course," Brett replied, "but on the weekends, it's just me and the volunteers."

"You pretty much run this place by yourself?" Gerald gave Brett a look of newfound respect. "That's dedication."

"The farm's been in the family for six generations," Brett replied as if that were explanation enough. "I always knew I'd come back here when my parents were ready to retire. I'd like to expand, honestly, but that'll have to wait a bit. I've got plans though." He opened the gate and released the lead ropes, sending the horses out into the paddock. "Let's get the rest."

"I bet your parents are proud to know the farm is doing so well under your management," Gerald said as he took another horse by the lead rope. He stumbled a bit when the horse bumped into him, and he turned an exasperated look on the animal.

"Don't let Misfit push you around," Brett warned lightly, patting the dapple gray mare on her white star. "She's a bossy mare, but she's a real trouper when it comes to putting up with the kids."

Gerald harrumphed and started walking, turning narrowed eyes on the horse when she sidled up near him again. "Uppity female, aren't you?" he muttered. He shook his head. She was still beautiful, and he had to give a silly smile and scratch just below her ear.

She tossed her head playfully and bumped him again, asking for more attention. "Careful," Brett warned a second time, "or you'll find yourself adopted."

"I thought I was doing the adopting," Gerald retorted, but he rubbed Misfit's chest as he'd seen Brett do with other horses. "She has spirit. I've always thought horses should have personalities just like people."

"Oh, they do," Brett assured him. "And yes, you can adopt them, but I've seen them adopt people too. They take it into their heads that someone is their human, and that's it. Turn her out. We've got more to get."

Gerald unhooked the lead and gave Misfit's shoulder a slight shove, but the horse bobbed her head and stayed put with a huff. Gerald put his hands on his hips. "Come on now. Don't you want to visit with the other horses?" he asked her.

Misfit blew loudly and shook her head, rubbing her nose against his chest.

"Adopted," Brett teased with a grin. He slapped Misfit's rump, and she danced away a few steps, turning to glare at him accusingly before moving right back and thumping Gerald's chest again.

Gerald looked between the mare and Brett. "Just like that? I didn't do anything!"

Brett shrugged. "Don't ask me. They have minds of their own. You can stay and get acquainted with her. I'll turn the rest of the horses out."

Gerald blinked a little stupidly as Brett walked off, only snapping out of it when Misfit snorted and bumped his shoulder with her nose. He turned to look at her, frowning a little. "Now what am I supposed to do with you?" he asked her. She bobbed her head up and down in reply, and

Gerald chuckled, reaching to comb his fingers through her almost-black mane.

She was really pretty, a dark grayish color, though he didn't know what to call it. Not brown, like a lot of the other horses. "All right, then, Misfit. I guess I'm all yours." The horse stamped one foot and nickered in apparent agreement, getting another laugh out of Gerald.

Brett shook his head in amused delight and went to finish emptying the stalls on the far side of the stable. He'd done it himself enough times. One more Sunday spent mucking stalls wouldn't kill him. After sending the rest of the horses out to pasture, Brett grabbed a pitchfork and the manure wagon and started shoveling dirty straw into the cart to be composted for sale.

It was a little while later when Gerald came wandering around looking for him. "Hey, wasn't I supposed to help?" he asked as he found Brett in the middle of the fragrant job.

"So go empty the cart for me." Brett grinned. "You'll see the big pile as soon as you go out the back door."

Gerald took the cart by the handle and trundled it out there. Brett wasn't kidding about the big pile. He frowned and tried to figure the best way to empty the cart and finally ended up turning it on its end, piling the straw on the side of the heap. It worked pretty well, and he headed back to Brett with the empty cart.

When Gerald came back, Brett offered him the pitchfork. "Your turn." He stepped back to supervise.

"Don't laugh if I fall on my ass," Gerald warned as he took the pitchfork and started scooping straw into the cart. "At least I have a change of clothes in the car," he muttered good-naturedly.

"You're welcome to use my shower if you get too filthy," Brett promised, grabbing a second pitchfork and getting to work in the next stall. The faster they got the manure cleared, the sooner they could eat lunch. He refused to let his eyes linger on the play of muscles beneath Gerald's T-shirt. His date last night hadn't been all that serious, but it didn't matter anyway. Gerald was straight, so there was no use pining over what he couldn't have.

On his part, Gerald figured the novelty would wear off really quickly, but he actually enjoyed the physical labor, if not the smell. It was much better than the dull monotonous habit of lifting weights in the gym. It only took them an hour, working together, and Brett was a lot quicker at it than he.

He stood leaning on the pitchfork as he waited for Brett to finish the last stall. "I think I need that shower, especially if we're grabbing a bite to eat somewhere."

"No problem," Brett replied with a smile, wiping his face with the back of his hand. "Grab your clean clothes, and we'll get cleaned up. What tickles your fancy for lunch? There's a Chinese takeout place or the usual fast food."

"I like Chinese," Gerald said as he took the pitchfork to the storage closet along with Brett. "Do I meet you at the big house or somewhere else?"

"The big house," Brett replied. "I've got two bathrooms, so you can use one, and I'll use the other, and we'll be ready for lunch in no time." He hung the pitchforks on their hooks and tipped the manure cart against the outside wall so it wouldn't gather water if it rained.

"Okay." Gerald headed toward his car, pulling his keys out of his pocket as he went. Once he was there, he popped open the trunk and started rummaging around for his gym bag, frowning because it had slid all the way to the back behind some of his Bankers Boxes.

Brett walked up to the house, pausing on the wraparound porch to wait for Gerald, toeing his boots off while he stood there. He smiled as he thought about the morning and about how enjoyable it had been to have someone working with him. He'd have to see about convincing

Gerald to hang out more often. He'd grown up in the area, but he'd been gone for enough years that most of his high school friends had moved on, and he found himself lonely at odd times.

Gerald closed the trunk with a thump and walked toward the porch, whistling quietly as he went. It was a good morning as far as he was concerned, manure and all. He smiled, chuckling to himself. Who would ever have thought he'd be out in the country shoveling horse shit on a Sunday morning? He stopped at the stairs and looked up at Brett.

"Got what you need?" Brett verified. "Leave your boots here on the porch, and come on inside."

Gerald sat on the porch swing and started unlacing the old hiking boots, tucking them underneath and out of the way. He stood up in his sock feet. "I'm ready for a shower," he said, rubbing the back of his neck.

"Come on then," Brett said, opening the screen door and leading Gerald inside. "The bathroom's right there," he added, pointing to a door off the hallway that led from the old-fashioned parlor toward the back of the house. "Take your time. There's plenty of hot water. That was the first improvement I made when I moved home!"

Gerald laughed and nodded. "All right." He got into the bathroom and shut the door, leaning back against it and sighing. What a weird situation. He almost wished he'd stayed as oblivious about Brett as he'd obviously been the past several weeks.

When the door shut in front of Gerald, Brett climbed the stairs to his bedroom and pulled out clean clothes before going into the connecting bathroom for his own shower. The hot water felt good, loosening muscles still not completely used to the renewed demands of this lifestyle. He wasn't sixteen anymore, able to muck stalls all day every day and not think anything of it. Usually he lingered in the shower, but today he found himself eager to rejoin Gerald, to see what new delights he'd discover through the other man's eyes.

GERALD finger-combed his hair, easy to do with it so short, and rolled up his dirty clothes to stuff into his small gym bag. He grabbed his cross trainers and opened the door to walk out into what he figured was the living room.

"Feeling better?" Brett asked when Gerald joined him.

"I smell better," Gerald joked. "Yeah, I feel fine. Hungry." He ran his hand through his hair again. It was a nervous habit.

"Well, let's go then," Brett said, pushing himself to his feet and grabbing his wallet and keys. "I'm getting hungry too."

"I'll just throw this in my car," Gerald said, lifting the bag. "And my boots."

"No need to stink your car up," Brett said. "Leave the boots. You can get them when you come back out the next time. Besides, you might want to put them on when you go bring Misfit back in after lunch before you go home."

Gerald actually brightened at that thought and nodded. "Yeah, yeah, that'll work." He dumped his bag in the floorboard of his car and walked after Brett, who was opening the door of an older Chevy truck.

When Gerald was settled next to him on the bench seat, Brett put the truck in gear and drove off the farm and down the road toward the Chinese buffet. "It's all you can eat," Brett said. "They lose money every time I go in."

"Eh, it all evens out. Besides, working like you do, you can eat whatever you want, I bet. I have to be careful," Gerald said with an irritated wave of his hand.

"Stick with me," Brett offered with a chuckle. "You'll be able to eat whatever you want in a matter of weeks."

"Lord. I don't even know what I'd want, it's been so long. I stick to salad, vegetables, chicken." He shrugged. "Occasionally ice cream, but that's rare."

Brett laughed. "Get the beef. It's wonderful and well worth the indulgence. You worked hard this morning."

"I'm not sure I know what beef tastes like anymore," Gerald muttered. "Being Chinese, it's going to be covered in sauce anyway. Is it a place you can order from the menu or is it just a buffet place?" He felt a little disconcerted, knowing it was physical work like what he did today that Brett faced every day. It put his own daily work into perspective. He wrinkled his nose as he decided he didn't quite match up.

"It's just a buffet, but it's huge, like six hot tables and several cold ones, so you can get whatever you want," Brett replied. "But the beef's my favorite." He parked the truck. It hadn't even taken them five minutes to get there. "Come on; see what catches your fancy."

Gerald looked at the bright red-and-green-painted pagoda-shaped building as he climbed out of the car. "Well, I'm certainly hungry enough to get my money's worth."

"Good." Brett shut his door. "Let's go eat."

Once settled in the restaurant with plates full of food, Gerald surveyed his choices. "I feel like I'm overindulging," he admitted as he dug in. "But it's really good. I think I'll take your advice and assume I'm calorie-negative today." He offered Brett a grin.

"Calorie-negative," Brett said with a chuckle. "Listen to you. So tell me, what does Gerald Saunders do when he isn't hanging around my stables? Are you a nutritionist?"

Gerald raised an eyebrow as he swallowed his mouthful. "No, I'm an accountant," he said. "Thus the exercise. I sit at a desk all day."

"I can't imagine," Brett said with a shake of his head. "I'd go crazy stuck at a desk all day. It's bad enough having to do the accounts for the farm once a week. Having to do it every day would drive me batty. Surely you've got something going on outside of work? Or am I really taking all your free time?"

Gerald tipped his head to one side as he poked through some sauce for a chunk of broccoli. "I tend to pick something to do every once in a while other than going to the gym. I learned to ski last year, but you actually have to go up into the mountains. I like this because I don't have to go far at all. And I love the horses." He shrugged a little. "Other than that, I'm really boring."

"I find that hard to believe." Brett laughed. "But I'll let you off for now. So you ski? It's the wrong season for it now, but I've got a cousin with a cabin up in the mountains. He lets me use it from time to time in the winter when I need a break from the city."

"I like skiing. I was pretty good at it," Gerald said, nodding. "These types of things are what I do instead of taking vacations. Kind of spreading the fun out."

"I can see that. A different kind of stress release." Brett finished his plate. "I'm going back for more. You want anything?"

Gerald pushed his mostly empty plate away. "I think I'll get some salad," he said, sliding out of the booth.

Brett shook his head. "You need more than rabbit food," he teased. "Unless you're done for the day."

Gerald followed along and perused the hot tables again. "Do you need more help? I'd like to see Misfit again before I go home."

"There's always more work to do," Brett replied honestly, "but I'm used to handling it myself on the weekends. You've already put me a good hour ahead of where I'd have been by myself, so don't feel obliged to stay. On the other hand, I wouldn't say no if you wanted to stay. It occasionally gets lonely with just the horses for company."

"I'm used to the quiet," Gerald admitted as he picked some rice noodles and stir-fry vegetables. "But I'd be happy to stick around."

"You'd think I'd be used to it too," Brett replied, heading back to the table with his plate full again. "But when I lived here before, as a kid, my parents and sister were always around, and when I was away, I almost always shared an apartment with somebody as a way to save money. It's been an adjustment being back out on the cove by myself."

"My parents are great, but we all like our space," Gerald said when they started eating again. "I talk to them pretty often, and we have dinner about once a week. Other than that, it's work and my own thing." He looked up and grinned. "But now I have Misfit."

"You certainly do," Brett agreed with an answering grin as he kept working on his plate. "And she'll take all the time you're willing to give her and more. But it's worth it."

"I can't believe I'm so tickled over a horse," Gerald muttered as his cheeks flushed a little. "You'd think I was a teenage girl instead of acting my age."

Brett laughed. "You ever watched the Kentucky Derby? Or the Olympic equestrian events? Those are no teenagers rooting for their favorites, I promise. They're men our age and older with large wallets and big cars. This isn't a poor man's hobby."

"Olympics, yeah," Gerald admitted. "And the Belmont. Not the Derby. I'm not worried about the money. I'm not rich, by any means, but I'm comfortable."

"I didn't mean it that way," Brett apologized. "I just meant you shouldn't compare yourself to a teenage girl just because you're interested in horses. And as much time as you're about to spend with Misfit, you won't be paying for many lessons. You'll earn them all in volunteer hours." He set his chopsticks aside. "Are you ready to head back?"

"After I get my fortune cookie," Gerald said as he snatched one up off the check. "I still feel a little silly about being so excited." Then he shrugged and laughed. "But I don't care."

"You'll get over it," Brett promised, snagging the other fortune cookie and dropping some cash on the bill. "Come on; Misfit's waiting for you."

"HEY, Brett. Jimmy said you were looking for me?" Gerald asked as he stopped outside the corral and started pulling off his gloves.

"Morning, Gerry," Brett said with a smile. "I've got a class of five-year-olds starting this morning, and I could use another pair of hands. Feel like being promoted?"

"Uh, sure," Gerald said, surprised by the use of a nickname and a bit slow to answer because of it. "I can deal with kids."

"Great. You're my new assistant," Brett declared, not noticing how Gerald stumbled a little over his reply. "We need to help them get their ponies saddled and bridled, since they've never done that before. Come on; I'll introduce you."

"Okay," Gerald said with a bemused smile. He'd only been riding himself for a little over two months, but if Brett needed help, he didn't mind giving him a hand.

Between the two of them, they helped the kids get the horses saddled and bridled and into the ring with no mishaps. When all the kids were standing next to their ponies, Brett smiled at them. "Okay, everybody. Ready to get started?"

A chorus of excited cries answered him. "Good. Mr. Gerry and I will help you mount up and then we'll see about getting started."

Gerald glanced to Brett upon hearing the nickname again before looking at the kids. They couldn't stop bouncing. While some of the kids were naturally excited, others were just so sweetly serious he wouldn't dare laugh. The little girls were the best, all prim and prissy, while the boys just wanted to ride like cowboys.

Watching the kids as he helped them mount, Brett stilled hands and adjusted grips, making sure the kids were ready to ride. Seeing one little girl fumbling unsteadily, Brett waved Gerald over. "Can you help out Sara? She looks a little nervous. Just walk beside her for a bit until she gains some confidence."

Gerald nodded. "Okay, just let me know if I do something wrong," he murmured before moving to Sara's side and patting her leg reassuringly.

The little girl smiled shyly at Mr. Gerry, hands twitching nervously on the reins, transmitting her unease to the pony below her. When the animal shifted restlessly, her panicked gaze flew to his face.

"It's okay, sweetheart," Gerald said gently, laying one hand over hers. "You have to hold the reins real still. Can you do that?"

She nodded slowly, her hands relaxing beneath the big, warm ones covering hers. Almost immediately, Honeycomb quieted down. "What do I do now?"

"The two things to remember with your hands are to keep still like this, right? And to pull just a little and then let loose. If you want to go, let loose a little more. To stop, pull a little. Just a little though, okay?" Gerald explained, looking up at the little girl.

"Okay," Sara agreed as the horses started walking at Brett's command. Her face lit up in quiet delight as she studiously kept her hands still, trying not to pull or do anything that might stop the horse from walking.

"Good job," Gerald praised. "Just like that."

"And ask your horses to halt," Brett said from the center of the ring.

Gerald looked down at the smiling rider. "Okay, now, remember what I said about pulling back just a little? Do that now," he said as he walked alongside.

Sara did as Mr. Gerry said. Honeycomb came to a stop with a shake of her head. "Why'd she do that?" the girl asked with a touch of panic in her voice.

"She's just saying, 'Okay, I did it,' pretty much," Gerald said, patting Sara's shoulder. "You did really well!"

"Oh, okay," Sara replied with a relieved sigh. Maybe she'd actually get the hang of this after all. She looked up to the bleachers and waved to her mother, dropping one of the reins as she did.

Gerald caught the rein before Honeycomb shifted. "Sara, don't drop the reins like that, okay? Honeycomb won't understand what you want," he explained calmly.

"Oh," Sara said, positioning her hand carefully on the rein again as Brett directed the students to turn the horses to the right and then to the left.

"Okay, this is easy," Gerald said. "If you want Honeycomb to go right," he pointed in that direction, "then you pull the rein on that side so her head points that way."

Sara nodded and did what Mr. Gerry said, tugging to the right. Honeycomb turned obediently. "And I pull the other way to go left?"

"Exactly! Great job," Gerald said with a grin.

Brett had everyone stop again as he set out a series of orange cones. "Okay, let's see who's up to an obstacle course," he challenged. "Weave in and out of the cones."

Gerald stepped back. "You can do it, Sara. Go ahead. Show Mr. Brett and your mom."

Nervously, Sara began guiding Honeycomb through the cones. The pony tried to wander toward Brett at one point, but Sara pulled determinedly on the reins and brought her back in line. When she finished, everyone applauded. "I did it!"

Gerald clapped too. "Great job, Sara!"

Brett smiled over at Gerald, thrilled with the way the other man was working with the kids. If this kept up, he might have to bring him into the ring for all the beginning classes. "Okay, who's next?"

After the lessons were done, Gerald was about to turn the corner of the barn when Sara ran up, took his hand, and led him over to her mother. He spoke with them both for a few minutes before they left, Sara smiling and waving. He waved back before walking back toward the stable.

"Nicely done," Brett said, meeting Gerald at the entrance to the stable. "Not everybody has the knack for dealing with the younger kids."

"Oh, I love kids," Gerald said. "I visit my nieces at least every other weekend."

"You have family nearby besides your parents?" Brett asked curiously.

"Oh yeah, everybody," Gerald said. He glanced at his watch. "I've got to get going," he said apologetically. "Meeting tonight for work."

"I'm sorry!" Brett exclaimed. "You should have said something. Go on. I'll see you later in the week."

"It's no trouble. I'm not late. But I will need a shower," Gerald said with a smile. "See you tomorrow?"

"Yeah, I'll be here," Brett promised. "Hope the meeting goes well."

"'Well' means not so boring that I fall asleep over my salad," Gerald said drolly as he walked backward toward the parking lot before he turned and walked to his car.

Three

"Mr. Gerry, Mr. Gerry, will you help me saddle Buckeye?"

Gerald turned around in place with a raised eyebrow, and then had to look down. Quite a bit. "Uh. Sure. You got a lesson?" he asked, peering down at the little girl already wearing her helmet and miniature cowboy boots. He didn't recognize her.

She nodded and led him to the pony that must have seemed immense to her, even though Gerald could probably have straddled its back with his feet touching the ground. Size, he supposed, was relative.

"You know me already," Gerald said. "What's your name?"

"I'm Patty. And I'm five!"

"Well. That's getting up there, isn't it?" he teased gently as she nodded. "Okay, so what equipment do you use?" he asked, figuring she'd be able to tell him. "I figure your saddle is smaller than one I'd use, huh?" he said, smiling down at her. Why she was asking him to help, he had no idea. But he didn't suppose he minded. Saddling a horse he could do after more than four months on the farm several times a week.

"Over here," Patty said, showing him a saddle half the size of the one he regularly used. "And the blankets too."

"I don't know," Gerald teased. "That's an awful tiny saddle for a big girl like you." But he picked it up in one hand, hefting it under his arm, and grabbed a blanket with the other hand.

"It's the one Mr. Brett tells me to use," she insisted. "It's perfect for Buckeye." She led him regally down the aisle to Buckeye's stall. "I'm not allowed to get him out by myself."

"Yes, I agree. Buckeye's a nice guy, but you're awfully short compared to him. He might not see you." Gerald walked into the stall and got the horse saddled and ready before leading him out of the stall, having worked the whole time under Patty's watchful eyes. "Ready to go?" he asked her.

"Yes," she said, holding out her hands for the reins. When he gave them to her, she carefully led the pony toward the ring with all the confidence of a girl twice her size.

Gerald watched her go, smiling and shaking his head. What an odd thing. He turned and stopped short, seeing Brett watching him. "Hey," Gerald greeted.

"Morning, Mr. Gerry," Brett replied with a drawl. "I see you're already in the thick of things today. Although I imagine saddling Buckeye's a little more pleasant than mucking stalls."

"Is that what I'm on the schedule for today?" Gerald asked.

"You're on the schedule for whatever you feel like doing," Brett retorted. "You've been around enough to know what needs to be done without me making you a list. Pick your poison, and I'll get the kids to do the rest."

Gerald jerked a thumb in the little girl's direction. "Hope it was okay for me to help her."

"It was fine. Patty knows what she's doing—she's been riding since she was three—but she's too small to do it by herself."

"Okay," Gerald said amiably. "You just tell me if I get in the way," he added as he pulled his gloves out of his belt. He didn't really think about it, but he dressed for dirty work without thinking about it these days: old jeans, T-shirt, work boots, gloves.

Brett shook his head. "You're not in the way." And it was the truth. In the past four months, the dark-haired man had become almost as much a fixture in the stable as Brett himself, there easily three evenings a week, sometimes four, and most of the day on Saturdays and Sundays. They'd fallen into an easy camaraderie, joking and teasing like they'd known each other for years instead of just for months. That was the magic of a shared passion. It brought together people of similar interests and temperament—when they were there for the horses, not for the status symbol—and gave them a bond far deeper than the passage of time would suggest. "Well, not unless you keep standing in the middle of the aisle blocking traffic."

Gerald blinked and turned where he stood to see one of the teenagers with a horse on a lead grinning. Flushing a little, Gerald moved to the side. "Yeah, well. I'll just get back to work. I've got a lesson at six."

"When it's time to get ready tonight," Brett called, catching Gerald's attention before he walked off, "saddle Misfit."

Gerald paused and turned to look over his shoulder. "What for?" he asked curiously.

Brett grabbed the nearest thing he could find—a curry comb—and chucked it at Gerald's head. "Idiot," he muttered affectionately. "So you can ride her at the lesson, of course."

Gerald ducked when the comb flew by, but his eyes were wide when he stood back up. His grin was huge too. "Really? That's great!"

"Goofball. Get to work or you won't be done in time for your lesson," Brett said with a shake of his head.

Gerald nodded, his grin undimmed as he headed off to get some work done. He didn't even mind that one of the only chores left was mucking stalls; there was too much air under his heels for him to notice.

About two hours later, Gerald finished cleaning up before heading to Misfit's stall. He stopped at the door as she met him at it, nodding her head as he got out an apple.

"You pig," Gerald said fondly as he cut the apple into chunks with his pocket knife. Misfit nipped at his hand, trying to get the fruit. "Hey! Not my fingers!"

"If you'd hold your hand flat and let her lift it off your palm, she wouldn't get your fingers," Brett scolded, coming to Gerald's side and stroking Misfit's forelock. She tossed her head regally, returning all her attention to Gerald. And the apple.

"Yeah, I know, but she gets in a hurry," Gerald complained, but he still fed Misfit the apple and rubbed her neck warmly before moving to hook a lead on the halter and lead her out of the stall.

Brett leaned back and watched as Gerald saddled her with competent hands, all the hesitation gone after months of practice, and he twitched the blankets into place with practiced ease and fitted the girth in just the right place around her belly. Her immaculately clean belly, Brett noted. Not an easy task given Misfit's penchant for rolling in the mud every chance she got. "She looks good. Being adopted obviously agrees with her."

Gerald looked up, smiling wryly. "She's spoiled," he muttered, but he stood and slung an arm over her neck in an adapted hug. Misfit bobbed her head as if in approval, and she didn't shy away.

Brett just chuckled. "Bring her in the ring when you're ready, and we'll get started."

"C'mon, Rotten," Gerald said, following along behind Brett. Misfit followed sedately though her tail flipped back and forth.

They got inside the ring, and Gerald mounted. "She's got a much more sensitive mouth than Tiny," Brett warned, "so she'll respond to a much lighter touch on the reins. She also responds much more quickly to your posture because I don't use her with the beginners who don't know what they're doing. If you lean forward, she'll speed up, and if you lean back, she'll slow down, even without a nudge of your heels or a pull on the reins."

Frowning ever so slightly as he concentrated, Gerald pulled on the reins to one side, and Misfit promptly shifted in that direction. Gerald's eyebrow perked. "Let's see if I don't dump myself on the ground," he said. He'd only done that once, thank God. Once was embarrassing enough.

"If you ride horses, you get thrown," Brett replied philosophically. "I've lost track of the number of times I've eaten dirt since I first learned to ride. Walk her around the ring a few times. Start, stop, ask her to turn. Get used to her, and let her get used to you."

Gerald nodded distractedly, giving Misfit very careful directions. Though she pranced a bit to the side a few times, for the most part she obeyed the tentative commands.

Brett let horse and rider work out their own communication. He could advise and guide, but ultimately, it came down to trust between the two actively involved in the process. When Misfit seemed to settle in, he spoke up. "Ready to try it at a trot?"

Glancing up, Gerald nodded, though he took a deep breath to settle himself. "Why am I nervous?" he asked with a soft laugh.

"I don't know," Brett replied seriously. "Why are you nervous?" If it was mostly just anticipation, that was fine, but if Gerald truly did not feel ready, he didn't want to push too hard.

Gerald swallowed. "I just want to do it right so I can ride her more after this," he admitted, looking up to meet Brett's eyes.

"The worst that can happen, and I wouldn't have put you up on her today if I didn't think you were ready, is that you aren't ready for her yet. So you'd ride Tiny for a few more weeks until you are ready for her.

I'm not setting you up to fail or for either of you to get hurt," Brett assured Gerald. "I want this to be fun for both of you."

Relaxing a little, Gerald nodded. He leaned over to slide his hand along Misfit's neck. "Let's go, girl," he said, indicating for her to walk. Once she was moving, he asked for a trot.

It was a little awkward at first to Brett's experienced eye, Gerald having trouble catching the much faster rhythm of Misfit's gait when compared to Tiny's loping strides, but after a few uncomfortable bounces—Misfit tossed her head in protest each time he came crashing down on her back—they managed to find their balance and move with reasonable grace around the ring.

Gerald let Misfit keep trotting as he got used to her movement, although he knew already he'd be sore tonight, just like the first few weeks when he'd first been learning to ride. Good thing he was using an English saddle now, he thought wryly. A saddle horn would have been murder. After several laps around the ring, Gerald slowed Misfit to a walk and finally to a stop next to Brett.

"Bet you're glad you're riding English these days," Brett joked when Misfit halted right next to him. "A couple of those bumps would've been really painful if you'd had a saddle horn in the way."

Gerald winced even though he'd been thinking the same thing. "I'll remember that in my hot bath tonight," he said, looking down at the other man from his higher vantage point. It used to strike him as odd, looking down at his teacher. But now he found he didn't mind the view. His lips twitched. "More practice time?" he asked.

"That's right," Brett agreed. "Do it again and again and again until you can do it without thinking. Oh, and pay attention to which diagonal you're on this time. You were on the inside instead of the outside last time."

"I was?" Gerald asked as he turned Misfit to start her walking again. "I think I was so focused on trotting at all that I didn't even think to look."

"It's fine," Brett assured him as Gerald and Misfit moved back to the edge of the ring. "She might get annoyed with you just because she's well enough trained to expect you to be on the correct diagonal, but you're not going to hurt her or yourself. You're much more likely to bother her bouncing around than posting on the wrong diagonal. Try it again."

"It's a lot to remember," Gerald said distractedly as Misfit started trotting again. He got with the motion much more quickly this time, and after some time he tried to check where he was posting, but it threw his motion off. After another round about the ring he pulled Misfit to a slow stop. "Going to need more practice."

"That's what we're here for," Brett replied easily. "You've got the hang of it until you think about it, and then it throws you off. Ride long enough, and you won't have to check anymore. You'll be able to feel from the way she's moving which foot is forward when. It just takes time and experience. Do you want me to tell you when you're off rather than having to look for yourself?"

"That would help," Gerald said with a nod as he turned Misfit about. She listened to him pretty well, not giving him trouble. Gerald could tell she was trained well, probably by Brett, he'd bet.

"Okay, get her to a trot, but don't start posting until I tell you," Brett directed. When Misfit was moving, he called, "Up, down, up, down," in time to her moving feet. As soon as Gerald was on the correct diagonal, he stopped, letting his student keep the pace on his own. Damn, he was a fine-looking man. Too bad he was straight.

Once Gerald was in the right motion, he could tell it was the correct one. It felt right, and Misfit seemed to relax under him too, though he couldn't have explained why he felt that. He trotted her around the ring several times before coming to a stop, a wide smile on his face. "That was great!"

"Now you just have to get used to figuring it out on your own," Brett said, returning the smile. He crossed the ring to fetch a long lunge line and whip. He snapped it to Misfit's bridle and returned to the middle of the ring. "Ready for something new?"

"Well, I'm not in the dirt yet, so I'll try it," Gerald answered.

Brett laughed. "Hold the pommel with one hand and Misfit's mane with the other. Don't worry about the reins. I'll guide her from here." When Gerald was situated, Brett shook the lunge whip at Misfit's heels, clucking to her at the same time. Gerald leaned forward instinctively, and that was all the encouragement Misfit needed to break into a gentle, rolling canter.

"Wow!" Gerald said after a few moments. "This is great!" Sometimes he wondered if he sounded like a little kid, but he just couldn't help it.

"Keep your heels down," Brett prompted as Misfit continued with her loping strides. "You don't want your feet to get caught in the stirrups."

Gerald corrected his stance, a little clumsily, but he managed it. "This isn't a trot," he said.

Brett laughed. "No, it's not. She's cantering. It's a faster gait, but once you get the hang of it, it's an easier one because it's a less jarring rhythm. You have to let your hips roll with her motion. A little like with a lover."

It was another long minute, but then Gerald fluidly relaxed into the movement, his midsection shifting as Brett had described. It didn't last long before he lost the repetitive motion, but he was already smiling.

Brett shortened the lunge line, bringing Misfit back to a walk. "Nicely done," he praised, coming up to stand beside Gerald's booted foot as the other man sagged a little in the saddle, "although we need to work on your stamina or there might be some disappointed ladies out there."

Gerald chuckled and shook his head, not really minding the comment. "I don't know that any ladies care since I devote my stamina to the guys instead," he said matter-of-factly.

Brett blinked a couple of times. "Well, isn't that nice to know?" he drawled before taking a step back and loosening the lunge line again with a firm reminder that he had a date tonight and therefore had no business coming on to his student. "Let's try it again."

Tipping his head to one side, Gerald realized Brett was teasing him. "You were right, you know," he said as Misfit started walking.

"Right about what?" Brett asked, having lost the thread of the conversation in the surprise revelation.

Gerald grinned as Misfit stretched into the canter. "It *is* like moving with a lover."

"Told you." Brett watched as Gerald picked up the movement much more easily this time. He let the other man find his own position. None of the little flaws were dangerous to Gerald or to Misfit, and Brett was of the opinion that too many directions all at once were distracting. Once Gerald was more comfortable, they could work on all the details.

BRETT leaned against the door to the stall where Gerald was busy mucking straw, enjoying the sight of muscles bunching beneath the sweat-soaked singlet he'd left on when he pulled off his dress shirt upon his arrival from work. Apparently he'd been in a hurry. It amused Brett so much that Gerald would come straight from work, pull on a pair of jeans, and get right to work like that. He'd found himself watching the other man more and more in the days since the matter-of-fact announcement that Gerald was gay. Damn, he wished he'd realized it sooner. Brett could think of a laundry list of things he'd have done differently if only he'd known.

"Enough work for one day," he declared, ready to have Gerald's company for himself. "It's time to ride."

Gerald glanced up and smiled, straightening and leaning on the pitchfork as he wiped his brow with the back of his forearm. "That's a first, you who always works telling someone else to take a break," he teased.

Brett shrugged. "As much as you're here helping me, I find myself running out of things to do. The work's done. It's time to ride."

"Well, I won't complain," Gerald said. He grabbed the old towel he'd thrown over the stall wall and used it to wipe off his face and neck. It was really hot in the barn, and while the horses were smart enough to stay outside, he apparently wasn't. He plucked at the soaked singlet. "Well, I knew I'd get sweaty today. Good thing I didn't change into an actual T-shirt. I'd have keeled over from heat exhaustion."

Brett thought it was a good thing as well, for an entirely different reason. The only thing sexier than a sweaty man in a singlet was a sweaty man with no shirt at all. "So take it off. It's just us here tonight. I'm certainly not going to complain if you're cooler without a shirt."

Gerald shrugged as he walked past with the pitchfork and latched the stall behind him. "So where do you want to ride? Remember I'm not on the level with you and Shah," he reminded.

"You choose," Brett replied. "We can do a lesson here in the ring or we can take a couple of horses out through the woods."

"I don't have a preference," Gerald said happily as he turned on the water at the spigot to wash his hands. "I just want to ride."

"Well then, saddle up Misfit, and I'll meet you in the ring." Brett laughed. "Let's see if you still remember how to canter. Have you been practicing at home?"

Gerald looked up from the water and blinked at him several times, confused. "How would I practice at…?" Then he perked up as his brain caught up, and he rolled his eyes. "Funny. Very funny."

"What?" Brett asked innocently. "For all I know, you could have a different guy for every night of the week."

"And one in nice pants for Sundays?" Gerald said drolly as he shut off the faucet and shook his hands out. "No," he said sweetly. "I've not been practicing. Sorry, Mr. Sutcliffe."

Brett cocked an eyebrow. "You know what happens to naughty boys who don't do their homework," he said sternly.

Gerald's lips twitched, and he cleared his throat. "No riding?" he tried.

"Worse than that," Brett threatened, grabbing a stray lead rope from where one of the kids had left it and running it through his hand.

Gerald's brows rose. "Uh…?" He blinked at Brett, trying to figure out what he might be hinting at. "Extra work in the barn?"

"Nope." Brett advanced on Gerald, the rope hanging loosely in his hands.

"No dinner?" Gerald guessed as his eyes grew wider.

"Not that either." Getting within arm's reach of Gerald, Brett threw the rope over his torso, pinning his arms and spinning him around as he swiftly put a knot in the soft cotton. "They get hog-tied and tickled."

Gerald immediately squawked and tried to get loose. "No tickling! No tickling!" he insisted.

"Why not?" Brett asked, fingers moving more quickly. "Can't take it?"

"I can't stand it!" Gerald insisted, jerking around, trying to get loose. And as soon as he didn't feel Brett's hands, he bolted.

"Hey!" Brett shouted, dashing after Gerald and tackling him to the ground. They both fell with a thump and a laugh. "I wasn't done with you yet!"

"No, please!" Gerald wheedled, rolling to his side. "Anything but tickling—anything!"

Brett was tempted to ask for a kiss, just to know what Gerald's mouth would feel like beneath his, but thoughts of Robbie held him back. They hadn't explicitly talked about not seeing anyone else, but Brett had considered it understood. And as long as that was the case, he couldn't bring himself to ask Gerald for what he really wanted. "That's a pretty broad offer," he drawled. "I could demand all kinds of sexual favors in exchange for not tickling." He got to his knees, rocked back onto his heels, and grinned down at the other man. "Or I could make you empty the manure carts for the rest of the month."

"There's only a few days left in the month," Gerald pointed out, relaxing with a huff. He deliberately ignored the other comment, although his body didn't.

"Fine, then you can empty the manure carts next month too," Brett joked, offering Gerald a hand. "Come on; get Misfit ready. I promised you a ride, and the state of Connecticut frowns on slave labor."

"Hey, it's not slave labor. You pay me eight dollars an hour," Gerald protested as he climbed up.

Brett paused. "What?" he asked in confusion. "How do you figure that?"

"Eight dollars an hour. It works out to a free riding lesson a week, about," Gerald said offhand as he stood still while Brett untied him.

Brett shook his head. "You accountants," he groused. "Always on about the numbers. Honestly, as much as you work, I shouldn't charge you for *any* lessons. I've forgotten how I ran this place without you."

"I just help out when I can. And it's not so much more than a lesson a week, really. And now that I ride several days a week, I try to keep it even," Gerald said with a shrug as they started toward the door.

"If it's really that important to you, then keep track," Brett agreed as they stepped outside into night air only marginally cooler than the air in the barn, "but like I said, you've more than earned all the rides you want as far as I'm concerned. So, you want to try a small jump tonight?"

"A jump?" Gerald's voice reflected his surprise. "I don't know how well I'll do, but I'll try it."

"Just a little one, a trotting pole really," Brett explained. "If you get the hang of that, we'll work up to a little X."

"WHAT did you think?" Brett asked as they walked Misfit back into the barn. "Want to try an X next time?"

Gerald's nose wrinkled. "I wasn't really comfortable with all that. I think I'd rather just ride."

"That's fine," Brett assured him, "although there's nothing quite like riding a full course. I want you to be comfortable, though. This is supposed to be fun for you."

"I think it's more fun to watch you and Shah," Gerald admitted as he led Misfit into her stall and grabbed a towel to start wiping her down. "I can feel the enjoyment just pouring off the two of you."

Brett smiled. "Yeah, we enjoy it. I find it's a wonderful way to relax at the end of a hard day."

"You always have hard days," Gerald said, giving him an amused smile.

"Which is why Shah gets so much exercise," Brett quipped. Leaning against the side of the barn, he sighed. "But I'm not going to get a ride in tonight, I'm afraid. Our annual barbecue and bonfire is coming up later this week, and I've got to get things ready for that. You are coming, aren't you?"

"Of course I am," Gerald said. "The kids have been all over me about it."

"Good," Brett said with a satisfied grin, anticipating spending the evening with Gerald in the relaxed, family atmosphere the bonfire always inspired. "It's the highlight of the summer for me."

"It sounds like a lot of fun. Should I bring anything?" Gerald asked as he finished up and stepped out of the stall.

"Just your smiling face. The farm provides everything else. I might put you to work that night. We always need willing hands to help keep the kids busy."

Gerald sketched a bow after closing the stall door. "At your service, *monsieur*."

Brett just grinned, not quite ready to tell Gerald how he'd like to be serviced. The thought of the dark man on his knees at Brett's feet—or on his hands and knees in Brett's bed—was far too appealing for comfort, especially since he had a boyfriend of sorts at the moment. "I'll remind you of that when the kids drive you crazy."

"I'll be sure to charge you for an extra hour," Gerald said almost seriously as he walked over and turned on the hose, soaking down the towel in his hand before turning the water back off.

"You can charge me for as many hours as you want," Brett said. "I swear, you work as many hours a week as some of my employees."

"No, I don't," Gerald disagreed mildly as he started wiping at his neck and arms with the wet towel.

Brett shook his head. "We aren't going to agree on this one, so there's no sense arguing," he said agreeably. "Just make sure you keep track of those hours. I don't want to cheat you out of lessons you've earned."

"Yes, sir," Gerald said before lifting the towel and burying his face in it to wipe away the sweat and caked-on dust.

Brett watched the progress of the towel with far more interest than was good for him, fighting the urge to reach for the towel and do it himself. He really needed to work off this attraction. He'd had no indication Gerald was interested, even if he were gay. Mentally, he calculated how long it would take to drive into town and visit Robbie, if the younger man was even available tonight. "You want a beer?" Brett offered instead, the words out before he could censor them.

"Sure," was Gerald's answer, coming out muffled from behind the towel. He uncovered his face to continue. "I just need to clean up a little," he said, jerking his thumb to the wash basin at the far end of the stables. "Then we can go wherever you like."

"I was thinking the porch, not out," Brett said sheepishly, looking toward the wide, wraparound porch longingly. "If that's all right with you. I'm not sure I'm up for a night on the town."

"Of course it's all right," Gerald said with a smile. "I'll be there in a few minutes."

"Great," Brett said, trying to think up an excuse to linger and watch as Gerald cleaned up in the hopes he'd pull off his sweaty singlet in the process. Nothing came to mind, though, so he reluctantly left the barn and headed for the house, leaving his muddy boots outside and slipping on a pair of Birkenstocks. He grabbed two beers and settled into the deep rocking chair on the porch, watching for Gerald across the yard between the house and barn.

Just like Gerald said, it was only a few minutes before he came out of the barn; he carried his singlet as he walked over to the trunk of his car, popped it open, and started rummaging.

Brett's mouth watered at the sight, eyes tracing the dark hair dusting Gerald's chest before he turned to the car and bent over, giving Brett an incredible view of the other man's ass outlined in tight denim. He took a gulp of his beer, trying to douse the heat inside him, but the cold liquid did nothing to cool him down. He averted his gaze, summoning an image of Robbie instead, of smooth, supple limbs and a slender, tight backside. The sound of footsteps drew Brett's attention, shattering the illusion and bringing him right back to his current dilemma.

Gerald had pulled on a dark green T-shirt, leaving it untucked and hugging his hips. "What are my choices?"

"A full bottle of Heineken or half of one," Brett quipped, holding the full bottle out for Gerald to take. He couldn't quite stop his eyes from traveling the breadth of the other man's chest.

"Choices, choices," Gerald said with a low laugh as he snagged the bottle and sat down next to him.

Brett propped his feet up on the porch rail in front of him, the motion rocking the chair back as far as it would go. Letting out a deep sigh of contentment, he stared up at the stars and tried not to think how much more comfortable it was having Gerald here than Robbie. His lover never wanted to just sit and enjoy the night. He had to be moving, either dancing or fucking or something. And apparently, Gerald was good with just sitting too, as he sat relaxed and content to be quiet.

Head falling back against the cushion on the chair, Brett let the sounds of the falling night wrap around him. It would be far too easy to get used to this, but he'd be damned if he wouldn't enjoy at least this much while he had it.

BRETT looked up from preparing the fire under the old grill by the lake on his property for the annual fall cookout. His smile widened when he saw the pickup truck full of the kids who rode at the stables pull to a stop near the lake. The kids piled out, shouting greetings and questions in his direction.

"Yes, you can swim," he told them with a smile. "Just don't go out past the ropes. It drops off sharply after that."

A group of riders topped the nearby hill, pausing and milling about for a moment before they started down toward the picnic area. Several tables were set up under the trees that lined the cove, as well as a couple of awnings to keep the sun off. About twenty yards away there were hitching posts set into the ground in a large grassy area not pounded down by so many feet.

The riders who stopped and dismounted were mostly instructors; they'd brought mounts to give rides for family members who came to the party, but not to the farm on a regular basis. There were also a few other volunteer members of the staff, including Gerald, who tied Misfit on a long lead so she could graze. As a group they moved over to the picnic area that was already well populated.

Gerald approached the grill, a large knapsack over his shoulder. "I was told to deliver this," he told Brett. "And Jimmy's got another."

"Thanks," Brett said with a smile, opening the bag to see dozens of ears of corn. "I'll get these on the grill as soon as the fire settles down to coals. They take longer to cook than the burgers and dogs."

A slightly younger man joined them before Brett could say anything else, giving the stable owner a circumspect squeeze around the waist. "Hey, Robbie," Brett said. "I wasn't sure you'd be able to make it."

"I got away from work early," the artfully tousled man replied. "I wanted to be here for your big shebang."

"Well, let me introduce you around. Robbie, this is Gerald Saunders. He helps out around the stables on the weekends and quite a few evenings. Gerry, this is Robbie Chauncey."

"Hi," Gerald greeted, looking him over curiously.

"I'm surrounded by horse lovers, aren't I?" Robbie asked with a dramatic sigh. "So what can I do to help, lover? Since I made it all the way out here."

"Nothing," Brett replied. "Just enjoy yourself. I've got plenty of willing hands already."

Gerald raised a brow and adjusted his baseball cap before glancing to Brett. "I'm going to help the kids set up the bonfire," he said, gesturing at the big stacks of wood and branches that had been dumped on the other side of the camp inside a cleared dirt circle. "You can help if you want," he offered to Robbie, making an attempt to include him.

"I wouldn't know where to start," Robbie replied with a light laugh. "City boy through and through, I'm afraid. Sometimes I wonder why Brett puts up with me." He draped his arms around Brett's waist and smirked at Gerald over the redhead's shoulder. He'd heard far too much about "Gerry" over the past three months not to want to make his claim as obvious as possible.

Gerald's lips twitched as he recognized Robbie's tactics. "If you need anything just yell," he told Brett before looking back at the man hanging onto him. "Enjoy the picnic." Then he turned and walked off toward the kids who started running about at his direction.

"He'd be glad to show you what to do," Brett offered, shrugging away from Robbie just a little. "I'm going to be busy here with the cooking for awhile. Or you can just relax down by the lake."

Robbie's eyes flicked to Gerald in his beaten-up jeans and old T-shirt, and he shook his head. "No, I want to stay here with you," he asserted. "I took the time to look nice for you, and I wouldn't want to ruin it."

"You look nice to me no matter what," Brett promised, wondering idly if he'd made a mistake inviting Robbie to the cookout. It wasn't exactly a stay-clean experience most of the time.

Smiling brightly, Robbie pressed his lips against Brett's in a blatant display. "You need something nice-looking around this farm," he teased. Sort of.

Brett frowned into the kiss. "Robbie, there are kids around," he scolded softly. "Let's save the kissing for later, when the younger crew has gone home."

Robbie huffed and took a step back, wrinkling his nose a little as a herd of youngsters stampeded by. "I'll hold you to that," he promised, hoping that would be sooner rather than later.

Brett sighed. Yeah, he'd definitely made a mistake. "Let me get the food ready," he suggested. "The sooner I get that done, the sooner the kids will be ready to leave." Of course, that didn't count the bonfire after dinner or the games the kids usually played, but he didn't see any reason to try Robbie's patience that much just yet.

Across the camp, Gerald helped some of the smaller kids pick up broken branches as he supervised the older students moving the cut pieces. He kept glancing over to the grill, wondering at the stiff set of Brett's shoulders. When Robbie turned, the petulant look on his face explained it. Gerald chuckled.

"What's funny, Mr. Gerry?" little Patty asked as she scooped up another branch.

"Ah. You all working so hard, you know? Makes me very proud of you," Gerald covered.

"Since we're working hard, can we ride Misfit later?" she piped. "Buckeye is here, but I ride him all the time."

"I don't know about that," Gerald said awkwardly as they walked with full arms toward the growing pile of wood. "We'll have to ask your teacher."

"Okay," she said as she tossed her armful down and then made a beeline toward the grill.

"Oh boy," Gerald murmured. He'd forgotten that Patty's teacher was Brett.

When she got to the grill, Patty had to push past Robbie. "Mr. Brett? Mr. Brett?" she asked, practically bouncing.

"What's up, Patty?" Brett asked, grinning down at one of his more apt pupils in the five-year-old class. "Having fun?"

"Oh, yes," she enthused. "Mr. Gerry says to ask you if I can ride Misfit later since I'm working so hard now."

Brett pretended to consider for a moment. "I don't know. She's an awfully big horse. Do you think you can handle her?"

She nodded so hard Brett thought her head might fly off, and her jostling made Robbie step back a little.

"Tell you what," Brett suggested. "After dinner, we can ride her together. How's that sound?"

"Yay!" Patty squealed, running back to tell Mr. Gerry.

"You're going to ride and smell like horse all night," Robbie said with a sniff.

"I rode out here already," Brett pointed out, trying to keep hold of his temper. "And that's the only way I have to get back to the house once the cookout's over. I told you this was a farm gathering. If you didn't want to be outside and around the horses, you shouldn't have come."

"I was hoping you'd spend some time with me if I came out here," Robbie pointed out.

"And I will," Brett promised, "just as soon as I finish cooking dinner and get the bonfire started. I'm the host, not just another guest. I have to make sure everything's taken care of."

"All right," Robbie said with a put-on sigh. "I'll just drag a chair over so we can still talk."

Brett didn't mention that Robbie would end up smelling like wood smoke if he did that. He didn't want a scene. Not here, anyway.

Hours later, tons of food was cooked and eaten, games were played, and kids got horseback rides and swimming time. The sun was low in the sky, and families were packing up to leave. The instructor who'd driven the kids down in the pickup was loading them into the bed, and a few other vehicles took off as well, leaving just a group of farm volunteers behind.

Brett sighed in relief as he swung down off Misfit's back. He loved the cookouts, loved listening to the kids laugh and squeal as he cantered them around the field, but it was tiring. His back ached from the odd position of having a child sitting in front of him, throwing off his motion just enough to make it uncomfortable. Loosening Misfit's girth and hooking her back to the grazing line, he turned and surveyed the remaining guests. Everyone seemed to be enjoying themselves, beer having replaced the soft drinks now that the little ones were gone. Well, almost everyone.

Robbie was sitting in a bag chair he'd claimed—no way was he sitting on one of the dirty picnic table benches—and he was tapping the arm impatiently. When he saw Brett climb off the horse, he was up and by him quickly. "Can we go now?"

"The party's just starting," Brett protested. "Come on, baby. Relax a little and have a beer. It's starting to get dark. We can slip back into the woods, neck a little if you want. And then when everyone's gone, we can go back to the house and make love all night long."

Frowning, Robbie shook his head. "I've waited all day, Brett, and I'm tired of being outside. The bugs will just come out after dark. Let's go back to the house and neck there."

"How many times do I have to tell you I can't leave until everyone else does?" Brett asked in frustration.

"You've got all these people who work for you out here to keep an eye on things," Robbie retorted. "You know, you've acted like you don't want me here all day, and frankly, I'm tired of it."

"Look, I don't want to fight about this," Brett said tiredly. "Why don't you go home, and I'll come by your place tomorrow? We can go to that club you like so much and hang out there. My treat, since you spent the day with me today."

Robbie looked somewhat mollified, though it was obvious he was still put out. "Fine. Take me up to the house then." He smiled slightly, a plan developing.

"Hey, boss," Jimmy called. "I'm going to drive up to the house and get more beer. Do you need anything else while I'm up there?"

"No," Brett replied, "but Robbie could use a ride, if you don't mind."

Robbie's lips compressed angrily, and he turned and stomped off to the truck without another word. Within a minute, he and the truck were gone.

Brett let out a long, relieved sigh. With Robbie gone, now maybe he'd be able to enjoy the rest of the cookout. He glanced around, wondering where Gerald had disappeared to. Seeing him by the bonfire, he walked over and joined him. "Sorry I haven't been around much tonight. Are you having a good time?"

Gerald turned his chin and lowered the beer bottle from his lips. "Yeah, it's been great," he answered as he studied Brett's face. The other man looked worn out. "You work really hard to make it good, especially for the kids," he observed.

"Without the kids, I wouldn't have a business," Brett replied practically. "I have some adult classes, yeah, but the kids are by far the bulk of my customers." He chuckled. "And I love it. Can you tell?"

"Yeah, it's obvious," Gerald said with a grin. "And the kids are great. Patty taught me the corn-hole toss."

"She's a champion," Brett laughed, enjoying the flicker of firelight over Gerald's face. "I don't think anyone's beaten her yet."

"I sure didn't," Gerald said with a laugh before tilting his bottle back and emptying it. "So what's next for the party? I actually expected marshmallows."

"We can break out the S'mores if you really want," Brett chuckled. "I think they got packed in one of the saddle bags. Otherwise, it's just sit around and enjoy the beer until it's gone or everyone decides to jump in the lake."

Gerald actually bounced a little. "I've always wanted to toast marshmallows over a real fire!"

"All right," Brett agreed, throwing up his hands in surrender. "Let me see if I can find them. If not, we'll have to wait for Jimmy to get back with the truck unless you want to run up to the house on Misfit."

He dug around in the saddlebags, finding a bag of marshmallows, but no graham crackers or chocolate bars. "Well, what do you want? Just marshmallows or the whole shebang?"

"I'm happy with just marshmallows," Gerald said, poking around part of the small brush pile yet to be added to the fire in search of a long, straight branch.

"Don't use one of those," Brett cautioned. "They'll catch on fire. Get a fresh one off a tree." He reached in his pocket and pulled out his knife. "Here, use this. And get me one too, if you don't mind."

"Okay," Gerald said agreeably, and he walked off into the sunset-lit bower to find a couple of branches he liked.

Brett opened the plastic sack and checked the fire, knocking a few coals away from the main blaze so they could roast the marshmallows rather than charring them. He knew some people liked the treats blackened, but not him. He liked them a light, golden brown. Just the color Gerald's skin had turned after spending the summer outside helping around the farm.

That skin soon appeared right under his eyes as Gerald crouched next to him and held out the branches, his long arms set off by the light blue T-shirt he wore. "How about these?" Gerald asked.

"They're fine," Brett said, not even looking at the branches. He was too caught up in wondering where that thought came from. "Here." He handed Gerald a marshmallow, his eyes never leaving the strong arms in front of him.

Settling happily cross-legged near the fire, Gerald jabbed the marshmallow with a small chuckle and soon had it carefully over the flames. "This is great!"

"It'll be even better if you don't burn it," Brett said with a laugh, guiding Gerald's hand away from the flames to the hot coals. "This way, it gets a nice crusty outside while turning hot and gooey inside. And it doesn't burn."

"Ah, see, you're still giving me lessons," Gerald teased, moving the stick as directed.

"Once a teacher, always a teacher," Brett said, sticking his marshmallow next to Gerald's until it was just the right color. Bringing the sticky mess to his mouth, he ate it right off the end of the branch.

Gerald followed suit, grinning as he sucked the gooey marshmallow off his fingers. "I never thought a horseback-riding lesson would lead to something like this," he said, reaching across Brett for another white sugar puff.

"You never know where things will lead," Brett agreed softly, his breath catching as Gerald's shoulder brushed against his chest. It was an innocent gesture, but the effect it had on him was far from unassuming.

"You said it," Gerald agreed, pushing the second marshmallow on his stick. He glanced up at Brett to see the firelight coloring his skin warmer and setting a sparkle in his eyes. A thought occurred. "Hey, where's Robbie? Won't he want a marshmallow?"

"He left," Brett said flatly, not wanting to discuss his disgruntled lover. "I don't think he realized how much work I'd have to put into today."

"I'm sorry," Gerald said genuinely. "I'm sure I could have done more to help." He offered Brett his toasted marshmallow.

Or Robbie could have, Brett thought uncharitably. "You were a huge help," he said aloud, "and you were here to have fun too, not just to work. Don't worry about it. It wasn't your fault at all."

The sound of the truck returning drew their attention. Jimmy jumped out of the cab and pulled down another cooler of beer. Several of the remaining volunteers grabbed a bottle, but several others called their goodbyes, taking the horses they'd rode in on and heading back to the barn.

Gerald traded Jimmy a hot marshmallow for two beers, and he offered Brett one. "Well, sit down and rest a bit then. Doesn't look like everyone's leaving just yet."

"Maybe not for a couple of hours," Brett said, taking the beer and swigging it down. "There's no end time for the cookout. People just drift off as they get tired."

"We had barbecues in the backyard for family reunions," Gerald confided. "But it was nothing like this."

"This is a Sutcliffe Cove tradition," Brett explained. "I remember coming out here with my grandparents when they were still running the farm, and it was already a huge event. It just seems to get bigger and better every year."

"There had to be more than a hundred people here today," Gerald said. "I figured you'd done this before to get it all pulled together."

"Oh yeah, for as many years as I can remember. Most of the time, even when I wasn't living nearby, I'd come home for this weekend to help out."

"I'd certainly have done the same," Gerald said. He reached over Brett's lap to snag another marshmallow from the bag. "I'm going to eat all these and regret it tomorrow," he muttered, this time poking two onto the stick so he could make one for Brett too.

"We'll just have to work it off you in the morning," Brett suggested. "You are coming by in the morning, aren't you?" The thought of starting a Sunday without Gerald's smiling face didn't appeal at all.

"Planned on it," Gerald said as he stuck the stick above the glowing coals. "Although I might sleep in a little later than usual after today," he said with a smile.

"You can crash in my guest room if you want," Brett offered. "I put clean sheets on it earlier in case anyone had too much to drink and couldn't drive home, but it looks like everyone's pretty sober. You're welcome to use it. It'll save you some time tonight and in the morning."

Gerald shivered ever so slightly despite how heated his front was from the fire. He looked at Brett for a long moment and told himself he was reading into the words something that wasn't there. Of course Brett wanted him there on Sundays; he always needed the help, though he'd never make Gerald feel guilty about missing. "That sounds great. Thanks."

"Do you need a blanket?" Brett asked solicitously, seeing the shiver run down Gerald's back. "I've got some in the truck. They're saddle blankets, but they're clean."

"Oh...." Gerald swallowed and scrambled for something to say. "No, just too close to the coals, I guess. My backside is a lot cooler." With a sigh, he was glad his face was already flushed, because it would have been after that bonehead comment.

"Turn around," Brett insisted. "No need to be shy. Or cold, for that matter."

Gerald cleared his throat and shuffled on the ground so he mostly faced away. He brought his two toasted marshmallows with him and started pulling one off the stick, frowning as the browned outer layer slipped off, leaving the creamy clump of filling on the wood.

Brett chuckled. "Here, let me get you another one."

"This one's fine," Gerald said. He just lifted the stick to his lips and ate the marshmallow off like it was on a skewer. As he moved on to the second marshmallow, the hot, sticky sugar smeared over his lips and cheek, and Gerald laughed.

Brett tried to stifle his groan at the sudden image of licking the mess off Gerald's face. He shouldn't be having these kinds of thoughts. He had a lover, for heaven's sake.

"Hey, boss, we're heading home," Jimmy called, interrupting Brett's lusty fantasy. "See you on Monday!"

"Night, Jimmy," Brett called back. "Thanks for all your help today."

Gerald waved as well as the rest of the instructors loaded up into the truck and left, having taken the horses back to the stables a few hours ago. Only Misfit and Zach, another of the stable's horses, stood in the nearby meadow, snuffling in the grass.

"I'll give you a hand cleaning up," Gerald said as they stood next to the dying fire.

"There's not much left to do," Brett replied. "Jimmy took the trash bags and coolers back in the truck. All that's left is the bag of marshmallows." He glanced around, searching for an excuse to keep Gerald out there a little bit longer. "Hey, you want to go swimming? The water stays warm all night long this time of year."

"I don't have any trunks with me," Gerald said, though he cast a longing glance toward the water. It would have felt great after being hot and sweaty all day.

"So? Just wear your shorts and then put your jeans back on when we're done and you can throw them in my washer tonight," Brett suggested. "It's not like I've got trunks out here either."

Gerald blinked a few times before shrugging, "Okay," he said. "Swimming sounds good."

Making sure the embers were contained enough that they wouldn't blow sparks, Brett kicked off his boots and pulled his T-shirt over his head. He stripped down to his briefs and started for the lake. "Coming?"

Gerald swallowed and wasted several seconds staring at the firm ass walking away. "Uh- huh," he grunted before shaking himself and getting undressed. He followed Brett out to the edge of the cove, forcing himself not to ogle. But he wanted to. Damn, he wanted to.

Brett waded into the water to the waist, turning to watch Gerald walking into the water after him, his tight boxer briefs allowing Brett to see the outline of a sizable package in the moonlight. Oh, fuck, he wanted to have the right to reach out and touch. To distract himself, Brett turned away and swam out deeper into the lake, his long, steady strokes taking him away from temptation.

The water was warm, just as Brett said. But being wet with the breeze blowing sent goose bumps over Gerald's skin, and he could feel his nipples tighten. Clearing his throat slightly, he walked farther into the water until he could submerge up to the neck. He started swimming out to the other man. It was light enough to see in the shadows, but not so much that details of a body would be clear in the water.

Diving beneath the ropes he used to mark the safe area for the kids, Brett kept going a little further, treading water as he turned back to wait for Gerald. Just as he'd warned the kids, the bottom fell sharply there, making it impossible to stand, but not so deep that an adult couldn't touch bottom. "So how much farther do you want to go?" he asked when Gerald joined him.

"I'm a good swimmer," Gerald said, peering across the dark water at the other man. "Do you come out here often?"

"Sometimes here, sometimes the actual cove," Brett replied, "but that's too far to swim from here. I've canoed it a few times, though."

"So it's a pretty big body of water," Gerald concluded, moving closer in the water.

"About forty acres, I think," Brett said, "although that might have changed a little since the original surveys were done."

"And all untouched woodland. It's a treasure, especially in this day and age," Gerald said, shifting to let himself float. His torso and belly crested the water to bob on the surface.

"That's just the lake. The farm itself is even bigger. My parents used to joke about being able to sell it for a fortune if they weren't worried about being haunted by the family." Brett laughed, keeping his hands moving steadily to resist the temptation to touch the golden skin that glowed softly in moonlight.

Gerald smiled and tipped his head. "It's so quiet. You'd think you'd hear the city."

Brett shook his head. "Not here. Maybe up at the stables, but we're pretty much in the heart of the farm right now. We get the light pollution still, but not much in the way of noise."

"Not even much light," Gerald said, looking up at the trees that sheltered the water. "Except for the moon." He flopped over onto his belly to swim a few strokes away into a pool of light, where he turned back over to float again. "Although I'm not sure if this helps me see or not."

It helped Brett see. All too well. Floating as he was, Gerald's groin just broke the surface, the wet cloth doing nothing to hide the shape of what it covered. Brett couldn't decide if the other man was half-hard or seriously well-endowed. Either way, it did nothing for his equilibrium. "You'd notice the light pollution without the moon," he said hoarsely. "You can see the big constellations, but not the fainter stars."

Gerald looked up at the stars, wetting his hair as he let the water buoy him up. "I can sometimes make out constellations at the house. Orion, usually. Cassiopeia. Sometimes the Big Dipper." He let the water relax him and sighed happily.

"You'll see more than that out here. The Pleiades, Ursa Major and Minor, Scorpius." Brett chuckled. "Can you tell I was fascinated by astronomy when I was a kid?"

"If you lived here, I can understand why," Gerald said before righting himself so he could look at Brett. "You should come out here more often, if you enjoy it so much. You work all the time, seems like."

"The summer's the worst because I've got parents trying to figure out what to do with their kids all day, so they stash them out here. Once school starts back up, my days are a lot lighter, and I'll have more time for myself."

"So another month or so," Gerald translated, since this weekend was the Fourth of July.

"Yes. Six weeks at the most, depending on when the different schools start," Brett said. "Of course, then it'll be time to start getting everything ready for winter, but even with that, I'll have more free time."

Gerald smiled. "It never ends," he said, echoing Brett's sentiment from a few months ago when he started spending more time at the farm. "But you love it." Gerald ran his hands through his hair, before letting himself slide under the water to soak it all and get rid of some of the dirt and sweat he'd accumulated the whole day.

"I do," Brett replied honestly. Seeing Gerald rubbing at his head made Brett realize how sweaty he still felt, even with the swim. Sinking beneath the surface, he wet his head completely, giving it a shake as he resurfaced. "I can't imagine doing anything else."

Gerald watched Brett rise from the water and had to swallow. He was already rubbing himself under the water, trying to relieve a little of the tension. With a sigh, he let off, knowing it wouldn't do any good. Maybe Brett wouldn't notice. He had a boyfriend, after all, a pretty one too, so why would Brett look at him?

As close as they were in the water, Brett hoped Gerald wouldn't notice the erection tenting his briefs. He ought to be ashamed of himself, perving over Gerald when he'd all but sent Robbie away. He sighed. "Ready to head back?" he asked.

"Sure," Gerald answered, stretching out his arms to start the swim back to shore, both happy and disappointed to have something else to focus on besides Brett. And Brett's body.

Brett followed behind, taking one last opportunity to ogle Gerald's backside as it flashed above the water occasionally as he kicked. As they reached the shallows and Gerald stood to walk the rest of the way out, Brett bit back a groan, hoping Gerald wouldn't look back and see that Brett had popped a woody.

Shaking himself to get off the worst of the water, Brett walked straight to his discarded clothes, using his T-shirt to dry his legs before he slipped off his briefs and pulled up his jeans, the thicker fabric forcing his cock into uneasy submission.

Gerald deliberately didn't look back. While he wasn't erect, his body was certainly interested in the sight that he shouldn't be seeing. He laughed at himself silently for that thought. Gerald trudged out of the water, letting it stream off him, very aware of how his soaked briefs clung to him.

Before he could even stop himself, Gerald's eyes slid to the side and he saw Brett push off his wet briefs, revealing quite a healthy erection that made Gerald's mouth go dry. Snapping his chin around quickly to not be caught looking, he slid his fingers under his own briefs and dragged them down his legs.

As dressed as he could get with soaked briefs and a damp T-shirt, Brett turned around to see if Gerald was ready to head back, only to get a view of the other man's bare ass. He bit his lip as his mouth watered and his knees threatened to buckle. Damn, Gerald was a good-looking man! He forced himself to turn away and head toward Zach, hoping Gerald would follow of his own accord. He had no idea how he'd be able to sleep tonight knowing that ass was in his guest bed.

Jerking up his jeans and fastening them, Gerald figured he wouldn't be *too* uncomfortable on the ride back. He grabbed his wet briefs and wrung them out before stuffing them in his back pocket as he walked over to Misfit.

"Ready to hit the sack?" Brett asked lightly, cursing himself as soon as the words left his mouth. The image of the two of them entwined in bed was far too intimate for comfort, especially in the saddle.

Gerald got up on Misfit before yawning. "It's been a long day," he agreed. "Thanks for letting me stay. A drive would be a pain right now."

"You're always welcome," Brett offered automatically. "If you're here late, that is, or whatever."

"Or whatever?" Gerald asked mildly, his voice tinged with amusement.

"Or you have an early lesson, or… whatever," Brett said lamely, trying to cover his embarrassment. "It's there if you need it."

Gerald smiled as they got the horses moving. "Okay," he said. And he watched Brett sway in the saddle all the way back to the barn, trying to not shift too much in his own damp jeans.

When they got back, Brett settled Zach as quickly as he could, then helped Gerald finish up with Misfit. "You remember where the shower is, right?"

"Yeah, I'm good." Gerald headed over to the car and popped the trunk, pulling out his duffel bag of extra clothes before joining Brett on the porch. He'd started keeping one handy, given how dirty he tended to get working at the farm.

"If you need anything, just let me know," Brett offered, starting toward the kitchen and the back stairs to his bedroom.

Once alone in his room, Brett stripped down and walked into the connecting bathroom, hearing the water start in the bathroom below. He groaned at the thought of Gerald naked downstairs, washing away the sweat and dirt from the day, skin glistening with droplets of water as he bathed. "Fuck," he muttered, turning on the taps and stepping beneath the burst of cold water. It did nothing to diminish his erection since the water heated too quickly to be a true cold shower.

Squirting shampoo into his palm, Brett lathered his hair quickly. He tried to ignore the desire to jerk off, but he was pretty sure that was a lost cause. Tilting his head back to rinse the suds away, Brett caught a few of them in his hand and wrapped it around his aching cock.

It took an embarrassingly small number of strokes before he came hard, the creamy strands mixing with the suds and water to disappear down the drain. With a muttered curse, he finished washing, dried off, and pulled on a pair of cut-off sweats and a T-shirt. His conscience demanded he go check on his guest. His libido agreed wholeheartedly.

Gerald had shut the door behind him in the bathroom before muttering, "Guess I can't ask for a helping hand." He sighed and started wriggling out of the jeans sticking to his clammy skin. A shower was going to feel good. He stood under the hot water, letting it sluice away the last of the grime and sweat. He had one hand braced on the wall as he soaked his hair; the other hand moved the bar of soap across his chest slowly. Thoughts of the man upstairs preoccupied him.

Gerald wondered why Robbie hadn't stayed. Brett sure hadn't been happy about it. Humming slightly in thought, Gerald stayed distracted as the steam built up in the room around him. Finally dragging himself out of the shower, Gerald got dressed in the shorts and T-shirt he'd had in the duffel even though he was still damp, and he opened the door, stepping out while still drying his hair.

"Need anything else?" Brett asked, trying to bite back the groan at the sight of a wet, tousled Gerald emerging from the bathroom. "The bedroom's right across the hall, and the kitchen's back through there. Feel free to raid the fridge during the night."

Gerald stopped still, blinking at the other man. Brett was flushed and damp. He looked relaxed, much more so than before. Gerald wondered if it was from the hot shower or… something else. He swallowed hard and lowered the towel to hold it strategically in front of himself. "Ah, thanks," he said weakly as he saw visions of Brett in the lake with that smile.

"Well, if you're sure you're okay, I'll head back upstairs," Brett said. His voice was a little hoarse. "Dawn comes early."

Brett climbed the steps slowly, wishing he could've come up with an excuse to linger downstairs a little longer, enjoying the smell of his shampoo wafting off Gerald's warm body, but his mind had gone completely blank. Short of propositioning the man, he had no idea what else to say.

Gerald watched raptly as Brett turned and climbed the stairs. He just couldn't pull his eyes away from that ass. Abruptly he turned and fled into the guest room, pushing the door closed behind him. He dropped the towel where he stood as he let his eyes get used to the darkened room. Some moonlight came in the window, so it didn't take much, and as he stepped toward the bed he didn't notice the door slide back open partway.

Climbing onto the quilt, Gerald flopped and rolled to his back. He wasn't seeing the dark ceiling; he was seeing Brett standing there on the stairs. Looking touchable. Looking fuckable. Looking like he'd just gotten off, and oh my God, had Brett done that in the shower upstairs while he'd been showering downstairs? Gerald groaned and slid his hand into his shorts.

He curled his palm around his cock, sighing as he tightened his fingers around it. He was so turned on. Something about Brett upstairs jacking off while he was in the house made him hot and bothered. Groaning again, Gerald lifted his hips up against his fist, and his eyes fell shut.

His breathing picked up as he used both hands to play with himself, doing everything that felt good. He needed to come. He'd not done it for a couple days, and now he needed it. Really needed it. Without thinking, Gerald visualized himself in the shower, working his cock as the water rained down. When he opened his eyes, Brett stood in the shower in front of him, mirroring his movements, both their cocks hard and red. Gerald's moan was long and low as he licked his lips.

Brett was stripping off upstairs when he heard a sound he was pretty sure he'd never forget. That moan couldn't be anything but a sound of pleasure. Oh, fuck! Gerald was downstairs getting himself off in Brett's guest bed. Tomorrow, when he went to change the sheets, they'd smell not just like Gerald, but like Gerald's come. Brett thought he might never wash them. The smell alone would be fantasy material for a month.

With a sudden guilty pang, he remembered Robbie. He couldn't fantasize about one man when he was seeing another. It wasn't right. When another stifled groan filtered up to him, Brett almost whimpered in sympathy.

Oblivious to being overheard, Gerald licked his palm and pulled on his cock harder, the muscles in his legs tense as he fucked his fist. Now it was just about getting there, about coming, and the vision of the shower dissipated as Gerald bit his lip on a choked gasp as he climaxed in several short spurts, panting heavily each time before letting out a shaky groan and sigh.

Trying to control his breathing, Gerald turned to his side and curled up, knowing he needed to get the towel and clean up before he messed up the sheets. But it could wait. A minute or two. He yawned. He'd get it in just a minute. With a sigh he fell into a doze.

Four

GERALD padded out into the house proper, following the sounds and smells to the kitchen. He stopped in the doorway and rubbed his eyes.

"Hungry?" Brett asked, looking up at the sound of footsteps in the hallway. "Pancakes'll be done soon, and there's coffee in the pot if you want some."

"Mmm. Coffee," Gerald said with a yawn. "What time is it?"

Brett shrugged. "Dawn. The horses don't understand the idea of a clock. They just know when the sun comes up."

"You do too, huh?" Gerald said, sitting down with a mug and blinking blearily.

"Not a lot of choice in the matter," Brett replied. "Either I do it, or they start doing damage. I'd rather get up early."

Gerald frowned. "Damage? Like what?"

"They start kicking at the stall doors or the fence lines," Brett explained. "Shah actually broke one down about eight months ago. I overslept, not back in the routine of the farm yet, and he made his disapproval most clear."

Both Gerald's brows flew up. "Wow. I get cranky in the mornings without coffee, but nothing like that."

"Yeah, well, that's what I get for keeping a stallion around, but he pays for the disruptions in stud fees," Brett replied.

"That's not disruption; that's property damage. Be sure to include that in your taxes as facility upkeep."

"Really?" Brett asked, surprised. "I've never thought about that before."

"Expense of conducting business," Gerald said with a shrug before taking another drink of coffee. "Doesn't your accountant tell you these things?"

"What accountant?" Brett asked.

Gerald stared at him, utterly appalled. "You don't have an accountant?" he asked as his coffee cup thumped to the table, and the liquid sloshed a little over the rim.

"No, I keep the books. Income, expenses, it's not that hard," Brett said.

It was a long moment before Gerald shook himself. "Did your par—?" He cut himself off. "Sorry. None of my business."

"Not that I'm aware of," Brett answered anyway. "As far as I know, all the records are in the office through there, although they did tell me copies of the year-end reports were all in a safe deposit box too, just in case anything ever happened here at the house."

Gerald had a seriously pained look on his face. He opened his mouth to say something, but closed it right back. "Okay," he murmured.

"What?" Brett asked. "Is something the matter?"

"It's just… how much are you missing in deductions?" Gerald blurted. "What about quarterly filing to reduce your tax burden? Investment in facilities and maintenance? Chargebacks against gross income…."

"Whoa!" Brett cried. "Over my head! Is all that stuff really necessary?"

"Yes!" Gerald retorted. "If your output exceeds input, you technically aren't making money so you'd get tax money back!"

"Fine," Brett said with a huff. "What do you charge?"

"Charge?" Gerald asked blankly. "Keeping a charge account can be a good way to track monthly expenses so you can project figures ahead a year."

"No," Brett groaned, rolling his eyes. "How much do you charge to handle someone's books? If you're really going to make me deal with all this stuff, you're going to do it for me. I don't know any other accountants, and I don't want to let a stranger handle this."

"I work in an office," Gerald objected. "I'm not an independent CPA. I wouldn't have any idea what to charge."

Brett frowned. "Can I request your services if I contact your office?"

Gerald's brow furrowed. "You don't need to do that. Just let me know what you need."

"I don't even know!" Brett exclaimed. "I thought I was doing just fine on my own."

"I'm not saying you're not doing a good job. Just that you might be missing out on so much." Gerald fretted.

"Well, could you glance over them, give me an idea of how much we're talking so I can decide if hiring an accountant would pay for itself in savings?" Brett asked.

Visibly relaxing, Gerald nodded. "That's no problem at all," he said. "But I'm afraid it will have to wait a couple weeks. I'm leaving Tuesday on vacation."

Brett's face fell. "I'll push the rest of this month's lessons off until next month, then," he said practically. "So where are you going?"

"St. Louis to visit my grandparents," Gerald said, picking up his coffee mug again. "The trip is long enough they can't make it, so I try to go a couple times a year."

"Wow, you're a long way from home," Brett commented. "What brought you up here?"

"Actually, this is home. My parents are here, and I've lived here all my life," Gerald said.

"And we've never met until now? Greenwich isn't that big!"

Gerald shrugged. "Who knows? I did go to New York for college."

Brett laughed. "And it's not like I've lived here much in the past ten years. I went and sowed my wild oats, as my grandmother used to say, until my parents were ready to retire. I suppose it isn't all that unbelievable." He pushed back his plate. "Ready to get to work?"

"Yeah," Gerald said with a nod. "I'll grab some clothes and meet you in the barn." He stood, gathered his dishes, and Brett's, and took them to the sink.

Brett nodded and headed out to get to work. When Gerald joined him a few minutes later, he'd already started loading the hay wagon so they could feed the horses.

Pausing several feet away, Gerald watched as Brett hefted the large bales, the smooth movements telling of long habit. He wondered how heavy those bales were. Hay was light, right? He felt somewhat apprehensive, studying the blocks. He'd broken one up before to help feed the horses, but he'd not actually picked one up.

And watching the muscles bunch under the often-washed, close-fitting fabric of Brett's shirt, Gerald would lay a good bet that those bales were heavier than they appeared. He fidgeted a little and sighed, pushing away thoughts about Brett's body creeping back from the night before. "How can I help?" he asked, needing to get his hands busy.

"Grab some bales and let's fill this wagon. The fuller it is, the fewer trips we have to make." As he spoke, he tossed another bale onto the cart with the ease of much practice.

"Ohhhhkay," Gerald drew out, eyeing a bale as he drew on his gloves. He squatted and slid his hands under the twine, using his legs to lift the bale. "Geez, Brett, this thing weighs a ton!" But he wrestled it over to the wagon.

Brett chuckled. "Yeah, I guess they do, but I've been tossing them around since I was old enough to lift them. I don't even think about it anymore."

"Reminds me of moving full Bankers Boxes," Gerald said as he got the bale up into the wagon. His eyes strayed to the side, watching Brett easily lift another bale and toss it on top of the one Gerald had just settled.

Brett laughed again. "C'mon," he urged, lifting the wagon and starting down the aisle. "Let's get the horses fed."

"That I know I can do," Gerald said as he followed along.

GERALD steered the car through traffic, annoyed that it was taking so long. He'd already been held up at the office longer than usual since it was his first day back after a two-week vacation; he was late for his self-appointed arrival time at the farm. He was in such a hurry that he'd passed on going home to change clothes since he still had his suitcase in his trunk. He'd just get changed at the farm. He'd long since started leaving his boots and gloves in one of the tack closets.

Despite his slight annoyance, he was cheered by the fact that he'd soon be back at Sutcliffe Cove. After only a few days away, he'd become aware that he was missing something. It was a few days later when walking with his grandmother at a lovely park that he realized it was the farm; he'd been spending so much time there that it had become a part of his life. Unexpected, for sure, but welcome once he accepted it as how it would be from now on.

Gerald had to snap out of his thoughts and hit the horn when another car cut him off, and he made himself focus on his driving.

Brett cursed under his breath when he caught himself staring down the lane to the highway for the tenth time already in the past twenty minutes. It was far too early for Gerald to show up, even if he left work early and came directly here. It was just that he'd become such a fixture at the farm. Brett hadn't realized how much until his friend left for two weeks of vacation. It was a planned, announced absence. He knew exactly when Gerald would be leaving and when he planned to return. He knew where he was going and who he was going to see. They'd talked about it before he left. It hadn't made his absence any easier.

"Stop acting like a girl with her first crush, Sutcliffe," he scolded himself softly as he made himself go back to mucking stalls. Misfit stuck her head out, looking at him expectantly. "I don't know when he'll get here, girl," he told her. "He's supposed to be here tonight, but that could be any time between now and midnight."

The worst part was that Robbie got a promotion at work and would be moving from the local office to the corporate headquarters in Atlanta. So on top of missing his friend, he was horny, a particularly bad combination where his temper was concerned. Never mind that he probably would have ended things before long after Robbie's display at the bonfire, but the man had still been good for releasing tension, and that hadn't happened.

It was almost an hour later by the time Gerald pulled into the parking lot and got out of the car, paying no mind to his dress shoes in the gravel as he straightened his jacket out of habit.

Brett refused to go out when he heard the car enter the lot. Misfit's excited whinny was the first sign that Gerald was finally here. Grinning from ear to ear, Brett walked out into the parking lot to greet his friend, stopping dead in his tracks when he got a good look at the other man.

Damn! Gerald was an attractive guy in jeans and a T-shirt, covered in dirt and sweat (or in a lot less), but in a suit, he was breathtaking. Letting out a low whistle, Brett crossed to the other man's side. "I'd hug you," he said, taking refuge in teasing and hoping his sudden erection wasn't too terribly obvious beneath his loose work jeans, "but I'm afraid I'll ruin your pretty suit."

Gerald turned his chin and laughed as a grin broke free. "Screw the suit, man," he said, slinging an arm around Brett's shoulders.

"God, I've missed you." Brett laughed, hugging Gerald tightly. "And I'm pretty sure I'm not the only one. Misfit's been even more crotchety than usual."

Closing his arms around the other man, Gerald squeezed in return. He was happy to see Brett, and it hit him then that the man had become probably the closest friend he had. "I missed you too, and that prima donna," he said before stepping back. He swallowed as he took in the sight of the man, and his gut clenched a little. Whoa.

"Go say hello to her before she kicks down the stall door," Brett insisted. "You can tell me all about your trip later. I'll even make you dinner, although I'm sure it won't compare to your grandmother's home cooking."

Gerald raised an eyebrow. "You don't have to do that," he objected mildly as he popped the trunk of his car and started digging into his suitcase. "But I wouldn't mind the time to visit. I realized about halfway through the trip that something was missing. Made me actually realize how much I'm out here."

"Well, the only other option is take-out Chinese," Brett replied, a smile tugging at his lips at the thought that Gerald had actually missed him. He scolded himself, reminding his overeager libido that Gerald was probably referring to Misfit. "The barn was empty without you hanging around all the time."

Gathering his clothes to his chest, Gerald shut the trunk and paused to look at Brett speculatively. "I wasn't talking just about Misfit," he said clearly. He was certainly glad Brett had noticed he was gone; he wanted Brett to know that Gerald had missed *him*, not just the horses.

Brett's grin widened. "In that case, I'll definitely cook you dinner." And if dinner and drinks led to something more, well, he certainly wouldn't complain.

Gerald's smile was wide. "You're on." He turned and made his way to the house, bouncing a little on the steps as he went in to change clothes.

Whistling happily, Brett went back to work, already anticipating dinner. He really did want to hear about Gerald's trip. He also wanted a chance at more. He'd held off before when he thought Gerald was straight and because of Robbie, but both of those reasons no longer applied.

Walking past Shah's stall, Brett grinned at his stallion. "I think one of us might be getting lucky tonight, old man, and it isn't going to be you."

Shah shook his mane at Brett as if to say he had no idea what the man was talking about. If he wanted to get lucky, he'd just jump the fence and join the mares.

WASHING his hands in the barn sink after feeding the horses, Gerald tipped his head from side to side as he stretched out a bit. He'd had a good visit with Misfit but just a short ride; he didn't want to overdo it on his first day back. And now he was looking forward to dinner… and Brett.

"Want to grab a shower while I get dinner going?" Brett asked Gerald, flipping off the lights in the stable. "It'll take me a good half an hour to have it done."

"Sure. I've got more clothes in the car," Gerald said, shutting off the water and peering through the dimly lit building as he walked out of the closet in a pair of clogs he used to get around after shedding his boots.

Brett tossed his own boots in the mudroom off his front porch and padded barefoot up the stairs to change clothes and wash up enough to cook. Thinking of his hopes for the rest of the evening, he decided he'd better take a quick shower, just in case. As the hot water ran down his shoulders, he refused to imagine Gerald in the downstairs bathroom in the same state.

Finished with his shower, Brett dressed quickly and went back downstairs to start cooking. He could hear the water still running in the guest bathroom and had to stop himself from imagining Gerald wet and naked. Robbie had been fun—not to mention convenient—but they hadn't had enough in common to make a real go of a relationship. Gerald, on the other hand.... Brett rolled his eyes at himself and started putting together the squash casserole. He'd throw a couple of steaks on the grill and that would be dinner. With a grin, he popped the top on a beer, wondering if Gerald would prefer wine instead. He'd have said no until he saw Gerald in a classy suit today. Now he wasn't so sure.

Gerald discovered once his eyes closed as he ducked his head under the water that he could see Brett inside his eyelids and the rugged sight made his belly cramp. His hand strayed to his cock, and he sighed after a slight rub. No reason to pursue it, he told himself, although his inner voice was weak. Brett was taken, he reminded himself. Just because he'd been gone two weeks didn't make things change. With a soft groan he let go of his half-hard cock and grabbed the soap.

After toweling off, Gerald finger-combed his hair and separated his clothes. He frowned a little when he didn't find boxer briefs and then shrugged. Wouldn't hurt him to go without for an evening. He pulled on a pair of soft khakis and ducked his head to slip the casual button-down shirt over his head, and he was ready. Barefoot, he walked out and around the corner to enter the kitchen.

"Feel like tossing a salad?" Brett asked when Gerald joined him. "And there's beer in the fridge, or I can open a bottle of wine if you'd rather."

"I prefer beer, but wine is okay if you want some," Gerald said as he changed directions to go to the fridge just to Brett's side. He hummed slightly in question as he bent over to look through the shelves for cans or bottles.

Brett held up his own beer, now almost empty. "No, beer's definitely my preference too." Deciding he needed another one right now, he crowded Gerald from behind, reaching around him to snag another longneck bottle. "At least where drinks are concerned."

Before Gerald knew it, his hand was gripping the fridge door hard as the press of Brett's body sent a bolt of arousal through him. He silently scolded himself and cleared his throat a little nervously before getting a bottle for himself and standing straight… which put him right up against Brett's solid body behind him.

Brett felt Gerald's surprise, but he made no move to push away, giving Brett the courage to lean even closer. "Actually," he mused, his breath fluttering against Gerald's ear, "I like my men a lot like my beer. Long, dark, and smooth."

Gerald shivered, and he sighed soundlessly as his body responded right away to the stimulus. No way was he moving, not yet. "You've got good taste then," he rasped, hoping Brett didn't think he was being vain.

"Very good taste," Brett agreed, his lips brushing the bristly skin of Gerald's cheek. He could still smell the aftershave the other man had used that morning, but the five o'clock shadow was definitely there in full force. He wasn't about to complain since his own scruff was far more than just a shadow.

Unconsciously purring, Gerald licked his bottom lip. His hand clutched at the cool glass bottle in his hand. "Maybe I should check just to make sure," he said boldly, his voice still deep and rough. By the tone of Brett's voice, Gerald was pretty sure Brett wasn't teasing.

"Maybe you should," Brett agreed huskily, bumping his hips against Gerald's as he set his beer on the counter, wanting both hands free. "Turn around."

Gerald shifted, the cool air of the open refrigerator sweeping down his bare feet as he turned to face Brett. His own pulse was racing, and he could feel the flush in his cheeks, but Gerald already knew he wanted this. Wanted something. Just to have a hint of what it would be like with Brett, if nothing else.

Brett slid his lips against Gerald's, wishing he hadn't drunk the beer earlier so he wouldn't have any taste on his tongue but Gerald's. He took his time, lingering over the slightly parted lips, licking at their curves, feeling Gerald's gasping breath wash over his moist lips. Gerald's pink tongue snaked out, more temptation than Brett could stand. He crushed their mouths together, invading forcefully, his arms going around Gerald's waist to pull their bodies together tightly. Inwardly, he crowed at the matching erection he could feel in Gerald's pants.

Gerald moaned into Brett's mouth, his eyes falling shut as he moved one hand to close over the back of Brett's neck while the other joined the effort to pull their bodies closer together. It was that hard bump of their bodies that dragged the wanting sound from him, and he swiveled from side to side, rubbing their groins together. Brett was just as hard as he was, and it made his own cock twitch.

"Gerry," Brett groaned against the other man's mouth. He tore his lips free, his forehead resting against Gerald's. He snatched the beer out of the other man's hand and put it on the counter next to his. He didn't want anything interfering with whatever happened next. "Why'd we wait so long to do this?" He didn't give Gerald a chance to reply, capturing his lips again in a continuation of the torrid kiss.

Pushing his tongue into Brett's mouth, Gerald explored and stroked as the heat tumbled through him, ratcheting up the tension and anticipation in the air around them. His hand left Brett's neck, combing down the other man's back and pulling the T-shirt free of his waistband so he could touch bare, warm skin at the base of his spine.

Brett took a couple of steps back, drawing Gerald with him so he could turn him out of the refrigerator and against the countertop, letting the fridge door swing shut. He sucked on the invading tongue eagerly as his hands mimicked Gerald's, one sliding beneath the soft cotton shirt, the other moving downward to grab a handful of strongly muscled ass.

Huffing out a surprised breath, Gerald went with the motion and didn't let go, diving back into the hot, wet kiss with enthusiasm. He arched under Brett's hands, moaning as he sucked on Brett's lower lip.

The timer buzzed, interrupting them. Brett moaned into the kiss, not wanting to break the contact. "Casserole," he murmured against Gerald's lips. "Oven."

Reluctantly pulling back from Brett's mouth, Gerald took two shaky steps to the side and wiped his lips with the back of his hand. He was a little shell-shocked, to be honest. He knew he'd wanted Brett, desired him and his body. But Gerald hadn't expected this strong of a response to him.

Brett's hands shook a little as he pulled the dish out of the oven, pleased to see it brown and bubbling. He set it on the stove and turned back to see the odd expression on Gerald's face. "You all right?" he asked. "Did I come on too strong?"

Gerald shook his head and laughed softly, perhaps a little nervously. "Just didn't expect it," he said with a small shrug.

"And now that you do expect it?" Brett pressed.

A whirl of thoughts went speeding through Gerald's analytical brain, weighing pros and cons, thinking of possible problems, reviewing how he came to this. Then he frowned. "What about Robbie? That guy you've been dating all these months?"

"He got a promotion while you were gone," Brett said. "He'll be moving to Atlanta in another week or so. We had a good time together, but it wasn't enough to keep him from taking the job or to convince me to move. He isn't in the picture anymore."

"And now all of a sudden I am?" Gerald asked, confused more than anything. Then a thought occurred. "Is this because I was wearing a suit when I got here?" he asked. "You want someone like him who looks nice and put together and formal like that?"

"What?" Brett asked. "What are you talking about? I realized how much I missed you while you were gone, how much of a fixture you've become in my life. You're far more a part of it than Robbie ever was, even before this kiss. It just took me until you were gone to see that."

Gerald realized he was reading too much into something insignificant. He smiled lopsidedly. "Sorry. Just surprised, is all. I feel the same way, actually. It's just that you've always been with him since I started coming here."

"Yeah, I guess I have." Brett shrugged. "We had a good time together, but it was never all that serious. He didn't ride and wasn't interested in learning." And if that hadn't been a clue how ultimately unsuited they were for each other, he didn't know what was. He just wished he'd recognized it sooner. "Of course, I thought you were straight until the first day you rode Misfit. You missed every hint I dropped."

Gerald actually flushed a little more. "I don't catch a lot of stuff like that. Doesn't occur to me, I guess." He whooshed his hand over the top of his head.

"I guess I'll have to stop being subtle then," Brett teased, crossing back to Gerald's side and kissing him lightly. "Is that obvious enough for you?"

Instead of answering verbally, Gerald tipped his head to catch Brett's lips again, this time in a more fervent kiss. They were both breathing a little harder when he finally broke away. "I'd say so," he drawled, his hands curled about Brett's waist.

"So we have two choices as far as I can tell," Brett mused, pulling back enough to breathe again. "We can go rescue the steaks from the grill and eat," his stomach rumbled loudly as if to illustrate the necessity of that at some point, "or we can leave them to burn and fuck each other silly."

Gerald laughed; it was clearly a happy sound. "Let's eat first. Otherwise we'll just have to stop later," he said with a raised brow. He had no idea what "later" would entail, but he was looking forward to having Brett close.

Brett groaned even as his stomach growled again. The thought of letting Gerald go when he finally had him in his arms was almost more than he could stand. Grinning suddenly, he kept an arm around the brunet's waist, dragging him along as he headed for the grill outside by the porch.

Gerald chuckled as Brett pulled him outside. "I'm not going anywhere, Brett, really," he said. He leaned to press his lips to the other man's ear. "I'm a little invested in sticking around," he murmured.

"Yeah, but you've been gone for two weeks, and I've waited almost five months to get my hands on you," Brett explained. "I'm not letting go anytime soon!"

Laughing again, Gerald leaned to steal another kiss. "Grill the steaks," he said as he pried himself loose. "I'll make it worth your while."

Brett pouted as he walked down the steps to the grill, ignoring the dogs who tangled around his ankles looking for a handout. His sister the vet had lectured him too many times about the dangers of table food for him to consider sneaking them anything, even when she wasn't around. Somehow she always knew.

Finally allowing himself the pleasure of watching Brett's ass in the close-fitting jeans he favored, Gerald found that he was really happy with this turn of events. He had a close friend who he was attracted to who felt the same way. He had a decent job that he liked. And he had Misfit to keep him on his toes. Although he thought Brett would be doing that as well.

Flipping the steaks on the grill, Brett turned back to look at the man sitting on his porch. Gerald had picked the same chair his mother always sat in to watch his father grill once she'd finished everything else inside, and the memory resonated within him. He knew it was way too soon to be thinking such thoughts, but the idea of having Gerald sitting there every night—or at least every time he grilled—appealed to something buried deep in his soul. He'd pushed the idea of permanence aside for the years he'd spent wandering around the country, working odd jobs here and there, because he always knew he'd return to Sutcliffe Cove.

In the time he'd been back, Brett had been so busy with his changes at the farm that he hadn't had time for more than the occasional one-night stand and then the casual thing he'd had with Robbie. Now, though, finding the time suddenly seemed of vital importance.

Noticing Brett's gaze on him, Gerald offered him a smile. "Anything I can help with?"

"Nah," Brett said with a shake of his head. "Just let them sit, flip them a few times, then eat."

"Want to eat out here? I'll bring the stuff from the kitchen," Gerald said as he unfolded himself from the comfortable chair.

"That'd be great, although you'll have to ignore the dogs," Brett told him. "They beg. I haven't given them anything even once since I've been home, but they still beg."

Gerald noted the two sitting at Brett's feet, giving him their rapt attention. "Yeah, okay," he said as he walked inside to get the casserole, beer, plates and flatware.

Brett flipped the steaks, amazed at how comfortable it was having Gerald there. It felt *right,* like it was meant to be. The thought scared him. What would happen if Gerald didn't feel the same way? Telling himself to stop jumping at shadows, he smiled when Gerald came back out. "How do you like your steak?"

"Whatever, as long as it's hot through," Gerald said, setting down the dishes and walking over to the grill with two plates.

"Then it should be just about done," Brett replied, flipping the steaks one more time. "Another minute or two and we can eat."

Gerald stood next to him, just watching, enjoying how easy this was. No nerves, no apprehension of being around a new person, because Brett… wasn't. Brett was a good friend already, and for him, that was more than enough. "If it's done right I won't need steak sauce," Gerald joked.

"Good thing," Brett retorted, "since I don't keep any at the house. My mom always said steak sauce was for people who didn't know how to cook beef."

"Ha! You understand!" Gerald crowed, bouncing in place. "Waitresses always give me a blank look when I tell them that."

"One more way we're perfect for each other," Brett rejoiced, the words slipping out before he could censor them.

A different, softer smile curved Gerald's lips. He turned and leaned against the house, standing next to the grill facing Brett. "Perfect?"

Brett shrugged diffidently. "My horses like you, my dogs like you, we share the same taste in beer and in steaks. Sounds pretty perfect to me." He didn't mention the incredible chemistry that exploded between them when they kissed earlier, but it was in the forefront of his mind.

"Mmm. No comment about how well we clicked tonight, I notice," Gerald said as he sat down at the table.

"I figured that went without saying," Brett said. He took the steaks up and carried the plates to the table, reveling in the freedom to lean over and kiss Gerald as he set one down in front of him.

Gerald's eyes were bright with pleasure when Brett parted from him. "I think I'm really going to enjoy this," he said, not taking his eyes off the other man.

"I'm glad to hear it." Brett took a seat and cut into the steak, glaring at the dogs when they whined pitifully at his feet. "Off the porch," he ordered firmly. "Your food's in your bowls in the barn."

Gerald chuckled. He turned in his seat, scratched their ears, then pushed and shooed them away. "Go on now," he said firmly, pointing toward the barn. Tails hanging, the dogs sulked off the porch.

"Damn, they make me feel guilty every time I do that," Brett said. "I know it's healthier for them, but it sure isn't easier for me."

"You're a big pushover," Gerald teased. "I've seen the kids do it to you in the barn with chores too."

"Yeah, I know." Brett sighed. "You'll just have to stay around and be the bad cop since I have no willpower."

"If it means I get more of your time to myself, I'll do it," Gerald agreed as they dug in. He'd wanted it before, really, just to visit and to learn more about horses. But now he craved that time, especially because Brett was his for more than just visiting.

"Keep looking at me like that, and I'll give you anything you ask for," Brett warned, his insides melting at the covetous look on Gerald's face. The thought that the other man wanted him still boggled his mind.

"Looking at you like what?" Gerald asked curiously, studying Brett as much as he wanted, now that he didn't have to worry about being caught at it.

"Like you want to eat me alive," Brett said hoarsely, desire curling wildly in his gut.

"Mmm. Good to know I telegraph things so much," Gerald commented as he cut up his steak and took another bite. "Duly noted."

Nonplussed, Brett returned to his steak, not quite sure what to make of Gerald's response. He'd been hoping for a little more… well, enthusiasm. Gerald only lasted several bites and a few minutes before pushing the plate away, standing, and pulling Brett up out of his chair and into his arms.

Gerald's action surprised Brett almost as much as the realization earlier in the evening of how badly he'd missed the man. He didn't have time to reflect on it, though, because he was in Gerald's arms being thoroughly kissed.

"I was teasing," Gerald murmured when their lips finally parted. "I do want to eat you alive." His hands dragged down Brett's sides familiarly.

"Have you had enough dinner?" Brett asked roughly, his voice breaking with desire. "Because I'm not hungry for steak anymore."

Gerald swallowed hard as his pulse sped. "It'll reheat," he agreed.

The epicure in Brett protested the abuse of good meat, but he had far more pressing needs at the moment. Like taking Gerald to bed and fucking him. Or maybe being fucked senseless himself. Or both. "The dogs can have it for all I care."

Gerald laughed breathlessly as he walked backward, pulling Brett along with him inside the house. "I'll buy you another steak." Seeing how much Brett wanted him was really turning him on, and he wanted to do something about it. "C'mere and touch me," Gerald invited bluntly.

"Where? How?" Brett asked. "Tell me what you like."

"Here? Or is there a bedroom somewhere you'd prefer?" Gerald asked, eyes sparkling with amusement. "You can touch me however you want. I'm sure I'll enjoy it."

"Bedroom," Brett declared shakily, wondering how he'd gone from being the one in control to being the one asking for advice. He hadn't gotten here by being tentative. It was time to remember that. "No lube down here."

"Definitely the bedroom then," Gerald said with a sober nod.

Brett led him through the rambling house to the back steps that led directly up to his bedroom. He'd remodeled soon after moving in, almost doubling the size of the room and giving him direct access to the main level. It was the one room in the house that bore his stamp. "Bedroom," he declared, turning to pull Gerald into his arms again.

"Good," Gerald rasped as their bodies bumped again. "Didn't know if you wanted to be stripped down in front of those windows downstairs, much less on the back porch," he said as his hands slid back under Brett's shirt to grasp at the heated skin.

"Nobody around for miles to see," Brett said with a shrug, "but the bed's more comfortable than the couch anyway. Neither of us are exactly small." He worked his hand between them, loosening a couple of buttons on Gerald's shirt before pulling it over his head. "And I won't be the only one stripped down."

Gerald certainly agreed, since the next moment his lips were on Brett's and his hands were unfastening Brett's jeans.

Brett unbuckled Gerald's belt, popped the button, and pulled down the zipper. He slid his hand inside, expecting to encounter fabric, but he only found hot, hard flesh. He groaned into the kiss, his knees turning to water at the thought that Gerald had gone commando for him.

"Aww, fuck," Gerald groaned, the rare profanity escaping him when Brett touched him. He unzipped Brett's jeans and started pushing at them. He needed them off. He needed his own pants off. Everything off, now!

Brett shimmied his jeans off his hips, pushing his briefs down too. He grabbed his T-shirt, ripping it over his head, reaching for Gerald even before it hit the ground. Later, he'd take time to look, to admire, but for now, he needed skin against skin. Nothing else would do.

Gerald wrapped himself around the other man, trying to touch as much as he could as they sealed their mouths together; the slide of their skin sending sparks along his nerve endings. He pulled away from Brett's lips and moved his mouth to the other man's neck, sucking and licking as he tasted it.

Brett's head fell back, baring his neck to more of the delicious scrape of Gerald's stubble across his flesh. He shuddered in delight, desire swamping him with its urgency. His hands clawed at Gerald's back, urging him on.

Dragging his lips and teeth along Brett's throat, Gerald bit down gently and sucked above the other man's collarbone as his hands explored Brett's chest, then belly, then the hard length that prodded his thigh. "Mmmm. Want this," he said throatily. "Want you."

"Yes," Brett hissed, arching into the provocative caress. "Anything you want."

"Good thing I'm such a good guy," Gerald muttered as he licked along the shell of Brett's ear. "Otherwise I'd take advantage." His hands moved to blatantly squeeze Brett's ass. "On the other hand…." He shifted and pushed Brett backward and down onto the bed and then climbed atop him without stopping his wet assault of Brett's now-swollen lips.

"Please," Brett begged. "Take advantage!" His hips tipped up, his body adding its own plea to his words.

Gerald smiled but tipped his head to one side as he looked down at his soon-to-be lover and forced himself to focus. "Seriously, for a minute. We have to be safe, you know. Is it okay for me to put my mouth on you? Or do we need to use something? Besides a condom."

"I'm clean," Brett assured him hoarsely. "I haven't had unprotected sex since I was too young to know better, and I've been tested regularly just to be safe. You can put your mouth wherever you want."

A soft smile spread on Gerald's lips. "I have physicals every year for the insurance at work," he said with a nod. "So we're both good." The smile pulled into a smirk as he started dragging his hands down all the flesh below him. "Scoot up," he said as he patted Brett's rump, wanting him all the way on the bed.

Brett shifted at Gerald's urging, lying back on the bed. "So," he asked, "top or bottom?"

Gerald gave him an evil grin. "Both," he said before swooping down to drag his tongue from Brett's balls to the tip of his cock.

Brett's hips bucked up at the unexpected contact. His eyes rolled back in his head, and it was all he could do not to come on the spot. "Warn a guy next time," he gasped.

"Where's the fun in that?" Gerald asked with a satisfied hum before lowering his head to suck Brett's cock between his lips.

Hard hands closed around his hips, reminding Brett that while Gerald looked damn good in a suit, he wasn't a man of leisure. The hot, wet suction left Brett groaning, wanting more, wanting to thrust long and hard into Gerald's throat, but the hands held him down. Fingers tangling in the sheets, he fought for control, trying to draw this out a little longer.

He wanted Gerald too badly for there to be much chance of success in that, though. "Close," he moaned. And Gerald responded by humming and increasing the suction, deliberately trying to push Brett over the edge while he watched.

It worked. The vibrations were enough to trigger Brett's climax, his release coming out of him in several long spurts, filling Gerald's mouth and dribbling down his chin. All the tension left his body as the suckling gentled, satiation filling him. Brett reminded himself firmly that his lover—they were lovers now, right?—was still unsatisfied. "So what can I do for you?" he husked.

Gerald crawled back up Brett's body to kiss him, the flavor of Brett's come still coating his tongue. "I'm not averse to the same in kind," he murmured once pulling back. "And I'd certainly enjoy nailing you into the mattress."

Brett sucked his flavor out of Gerald's mouth, incredibly turned on by the fact that Gerald had let him come down his throat. "You won't hear me complaining either way," he replied, "but it's been awhile since I've bottomed, so nail me carefully at first, yeah?"

"I can do careful," Gerald said as he dipped his head to drop soft kisses along his cheekbones and jaw. "Want to please you as much as please myself."

"Lube's in the drawer by the bed," Brett offered, legs parting in silent offering as he arched into the gentle caress. He wished he'd shaved that morning so his whiskers didn't interfere with the feeling of Gerald's lips against his skin. A grin broke out on his face. He'd have to buy a new razor if he was going to be shaving every day.

Gerald shifted to the side to pull open the drawer. "What's the grin for?" he asked. "Something besides the obvious?" His eyes glinted with humor.

"Just thinking I might have to start shaving more often now that I'll be seeing my lover on more than just rare occasions," Brett admitted.

"I certainly hope it's more than rare occasions," Gerald said. "But I love the feel of your scruff against my skin." He dipped his head to rub their cheeks together.

"Well then," Brett said with a grin. "Just enough to keep from looking totally disreputable."

Gerald smiled and leaned to pull out a tube of lubricant and looked back at Brett. "Condom or no?" he asked. It was a big leap of faith, going without.

"Only if you really want one," Brett replied, knowing he was taking a chance, but he'd seen enough of Gerald, talked to him enough over the past months to know he wasn't a huge risk taker, at least not in a way that was likely to get him sick. "I'm sure I'm clean, but I'll understand if you'd rather wait until we can get tested again. I'm not playing around with this. I'm not going to do something that might hurt you."

Gerald nodded, sure he could trust Brett. "I'd never play fast and loose. Not with something this important." He snagged a condom, pushed the drawer shut, and crawled back over to kiss Brett sweetly. "I just don't want it to be a point of tension. The only pressure I want between us is what we're feeling when I'm pushing into you."

"That's a pressure I'm looking forward to feeling," Brett replied with a grin. "So how soon am I going to get to feel it?"

Popping open the tube, Gerald squeezed a generous amount onto his fingers before reaching between Brett's thighs to smear the gel liberally within the crease of his buttocks. "You asked me to be careful," he reminded as he started to tease the hidden entrance.

"Doesn't mean you can't start," Brett rasped, parting his legs wider to give Gerald easier access. "God, that feels good!"

Gerald chuckled lowly and leaned to lap at Brett's taut balls as he slowly slid a long finger into him. Any words died in Brett's throat, only a long, needy moan escaping his lips as he felt the slight burn of muscles stretching.

As Gerald took his time preparing him, he also watched Brett's face and the emotions playing across them. Brett was so incredibly open; he lived so totally in the moment. While he processed those thoughts, Gerald leaned to suck Brett's half-hard cock back into his mouth as he carefully wedged a third finger into his ass.

Brett squirmed and writhed as the burn peaked and then ebbed, leaving him instead with that delicious feeling of being stretched that preceded a long, hard ride. "I'm ready," he moaned.

Gerald let out a shaky breath. He was hard and aching, and his hands shook as he rolled on the condom and moved between Brett's knees. "I sure hope I am," he said fervently as he hitched one of Brett's legs up against him and started to push against the slick hole.

Brett consciously reminded himself to relax as Gerald's thick cock stretched him even more than his fingers, but then the cock head brushed Brett's prostate and the jolt of pleasure overruled everything else. "Right there!" he gasped, knuckles turning white as he gripped the covers.

Gerald groaned and shifted his hips, pulling out and pushing in just the same way to start a rhythm that shook them both as he thrust.

Brett thrashed beneath him, speared firmly by Gerald's cock. The feeling of fullness struck him as so incredibly right that it stole what little breath remained, leaving him light-headed, his cock swelling again as Gerald continued to tease him.

"C'mon," Gerald said persuasively as he kept up the slow, steady movement while reaching to encircle Brett's cock and stroke it.

"I will," Brett promised, the shaft twitching beneath the encouraging touch, "but it won't be fast. I'm not eighteen anymore."

Gerald chuckled. "That's not what I meant, but I don't mind." He groaned lowly as he kept sinking into Brett's heat. "Touch yourself for me. That's what I meant."

Brett slipped one hand around his cock, the other moving to tweak a pink nipple, showing Gerald how he preferred to be touched. The combination of Gerald's gaze, his own touch, and the feeling of the hard cock moving inside him brought him erect again far sooner than he would've thought possible.

His breaths growing short, Gerald moved to grip Brett's hips as he began to thrust a little harder. "Have I been careful enough?" he asked in a strained voice.

"Yes, Gerry," Brett gasped. "Nail me to the mattress, lover, so I feel you tomorrow."

"Oh hell," Gerald swore, the inflammatory words getting him right in the gut. With soft grunts, he started really fucking Brett, gasping with each thud of their bodies together. "Oh… oh fuck… it's good.…"

Brett moaned with each pass of Gerald's cock over his prostate, the force behind each thrust rocking his body on the bed. He abandoned his nipple in favor of bracing himself against the headboard to keep his neck from getting bent all out of shape as Gerald pushed him up the bed with each inward movement. An incomprehensible mixture of curses, pleas, and Gerald's name tumbled from his lips as his body neared its peak again.

Gerald's hips stopped moving, and he groaned aloud as everything in him contracted and he came. His eyes rolled back and he clutched at Brett as he shuddered all over. Hearing Gerald's groans—the same ones he'd overheard that night weeks ago—was enough to trigger Brett's second orgasm, and thick strands of come spurted over his belly and chest, tangible proof of just how well Gerald had pleased him.

Gerald shuddered against Brett, opened his glazed eyes, and saw the thrilled agony and rapture written across his lover's face. It was a gorgeous sight. He carefully lowered himself between Brett's thighs and kissed him slowly.

The lazy, almost loving kiss was the perfect end to a perfect round of sex. Brett sighed into the union of mouths, his body relaxing beneath Gerald's weight that pressed him tightly down into the mattress. Languidly, he draped his arms around Gerald's shoulders, not really holding him in place, but definitely making clear how welcome he was.

Sighing happily as their mouths parted, Gerald let his chin drop lightly to Brett's chest, rubbing his forehead against the other man's bristly cheek. He was more than satisfied, and a smile curved his lips as he soaked in Brett's heat.

Brett's arms tightened as Gerald broke the kiss, but loosened again as soon as he realized the other man wasn't moving away, just getting comfortable. As far as Brett was concerned, they could just stay there forever.

They had lain there quietly for long minutes before Gerald rubbed his lips against Brett's throat. "Bathroom," he murmured, and he rolled out of bed and disappeared into the next room to dispose of the condom.

When he returned just a minute later, he climbed back into the bed next to Brett, who wrapped his arms around him and pulled him close. "I should probably go," Gerald murmured. "Getting late. Work tomorrow."

Brett's arms tightened again, this time with no intention of loosening. "You've got your bag in your car," he murmured. "Stay?"

Gerald moved just enough to look up into Brett's eyes, and he smiled warmly. "Sure. As long as I'm wanted," he added. He wouldn't impose on Brett without being invited.

Brett pulled Gerald's head back down to his, kissing him thoroughly. "You're definitely wanted."

Five

GERALD finished up his spaghetti and pushed the plate away. "So. Where are the business ledgers?"

Brett frowned. "You want to work on those tonight?" He'd had other things in mind when he'd suggested Gerald stay for dinner.

"Well, I figured it was as good a time as any," Gerald said as he stood and picked up his plate and the empty bowl from the table. "I brought my laptop." He stopped and looked at Brett with a raised brow. "Did you have other plans?"

"Oh, no," Brett replied quickly. "You can set up in the den or the dining room or wherever you'll be most comfortable, but I'm not letting you get away so quickly. I've barely even gotten a kiss tonight! And while working on my books wasn't part of my plans, kissing you definitely was."

Gerald smiled, leaned over, and dropped a quick kiss on his lips. "Done with your plate?" he asked once he straightened.

"Yeah," Brett replied, only partially mollified by the kiss. After just two weeks, he'd figured out pretty quickly that he couldn't get enough of Gerald's time and attention. Having him work here was preferable to having him leave, but it wasn't what Brett really wanted. Still, he had some work of his own to do—supply orders and the like—that he'd been putting off to spend time with his sexy new lover. It was probably time to take care of those while Gerald looked at the ledgers for the farm. "I'll get the books. Where do you want to work? And do you mind if I join you?"

"I thought I'd sit here at the table," Gerald said as he rinsed the dishes in the sink. "And of course I don't mind if you join me."

Brett smiled. "Let me just get the ledgers then, and you can get started while I reorder the supplies. I should have done it earlier this week, but there's been a few other things going on." They'd had a rough night a week ago when Brett spent the entire night in the barn with one of the horses who went down and wouldn't stand back up again. Finally, around dawn, she'd shaken her head and stood up like nothing had happened, but the night was gone, along with his chances for any sleep.

"Okay," Gerald said. "I'll run out to the car and get my laptop." He returned in less than five minutes, carrying a canvas case, and chose to sit at the kitchen table with his back to the wall so he was out of Brett's way.

A moment later, Brett came back into the kitchen, a huge leather-bound ledger in his hand. "Here's this year's stuff," he said, setting it down next to Gerald's computer. "Do you want the previous years' books as well?"

"No, not yet. Let me get a feel for what you've got here. Then I'll want to look at past taxes," Gerald said distractedly as he started to page through the book. Then he wrinkled his nose and leaned over to dig in the bag. He sat up with a small leather case. Snapping it open, he pulled out a pair of metal-rimmed glasses and slid them on before going back to reading the ledger.

Brett looked up from the seed catalog he'd been perusing at the sound of Gerald rustling his bag. He bit his lip to hold back a groan at the sight of the thin metal glasses on Gerald's face. He'd never thought he had a thing for glasses before, but he'd apparently just developed a new fetish. "I didn't know you wore glasses," Brett said, his voice husky with desire.

"Just for close work," Gerald said, glancing up, then back down at the books, then back up just as quickly as the tone of Brett's voice sank in. His lips curved in amusement.

"And tonight when I'm fucking you," Brett declared firmly, images of staring at Gerald's face adorned with glasses as they made love enough to have him half-hard already.

Gerald laughed in surprise. "Are you kidding?"

Brett stood up and moved to Gerald's side, capturing his lips in a torrid kiss. "Hell, no, Gerry, I'm not kidding," he replied when he lifted his head again.

Gerald stared up at him, arrested by the look on Brett's face and the intensity in his eyes. "Well, I'll wear them anytime you want, if they get me this kind of reaction."

"Only in private," Brett said. "I don't want anyone else seeing you with them on. Somebody might try to steal you from me."

Charmed, Gerald reached for Brett's hand so he could tug him down to give him a soft kiss. "Not going to happen," he murmured when their lips parted.

"Can the books wait a couple of hours?" Brett grunted as he slid his hand through Gerald's hair. "Because I don't think I can."

Gerald grinned. "It's going to take a couple hours?" He leaned forward and slid his hands down Brett's thighs.

"Once isn't going to be enough," Brett informed him bluntly, pulling Gerald to his feet.

"Damn. You really *do* like the glasses," Gerald murmured.

"Yeah," Brett sighed, "I *really* do." He hooked his thumbs through Gerald's belt loops, keeping him close as he backed him toward the stairs that led to the master suite. "I really, *really* do."

"I guess you know how I feel when I see you riding Shah," Gerald murmured as he followed along while dipping his head to kiss along Brett's neck.

Brett grinned and pushed Gerald up the stairs ahead of him. "I bet he could carry us both."

"Jesus," Gerald said under his breath as a shot of heat aroused him to the point his slacks were strained across the front. He hurried up the stairs into the bedroom and started unbuttoning his shirt.

Brett raced up behind him, stripping his own clothes off as he crossed the threshold. He tackled Gerald onto the bed, tugging at his pants, but careful not to dislodge the glasses. He wanted to drive into Gerald, staring down at the handsome face adorned with wire frames.

Gerald went down with a gasp, his mostly unbuttoned shirt still on his shoulders, and he helped Brett unfasten his pants and shove them down as much as he could while lying on them. He peered up at Brett through his glasses, and the heat glazing the other man's eyes just made Gerald want him more. He arched his back so Brett could yank the fabric down his thighs.

Stripping Gerald out of his pants and briefs, Brett fell on his chest, sucking and biting at the dark nipples, wanting Gerald as frantic as he was. He only hoped his lover caught up quickly, because he wasn't going to be able to wait long. God, he was so thankful they'd gotten tested last week, and condoms weren't a concern now. He could jump Gerald whenever he wanted. And fuck, how he *wanted*. Wanted *now*.

"Brett...." Gerald breathed as he gripped his lover's arms, spreading his legs so their bodies fit together. He was already hard, and he gasped each time Brett's teeth sank into his skin. He lifted his hips to try to grind against Brett's thigh.

"Want you," Brett gasped, lifting his head and staring down at the dark eyes framed by the lenses. "Need you now."

Gerald groaned, and his eyes rolled back as his fingers clenched. He wrapped one long leg around Brett's waist. "Please. Please, Brett."

After scrambling for the drawer to grab the lube, Brett coated his fingers and stretched Gerald roughly. He knew he was rushing, but he couldn't wait. "Ready?" he pleaded.

"Yeah," Gerald gasped, spreading his knees and rolling back so Brett could press close. "So fucking turned on," he rasped.

Scooting up onto his knees, Brett pulled Gerald's ankles over his shoulders, dragging his lover's hips up onto his thighs so he was completely open to Brett's invasion.

The clinging heat surrounded Brett immediately, squeezing him tight. He grabbed Gerald's cock, sliding his palm up and down its length, trying to push him over the edge as soon as possible.

Gerald huffed out a helpless laugh. "You're gonna make me come in like two damn minutes!" He couldn't stop squirming around the cock pinning him in place.

"Then I'll just have to make you come again," Brett rasped, although he wasn't sure he'd last much longer than Gerald.

Grunting in effort to hold off orgasm as Brett did everything he could imagine to make him lose control, Gerald's eyes suddenly focused on Brett through the glasses as he choked on a breath. "Oh fuck!" Gerald exclaimed, and his eyes glazed over as his cock contracted, and he came all over his belly.

The spasming muscles nearly broke Brett's control, but he held back, stopping his climax by force of will and more than a little luck. He kept thrusting as Gerald went limp beneath him, his hand never stopping its insistent stroking. "We're not done," Brett drawled, pulling out so he could lick the hot streaks of come off Gerald's belly. "Nowhere near done."

Still shuddering, Gerald moaned as he looked down at Brett's tongue lapping up his come. "Oh fuck," he whispered as his cock immediately twitched. "That's so... sexy."

Brett's laugh was deep and dark. "So what else is sexy?" he prodded. "What can I do to make you hard and begging again? After all, I promised you a couple of hours."

"Watching you as you fuck me is really damn sexy," Gerald said, still flushed and still aroused. It was only at times like this that he talked dirty. "Watching you as I fuck myself on you is even better."

"You want that now?" Brett teased. "Or do you need something else first?" He slid his fingers between Gerald's parted cheeks. "Let me taste all of you, baby, then you can ride me to oblivion."

Gerald's eyes went really big as what Brett said sunk in. "You want to...?" He looked totally bowled over.

"I want to stick my tongue so far up your ass that you could come from that alone." Brett's voice broke with lust. "Will you let me?"

Unable to get another word out, Gerald reached for both knees and spread them, exposing himself. Just the thought sent him up into flames again, as well as knowing he wouldn't have to be empty and aching like he was now.

Brett slid to the edge of the bed, kneeling on the floor next to the mattress, pulling Gerald so his ass rested right on the edge of the bed, exactly at eye level. He nipped at the curve of one taut cheek, then the other before parting them to reveal his target. Nuzzling around the base of Gerald's reviving cock, he licked his way down over heavy balls to the little pink pucker that clenched in anticipation. "I'm gonna make you feel so good," Brett promised.

Gerald hoped his whimper wasn't audible. His head spun as he nearly drowned in the heat Brett caused. His thighs shook as he tensed in anticipation. What Brett was going to do… oh fuck. "If you say so," he said shakily. "I trust you."

Brett froze, his tongue poised to lick at the smooth skin. "Nobody's ever rimmed you before?" he asked incredulously. "What kind of selfish lovers have you had?" Without waiting for a reply, he licked a long, wet strip from stem to stern before settling on Gerald's entrance, his tongue playing along the outer edge.

"I don't know!" Gerald yelped helplessly as he felt the wet swath of tongue. "I've not done it either," he said weakly. But damn, he thought he might be willing to try.

Brett hoped he'd be able to change Gerald's mind about that too, but in the meantime, he had a lover to drive wild. He took his time, despite his own throbbing cock, licking and sucking at the tight hole until Gerald whimpered and writhed above him. Brett kept his eyes trained on Gerald's passion-darkened eyes, highlighted by those damn sexy glasses. When Gerald was mewling with pleasure, Brett pointed his tongue and stabbed it as deep as he could.

The long, slow, rising heat of the continued attention threatened to send Gerald out of his mind—he was already seeing stars—and he could not imagine how anything could be so hot. Watching Brett suck and lick at his hole was like nothing Gerald had ever seen before, and it did the trick of making him hard again. Seriously so, and he couldn't hold still under that tenacious tongue. And when he felt it slide inside him, he gave a broken cry of obvious pleasure.

Urged on by Gerald's wordless encouragement, Brett fucked his eager lover with his tongue, working the hole until it was slick and loose and desperation was clear on Gerald's face. Pushing to his feet, Brett shuffled close and slammed home, driving into his lover's ass until his balls slapped what he'd just been licking.

Gerald's shout echoed in his own ears, followed by a near sob as the tension inside him kept twisting tighter and tighter until it was so much he could barely stand it. He was so far gone in it that his hands clenched white-knuckled in the sheets. He couldn't even form the thought to jerk himself off and end the torture ripping through him.

Brett tried to hold on to his control, but all he could manage was to pound Gerald into the mattress, bending him almost double as he leaned forward to nip at peaked nipples and then up toward Gerald's mouth, hoping his lover would kiss him.

His body being manipulated got enough of Gerald's attention that he opened his eyes to stare at his lover. Licking his own swollen lips, Gerald released the sheets with one hand as he gasped with each thrust and slid his fingers along Brett's cheek.

"Come on, baby," Brett urged, his hips thumping rhythmically against Gerald. "Come for me, just from my cock fucking you long and hard."

Gerald grasped at Brett's shoulder as he shuddered, and he bit at his lip as he remained on edge. He'd not tried to come twice so closely together in a long time; even with Brett's attentions, Gerald was usually pretty much done after one round. But tonight, the sheer impact and intensity of being rimmed roused him to a fever pitch. Shifting his hips to try to gain some little bit more that would be enough, Gerald moaned.

"What do you need, baby?" Brett asked hoarsely as Gerald thrashed beneath him. "Come for me so I can fill you up so full you overflow. I want to lick you clean."

Brett using his tongue on him turned Gerald on like crazy; Brett promising it again after coming inside him did Gerald in. He gasped and cried aloud, finally finding the presence of mind to clutch at his erection and squeeze just as the cock driving into him rubbed against the sweet spot inside him. The shockwaves catapulted him into orgasm; his cock contracted, and Gerald wailed.

Brett came hard as Gerald's body spasmed around him a second time. Giving up his struggle for control, he spent himself deep in

Gerald's ass, thrusting through his climax until he was completely spent. Sinking back to his knees, Brett nuzzled Gerald's now-limp cock, then proceeded to make good on his promise, licking gently at Gerald's well-stretched hole.

Gerald gasped and shuddered; he moved his hands to hold onto his shaking legs. "Bre… Brett… too much!" He moaned and another shudder rippled through him, extending the orgasm.

"Do you really want me to stop?" Brett asked against Gerald's inner thigh. "I will, if that's what you want."

The whimpers that formed Gerald's response were soft, but he kept his legs spread and even lifted his hips. He'd never felt this much at once before, and he was drunk on it. He didn't want it to end. Smiling, Brett returned to what he was doing, slowly, tenderly licking Gerald clean, drawing out their lovemaking that much longer.

Gerald slowly started relaxing as the energy seeped out of him and the sensations calmed, the gentle lapping a reminder of the explosive pleasure he'd just received. "Brett," he whispered, propping himself up on one elbow.

"Yes, baby?" Brett asked softly, lifting his head to meet Gerald's eyes.

Unable to put anything into words, Gerald simply lifted his arms to wordlessly ask Brett to come close. The endearment echoed in his head, and he felt like he'd come home to stay.

Brett crawled up on the bed next to Gerald, rolling him so they lay properly before cuddling his lover against him, arms and legs entwined. Gerald sighed shakily and curled into him, basking in the warmth of their bodies as they held each other.

GERALD was back at the ledgers later in the evening, wearing running shorts from his gym bag, the unbuttoned dress shirt, smudged glasses, and mussed hair. He read along, checking items against a list he'd made, tapping at the keyboard periodically, humming quietly.

Brett sat across from him studiously refusing to look at his lover. The sight of Gerald there, so obviously recently well-fucked, was more of a temptation than any man should be expected to resist. A part of him wanted to take Gerald back to bed and fuck him again. Another part simply marveled at the ease he felt sitting there. Sure, the glasses were still an incredible turn-on, but Brett pretty much stayed turned on around Gerald even without them. More than that, he was amazed at how incredibly right it felt to have Gerald there with him, doing ordinary things.

"Stay tonight?" The request was out even before Brett realized the desire had formed.

The typing stopped. "Okay," Gerald said amiably, pleased to be asked. It felt good to be with Brett, and it was no more difficult to drive into work from here than from home. Except tonight, he didn't have clothes for tomorrow. "I'll have to leave pretty early, but you'll be up anyway."

"Yeah," Brett agreed, more than a little bemused by the simplicity of Gerald's reply. Did nothing faze the man? Other than rimming, anyway? "Work starts here far earlier than it does anywhere else."

"Yeah, I remember," Gerald said, smiling at him across the table. "I get up early, but not usually at the crack of dawn," he teased.

Brett shrugged. "The horses get hungry. That's the way a farm works."

"I understand," Gerald said, accepting the statement like any other irrefutable truth. "I'd help out in the stables, but I'll need to go home and get clothes for work."

The sudden desire to have Gerald there every morning left Brett nearly speechless. He nodded dumbly in reply to Gerald's comment, his mind whirling as he tried to figure out how to suggest his lover bring clothes so he wouldn't have to leave so early the next time he stayed.

Gerald frowned as an odd look crossed Brett's face. "Brett?"

"Huh?" Brett said, returning to the moment and pushing aside the desire as far too sudden to mention just yet.

"You just got the weirdest look on your face. If there's something you forgot, I can go ahead home," Gerald offered, his own brow creased in concern.

"No, not at all," Brett replied hastily. "Just a stray thought, that's all. I'd really like it if you stayed."

Gerald's charmed smile returned. "Me too. Maybe half an hour, and I'll be at a stopping point with this," he said as he tapped the pencil against his cheek.

"Take your time," Brett answered automatically. "I've always got paperwork to do."

Gerald nodded, happy that Brett seemed okay, and he went back to the ledgers and laptop, ready to be done so they could spend some more time together before bed.

Brett's mind raced as he completed the standard supply orders, filling in the columns without conscious thought. He hadn't gone looking for it, but it seemed fate had dropped everything he'd never dreamed he'd have right in his lap. He just had to figure out if Gerald felt the same way.

The only problem was that Gerald always seemed fine with whatever Brett suggested. He just didn't know what to make of it, and it made him leery of suggesting things outright for fear Gerald would simply go along, regardless of what he really wanted.

Gerald was relieved when he finished what he had to; it was getting more and more difficult to block out the memories of earlier that evening. What Brett had done…. He shivered a little and set his pencil down.

"All finished?" Brett asked, the click of the pencil hitting the table drawing his attention. He closed the book and pushed it aside, stretching his back carefully.

"Yeah," Gerald said as he closed the laptop and the ledgers and slid the computer back into its bag. Then he picked up the glasses case, glancing up at Brett with a small smile.

"Go ahead and put them away," Brett said with a grin. "I'm not sure even your sexy glasses are enough to get me up again tonight."

Gerald chuckled and took the glasses off, tucked them away, and zipped up his briefcase. He stood up and walked around the table to stand next to Brett, his mind refocusing on what he'd promised himself in exchange for actually laying the groundwork for a good study of the farm's books. "Well, I would have said the same thing after the first time you got me off earlier. The second was unbelievable." He leaned over Brett's shoulder to let his warm breath gust over his lover's ear. "And you've had time to recover."

The tickle of air sent a shiver down Brett's back, goose bumps raising on his skin as he looked up at Gerald in surprise. "Are you suggesting…?"

"I'm not *suggesting* anything," Gerald drawled as he drew Brett up out of the chair to stand chest to chest with him. "But I'm certainly going to *do* something. Come on." He took Brett by the hand and led him toward the stairs, turning off the kitchen light as he went.

Brett followed obediently, wondering what in the world Gerald had in store for him. Despite his earlier assertion, his cock twitched with interest beneath his sweats. Gerald went up the stairs and into the master suite, but he didn't stop at the bed. He kept going until they were in the bathroom, where he leaned over the large, old-fashioned claw-foot tub and turned on the hot water.

Brett watched, amused, as Gerald bustled around his bathroom, opening cabinets until he found a bottle of bath oil left over from when his parents still lived here and poured some in the steaming water. "Going to pamper me?" Brett teased.

"Yes," Gerald said blithely. "You certainly took care of me earlier this evening." He sent Brett a significant look. "So strip," he ordered.

Surprised—an emotion that was becoming rather frequent with Gerald around—Brett did as he was told, pulling off the sweats he'd donned after they got up earlier and dropping the thin T-shirt to the floor.

"Into the bath." Gerald pointed as he waited, admiring the view of Brett's ass. It was, in Gerald's opinion, one of his best assets. He snickered quietly. *Asset.*

"What's so funny?" Brett asked as he climbed into the tub and sank into the hot water. It felt wonderful on muscles taxed by their extracurricular activities on top of his usual day's work.

"I was admiring your best asset," Gerald admitted as he snagged a washcloth from the shelf and pulled the straight-backed chair from the corner over next to the tub.

Brett's eyebrows flew up. "And what's that?" he asked, sputtering slightly.

Gerald leaned over to drag the cloth through the water. "Your ass," he said, as if it were something commonplace to think about.

Now Brett sputtered for real. "My ass?" he repeated with a shake of his head. "Baby, you have too much going on in that head of yours."

"Mmm," Gerald commented as he lifted the dripping cloth and dragged it over Brett's shoulders. "It's a seriously fine ass."

Brett told himself the color staining his cheeks was a reaction to the steam rising from the rapidly filling tub. "Aren't you joining me?" he asked, trying to change the subject.

"So I can feel that fine ass up close?" Gerald asked innocently, sliding the cloth around Brett's throat.

"If you want," Brett replied in a strangled voice, his face flushing even darker.

Gerald chuckled. "What's the matter? Water too hot?" he teased. "Wouldn't want that ass to be uncomfortable." The cloth strayed down Brett's chest.

Brett just shook his head, too embarrassed to admit how uncomfortable Gerald's frank perusal made him. It wasn't false modesty; just a man's discomfort with being so openly appraised.

Gerald's fingers wrapped in the cloth coasted over Brett's belly. "You know the first time I noticed that ass? Noticed *you*?"

"When?" Brett asked softly, his body thrilling to Gerald's touch even as his mind still squirmed.

"The first time I saw you riding Shah," Gerald purred, moving to kiss Brett's jaw just below his earlobe. "Puts that ass on fine display. I got hard standing right there watching."

Brett's head tipped sideways. "That was months ago!" he protested, remembering.

"Yeah," Gerald admitted as he drew the cloth over Brett's groin as his other hand moved to cup his shoulder.

Brett wanted to ask what had taken Gerald so long then, but the hand on his cock distracted him, and his hips lifted off the bottom of the tub.

Gerald slid the cloth between his thighs and moved it back and forth behind Brett's balls as he watched the relaxed cock straighten.

"That was the day you pretty much told me you liked men," Gerald said. "The day you told me you had someone. So I contented myself with watching," he murmured, sliding the cloth over one thigh and under it to rub the body part in question.

"If I'd known I could have this, I'd have dropped him in an instant," Brett admitted. "But I thought you were straight."

Gerald hummed a little. "Hadn't come up before then. No reason to mention it."

"I suppose not."

Gerald leaned to place a simple kiss on Brett's shoulder. "Does it matter now?" He moved the soaked cloth back up to Brett's chest.

"I suppose not," Brett repeated. "We're here, and the months in between weren't wasted. We became friends, and that makes this so much more comfortable now."

"Comfortable," Gerald echoed. "Yeah." He fell silent then as he used the washcloth to rub Brett all over, including every finger and toe, then lingering between his thighs. He released the cloth and smoothed his fingers over Brett's cock as he leaned over the edge of the tub to seek a kiss.

Deciding the conversation was finished, Brett returned the kiss, his body reacting to the touch without his conscious choice. Gerald shifted to the edge of the chair to cup Brett's cheek with his other hand, deepening the kiss and dipping his tongue farther into his lover's mouth.

The kiss was wonderful, and the touch of Gerald's hand arousing, but Brett wanted more. He pulled back and focused on Gerald's sparking eyes. "Either you need to join me in here, or we need to move to the bed, because I want to feel you against me."

"There's not enough room in this tub for both of us," Gerald murmured, pulling his hand out of the water.

Brett rose to his feet, deciding right then that he needed to get a bigger tub. He wasn't about to forgo the pleasure of sharing a bath with Gerald forever. "I guess it's the bed then," he said, reaching for a towel.

Gerald beat him to it and started drying Brett's body himself, taking advantage of the opportunity to grope and squeeze as he went—paying special attention to Brett's ass, of course. Brett was on a long, slow simmer by the time Gerald finished with the towel. Brett shivered—from desire, not cold—and stepped from the tub, pressing close to his lover's partially clad form. "You're wearing too much clothing."

"Compared to you, maybe." Gerald chuckled, looking down at his boxers and half-buttoned shirt. But he pulled the shirt over his head and dropped it to the floor before pushing his shorts over his hips and letting them fall.

"Much better," Brett declared, rubbing against all that bare skin. "Much, much better."

Gerald grinned and rubbed back, even hitching his relaxed cock against Brett's thigh. "I think I'll take this opportunity to drive you out of your mind. You'll sleep very, very well."

"I'm all yours, baby," Brett promised, cock twitching in happy anticipation. "Take me to bed and drive me wild."

Taking Brett by the hand, Gerald led him back out into the bedroom and to the bed, gently pushing him down onto the mattress. He settled on his side next to Brett and slid one hand from throat to belly. "So, we've been together a couple weeks now, and we established tonight that you've got more experience than I do. Now I want to know: What drives you out of your mind? Besides my glasses, of course."

"Having somebody play with my ass," Brett replied, face flushing again. "Not much turns me on like a prostate massage. Except your glasses, of course."

"See, I knew you'd get off on my ogling your ass," Gerald said with a grin. He rolled and grabbed the bottle of lubricant off the nightstand. "Want to watch?"

"Hell, yes," Brett replied, spreading his legs. "Unless you'd really rather I turn over."

"No," Gerald said as he scooted closer. "If you're watching I can also kiss you." He popped open the tube and drizzled a generous amount on his fingers.

"I won't say no to that," Brett husked.

Gerald shifted to brush his lips lightly over Brett's as he slid his fingers under Brett's balls to rub at the sensitive skin hidden there before sweeping the slick digits over the twisting flesh, over and over, deliberately teasing just as he did with tiny flicks of his tongue.

Brett tried to catch Gerald's mouth with his, but each time he lifted his head in the attempt, Gerald pulled away with a shake of his head. Finally Brett subsided, accepting he'd simply have to wait for Gerald to give him what he wanted.

"Good boy," Gerald breathed as he rubbed his thumb against the giving opening, slowly caressing in circles just around the edges.

Brett pulled his knees back, opening himself completely to Gerald's touch, the bit of praise giving him an unexpected thrill. Gerald purred against his ear, nipping at the lobe as he pushed his thumb inside, just to pull right back out, only to repeat it over and over.

Brett trembled, his body aching to be filled. He knew he wasn't going to get Gerald's cock again tonight, but he could get more than just that fleeting touch. "Please," he begged.

The thumb sank deeper, moving around to rub the entire passage. Then it withdrew completely. After a couple heartbeats, a longer finger slid in and kept going until Gerald's knuckles rubbed Brett's entrance.

Brett didn't even try to bite back the cry that tore from his throat at the feeling of the long finger inside him. "So good," he panted.

Gerald went back to kissing gently along Brett's jaw as he played with his ass, but he deliberately avoided the spongy bump that would send shocks of sensation into his lover. After a short time, Gerald pulled free and slid two crossed fingers into the tight heat.

Brett writhed on the bed, trying to get the fingers deeper, in just the right spot, but Gerald stayed one step ahead of him, slapping him lightly on the thigh. "You'll get what you want," he murmured in Brett's ear. "Just not yet. Not until you can't stand it anymore and the only word in your head is my name." To make his point, he dragged his fingers over the right spot for a mere second.

"Gerry!" Brett shouted as fireworks went off behind his eyelids, only to recede when Gerald's fingers slipped away from his prostate.

A third finger joined the first two, delving deep and twisting, and without warning Gerald began to rub over Brett's prostate slow and steady.

Brett trembled, the sudden, repetitive massage overtaxing his senses. He cried out again, some mangled sound that should have been Gerald's name but didn't quite make it. The soft, gentle manipulation was enough to fill him with a heated buzzing that propelled him toward climax, but wasn't enough to push him over the edge.

The corkscrew of fingers inside him left Brett twisting against the delicious friction. He needed more, needed harder, faster, fuller. He sobbed Gerald's name again and again.

"So handsome," Gerald whispered as he claimed Brett's lips and began churning his fingers in and out, truly fucking Brett with them, pressing hard against his prostate every time.

Brett didn't give a flying fuck about handsome. He just cared that Gerald was finally reaming him hard, driving him wild with need. He thrashed on the bed, feet planted to thrust up into the plunging fingers, vision darkening around the edges as he fought for his release.

"C'mon, lover," Gerald breathed against his ear, doing his best to give Brett what he needed. His face was flushed, and Gerald could tell he was on the edge. Looking down at the swollen, deep red cock standing from Brett's belly, he leaned over to lap at the liquid dripping from the head.

That was all it took. Brett groaned and shuddered through his release, the sensations going on and on and on until he was gasping for breath and his muscles were trembling with exhaustion. And still the tremors rocked him. Gerald continued to lick and suck at the twitching cock, catching come on his tongue as he kept screwing his fingers into Brett, extending the orgasm until Brett practically collapsed. As his lover shivered, Gerald pulled his fingers away and helped him lower his legs to the bed.

It took several long minutes for Brett to come down from his high as his ass continued to clench in echoing sympathy. Gerald's hand tenderly stroking across his chest finally woke Brett enough to open his eyes and meet his lover's smiling gaze. "You pack quite a punch," Brett said, his voice still husky and breathless.

"Just for you," Gerald said.

"Good," Brett declared firmly, the wave of possessiveness that swamped him enough to make him pull Gerald down next to him and into a tight embrace. As far as he was concerned, they didn't ever need to move again.

BUSTLING around the kitchen, the slim dark-haired man gathered fixings for coffee and pulled out home-baked cookies, setting it all out on the table. "Now tell us, Brett, how are you? You don't usually go so long without visiting." He propped one hand on his slim hip.

"What Jeff says is right, Brett. We've missed you," a white-haired heavy-set man sitting across the table from Brett said.

"I've been busy," Brett admitted with a slight flush. "I have a new student at the stable who's taking a lot of my time."

"You spend too much time with your students and not enough time with potential lovers, Brett," Jeff scolded as he sat down. "Isn't that right, Bruce?" The older man just nodded as he munched on a cookie.

Brett couldn't stop the laugh that escaped him. "You haven't seen my student."

Jeff and Bruce exchanged glances. "Well then," Bruce drawled. "Do tell."

"Yes, do tell," Jeff added as he offered Brett the cookie plate.

"His name's Gerald Saunders and he's… special," Brett said slowly, trying to describe his new lover to his longtime friends. "He's an accountant, very laid-back. Absolutely gorgeous. And all mine."

Jeff grinned. "All yours, is he?"

"Does he know that?" Bruce rumbled curiously, wrinkles creasing at his eyes.

Brett shrugged. "Neither one of us is seeing anyone else," he said. "And we're together for at least a few hours almost every night, and he's around all day on the weekends."

"How do you know he's not seeing anyone else?" Bruce asked as Jeff filled up the coffee mugs. "Could be going home to someone at night."

"Bruce," Jeff scolded.

"If he's going home to someone as late as he leaves me, that someone is as clueless as they come," Brett retorted. "And some nights, he doesn't go home at all."

"Doesn't go home?" Jeff asked in surprise. "That's never happened before. Or at least you haven't told us if it did. You usually send them on their way because of the farm."

Brett shrugged diffidently. "Yeah, well, he helps with the farm," he explained helplessly. "I told you. He's special."

Bruce chuckled. "Likes the farm, does he? Well, Brett, you may have found you a good one then."

"So tell us more about him. Is he hot in bed?" Jeff asked, leaning forward to get the gossip.

"Jeff!" Brett protested, his face flaming, which was already a response in itself. But Bruce's matching expectant expression meant they wouldn't let him get away with avoiding an answer. Brett sighed. "Amazing."

Bruce chortled. "It's about time. I never did think that young man you had for awhile could do it for you for long."

"He was a lot of fun, and we had a good time together," Brett defended. "It was never meant to be permanent, just a way to release some tension for both of us. Gerry's different, though. He's, damn, I've got to find a better word for it. Special. He found the farm before I started seeing Robbie and started spending a lot of time there before I even realized he was gay. Then we became friends, and only recently lovers. The sex is mind-blowing, but it's so much more than that."

"You're taken with him," Jeff said knowingly, waving a cookie at him. "I don't think I've ever heard you describe someone like this."

"I don't think I've ever felt this way about someone," Brett replied.

"Serious stuff, Brett," Bruce said. "How's he feel about all this?"

"That's the problem," Brett admitted. "I can't tell. He doesn't talk about it. And when I try, we always seem to get sidetracked. He's always affable, always laid-back. I'll suggest he stay, and he always agrees, but he never asks, never seems upset if I don't mention it for some reason. It's like he isn't thinking beyond the moment, yet I've never been happier than when we're together. It's just when we're apart that I'm not so sure he wants the same things I do."

Jeff looked thoughtful. "Well, could be he's not serious." Then he yelped and glared at Bruce, who had kicked him under the table.

"Sidetracked, hmm? Maybe he's happy with things the way they are," Bruce suggested. "Serious," he looked pointedly at Jeff, "but not sure what to do about it."

"I know he's serious about it," Brett agreed, thinking of the decision to get tested and forego condoms. "As for knowing what to do about it, I don't know. I'll make comments about the drive to his house and then out to the farm, and he'll just shrug and say it's no big deal. He doesn't seem to catch any of my hints."

"Has he always been like that? Sort of dense? Or could he be blowing you off?" Jeff piped up.

"He missed all my lines the first day we met," Brett mused. "I thought he was straight for months."

Bruce frowned. "But he's an accountant, an intelligent guy. How can he be that dense?"

Jeff shrugged. "Two plus two always equals four. No reason to think differently."

"I want to meet this 'special' Gerald. Bring him for dinner next week," Bruce said.

Six

"So instead of eating here Saturday night," Brett suggested casually as he and Gerald finished up their chores around the stables, "what if we went out?"

Gerald glanced up from where he was forking hay. He was hot and sweaty, his jeans were a mess, and his boots were worse. He had heavy work gloves on his hands, so when he'd wiped his brow, it was with the back of his forearm, which left his hair ruffled and a little messy. He tossed more straw onto the ground in the stall. "What if?"

"I had dinner with a couple of friends of mine the other night, and they suggested the four of us should have dinner sometime," Brett explained, not sure quite what to make of Gerald's answer, "so I thought maybe we could go out somewhere to dinner with them on Saturday."

"Okay," Gerald agreed pleasantly as he scraped the last of the hay out of the cart and set the pitchfork aside.

And there was that incredible, wonderful, annoying affability again, Brett thought, hiding a grimace. He wanted Gerald to ask more questions or express some curiosity. The easy acceptance gave Brett no way to judge his way forward. "You need a shower," he told Gerald, pushing aside dinner with Bruce and Jeff for now in favor of other more immediate concerns. "Are you staying tonight?"

Gerald smiled, glad that Brett asked. He liked being here a lot more than being at home alone. "Sure," he answered, pulling off his gloves.

Brett wanted to beat his head against the wall. While he was thrilled with Gerald's answer—he certainly wanted his lover to stay—he wished he could get some indication of whether Gerald had intended to stay or whether it was a spur-of-the-moment decision. "Let's get cleaned up then," Brett suggested, "and I'll see what I can scrounge up for dinner. I haven't made it to the store yet this week."

"I could run out and get some stuff if you want," Gerald offered, grabbing up the pitchfork as he walked to put everything away.

"After you clean up," Brett reminded him. "They won't let you in the store smelling like the manure pile. But yeah, that would be great, if you don't mind. There's cash on the desk, or—"

"Brett, you feed me like six days a week; I can handle some groceries," Gerald said, shaking his head as he sat down outside the tack closet to pull off his work boots.

Brett shrugged. "You don't have to," he said weakly.

"I know I don't have to," Gerald answered as he stood up and put his hands on his hips as he watched his lover. "But what kind of house guest would I be if I didn't chip in? See you at the house." Then he turned and padded out in his sock feet, whistling as he walked away.

Brett stood there in shock. *Guest.* After all the months of working side by side and the weeks they'd been lovers, Gerald still considered himself a guest. Slowly, mind reeling, Brett walked over to Shah's stall, rubbing the stallion's nose when he butted his head against Brett's chest. "You've got it easy, old man," he said hoarsely. "Just wait until the ladies are in heat and then do your thing. What the fuck am I doing wrong? How can he not realize how crazy I am for him? He stopped being a guest about the same time he started leaving stuff in my bathroom. Why doesn't he see that?"

Shah just snuffled in reply.

GERALD washed the dishes, his self-appointed chore since Brett did all the cooking, and kept his eye on the other man. Brett had been oddly distracted through dinner, enough so that Gerald wondered if Brett had gotten some bad news while he was at the store. He frowned a little. He didn't like Brett being unhappy or worried, not one bit. Decided, he finished the dishes, rinsed and dried his hands, and walked over to the kitchen table where Brett supposedly worked on a leather-goods order.

"Hey, you okay?"

"Huh?" Brett asked, looking up in confusion. "Oh, yeah, I'm fine." He didn't know how to talk about what bothered him. "Just trying to do the math in my head because I'm too lazy to get a calculator out of the office."

Gerald glanced down at the order form that didn't have a mark on it. "Want some help?" he offered, studying Brett's face.

Brett grimaced and tossed the catalog and order form aside. "Not really," he groused. "I'm too tired to even know what I need."

Chest aching a little to see Brett so down, Gerald crouched next to him. "Something wrong? Did you get some bad news while I was gone?" he asked in concern.

Brett shook his head. "It's nothing a good night's sleep won't fix," he lied, although he hoped a night in Gerald's arms would at least give him a better sense of perspective on the whole issue. He almost wished Gerald wasn't staying so he could call Bruce and Jeff, but he wasn't about to ask his lover to leave after hinting at him to stay earlier.

Gerald glanced at the clock on the wall. It wasn't even eight. "Think you're coming down with something?" he asked worriedly. He put his palm across Brett's forehead, and then the backs of his fingers against Brett's cheek.

It was so totally the gesture of a lover that Brett grew even more confused. He wanted to rant and rail and demand an explanation, but that surely wouldn't help anything. He sighed. "I'm sorry, Gerry," he said. "I don't know what my problem is tonight. I'm not very good company, I'm afraid."

"It's okay. I'm just worried a little is all," Gerald said as he lowered himself to one knee, set his hands on Brett's knee, and propped his chin there to look up at the other man.

Summoning a smile, Brett tried to push aside his confusion and concern. "There's probably something mindless on TV. We could sit on the couch and neck like teenagers until bedtime."

Gerald nodded. "Okay," he said, hoping to be reassuring. He wanted Brett out of this funk. It just wasn't good for him.

Keeping his smile firmly in place, Brett pushed his chair out from the table and walked into the living room, leaving the lamps off but using the remote to switch on the television. He flipped through the channels until he found *Ocean's Eleven*. "How's this?" he asked, flopping down on the couch.

"Fine," Gerald said. He really didn't care; he planned to focus his attention on Brett. He sat down on the couch and scooted close.

Brett was pretty sure if he heard that word one more time, he'd run away screaming. But he suppressed the urge a little longer and relaxed against the back of the couch, his mind replaying their conversations, trying to read layers of meaning into them.

Gerald frowned as Brett didn't relax and shifted to lie against the opposite end of the couch. "C'mere," he invited, holding out his arms so Brett could lie against him.

Even more confused, Brett moved as Gerald suggested, stretching out against his lover, his back against Gerald's chest, Gerald's arms around his waist. As he got settled, Gerald pressed soft kisses to Brett's forehead and squeezed him slightly, trying to offer comfort of some kind, best he knew how.

Brett stifled another frustrated sigh. How could Gerald be so casual one minute and so attentive the next? Whatever the answer, he wasn't going to figure it out tonight, and the butterfly kisses were relaxing, lulling him to the point that he could set aside his worries for the moment.

Gerald smoothed his hand back and forth over Brett's belly, holding him close. He hoped Brett would feel better soon; he also hoped he wasn't somehow the cause of the problem. But Brett wouldn't have asked him to stay if he was unhappy with him, right? He laid his cheek upon Brett's head and sighed, feeling a warm wave of possessiveness washing through him.

The comfort of Gerald's cheek against his head eased some of Brett's worry. They weren't going straight from dinner to bed, but Gerald didn't seem concerned, didn't seem anxious to either get to the action or get out of there, so he had to feel something for Brett besides just lust. Telling himself he was being ridiculous, Brett turned on his side a little so he could wrap one arm around Gerald's waist while he watched the movie. The fingers of his other hand sought his lover's, entwining with them gently.

Relaxing as Brett did, Gerald held him quietly as time passed, eventually turning his chin to press a kiss to the mussed reddish-blond hair.

"I'm all sweaty," Brett warned, though he didn't pull away. It would hardly be the first time he and Gerald had made love straight from the stables without the benefit of a shower first.

Gerald chuckled. "So?"

"So I just thought I'd warn you, that's all," Brett replied, feeling things slide back into place. He might not know everything on Gerald's mind, but the slowly filling erection against his hip reassured him. Gerald definitely still wanted him.

"I love it when you're sweaty," Gerald murmured as he slid his lips to Brett's ear.

"I don't know why," Brett snorted, tilting his head to give Gerald better access to his neck. "I stink to high heaven, but if that's what floats your boat, far be it from me to protest."

"You may stink after mucking stalls, but any other time...." Gerald hummed lowly. "You smell warm and spicy. Hard for me to resist."

Brett raised an eyebrow. "Did somebody ask you to?"

Gerald smiled and shook his head. "Wouldn't try, anyway." He held Brett close, deciding this was about as good as it got.

"Good." Brett snuggled closer to Gerald, his arms tightening their grip as the film played on in the background. It wasn't some huge declaration, but he thought maybe he didn't need one after all.

GERALD walked up the stairs behind Brett, pleased with the way the evening was going so far. They'd gone riding that morning after some lessons, then worked in the barn awhile before going to the house, where Brett had made love to him until he had practically passed out. Then after a short nap and shower, here they were, and he was about to meet a couple of Brett's friends.

When the door opened, he couldn't help but smile.

"Welcome to Chez Laramie!" the slight man sang out with a wide grin.

"Jeff," Brett scolded, "you'll scare Gerry off before he ever gets a chance to know you."

"Nonsense! He's standing there smiling at me already," Jeff said with a wave. "Come in, come in, both of you."

Gerald followed Brett into the renovated historic house and stopped in the foyer as Jeff closed the huge door. "I asked Brett what to bring, and he just looked at me, so I brought a bottle of wine."

Jeff sidled up along beside him and oohed over the bottle. "Bruce! Brett picked a good one!"

"Jeff," Bruce scolded. "Turn it down a notch, love." He turned to Gerald. "Bruce Laramie. Nice to meet you."

"Gerald Saunders." He shook Bruce's hand and smiled. "I feel very welcome already."

"Ooh, and charming too! No wonder you're keeping Gerry to yourself, Brett," Jeff said cheerfully. Gerald raised an eyebrow and glanced to Brett in silent recognition of the nickname.

Brett sighed and rolled his eyes, eliciting smiles from Gerald and Bruce and a huff from Jeff. "And if you don't watch yourself, I'll take him home again and not bring him to visit anymore."

Jeff turned on a spectacular pout. "Come on, Gerry. Let's go to the kitchen," he said petulantly, curling his arm through Gerald's and pulling him away. Gerald looked back over his shoulder at Brett, grinning as he left the room.

"Good Lord, Bruce," Brett laughed when Jeff and Gerald left the room. "What did you put in his drink?"

"Not in his drink, but it won't be long before I put something on his finger. You haven't had the TV on today, have you?" Bruce said.

Brett shook his head. "No. Why?"

Bruce grinned. "We're celebrating. The state Supreme Court announced its decision on gay marriage. Jeff and I are getting married next month. I asked him this morning as soon as we saw the news."

"That's wonderful!" Brett exclaimed. "I know how long you've waited for this! We're definitely celebrating tonight!"

"That's right, so that's why Jeff is over the moon. Just be prepared, because I've not seen him this giddy since he ate three cones of cotton candy at the fair in half an hour." Bruce shook his head and led the way to the kitchen where Jeff was holding court.

Gerald half-sat on a barstool, watching Jeff with great amusement as the other man talked and gestured. He was answering a question as Brett and Bruce joined them. "… no, I didn't know that."

"Didn't know what?" Brett asked, moving to Gerald's side and draping his arm around his lover's shoulders.

Gerald's eyes danced as he turned them on his lover. "That you used to skate in the roller derby."

Brett flushed six shades of scarlet. "Are you telling him all my secrets?" he asked, mock-horrified. "Next you'll be telling him about my father walking in on me as I was getting my first blow job!"

"Really?" Jeff squeaked, which drew laughter from both Gerald and Bruce. "You never told me that!"

Brett flushed even darker. "Yeah, well, I didn't mean to tell you now either."

Gerald chuckled and slid his arm around Brett's waist. "I promise I won't tell."

Beyond embarrassed, Brett just shrugged. "Nobody to tell now that you know," he replied. "The guy's long gone, my dad's gotten over it, and the only other two people who'd care are these two jokers."

"That's because we love you, Brett," Jeff said as he leaned forward impulsively and kissed him on the cheek.

"Now, Jeff, none of that. You'll give Gerry the wrong idea," Bruce said in his booming voice.

Jeff made a discontented noise and waved his hand. "Fine then. You get some drinks, and I'll check the oven."

"Come on, Gerry, this is a help-yourself household," Bruce said, indicating the refrigerator. "Glasses are in the cabinet to the left of the sink.

Still smiling, Gerald slid from his seat to fetch glasses, pulled down four, and then took two to the refrigerator while Jeff chattered on happily.

Bruce watched with a smile as Gerald dropped a couple of ice cubes in each glass, taking the whiskey off the counter and pouring two fingers into each one. He knew exactly how to make Brett's drink, which told Bruce all he needed to know.

"Now, Brett, be useful and set the table or you'll set a bad precedent for Gerry. He should know right now that no one is ever a guest in this house, just family," Jeff pronounced.

Brett laughed and set about pulling dishes out for dinner. "So what are we having?" he asked so he'd know what silverware to put out.

"Bruce's favorite. Chicken enchiladas," Jeff said as he pulled a bubbling dish out of the oven.

Gerald put the two glasses on the bar. "Anything I can do to help?"

Bruce clapped him on the shoulder. "I'll warn you, anything is likely to happen when you ask that of my Jeff here."

"Now who's going to give him the wrong idea?" Jeff retorted from the stove. "I'll have you know there are certain things I'll never ask for from anyone but you."

Gerald watched the animated discussion, totally able to understand why these two were so special to Brett. He thought they would be to him as well, without question.

"Now, now, don't get your back up," Bruce said with a wagging finger. "We're celebrating tonight."

"What are we celebrating?" Gerald asked as he sat down where Jeff pointed.

"We're getting married!" Jeff crowed. "Next month. You have to help us convince Brett to be our best man."

Gerald blinked, totally surprised. "Married?"

"That's right, married," Bruce confirmed as they all sat down with the food in place. "Lucky man, I am."

"Apparently the state Supreme Court ruled today that gay marriage is legal under the constitution," Brett explained to Gerald. "I hadn't heard until we got here either."

"Wow," Gerald said, still off balance. "That's... great! Congratulations," he offered genuinely.

Jeff kissed Bruce's cheek before sitting down next to him. "So now, as I said, I need your help to get Brett to stand up with us."

Gerald looked at Brett speculatively. "Somehow I don't think he'll need much convincing."

"No convincing," Brett replied immediately, although the thought of having to dig out his suit was rather alarming, "but you could *ask* instead of trying to inveigle my boyfriend into it."

"Oh, I think your man would have helped if it came right down to it. Wouldn't you have, Gerry?" Jeff said sweetly.

"Of course I would," Gerald answered automatically, looking back and forth between Jeff and Bruce, starting to recognize the dynamic between them. It was so loving; they were so obviously committed to each other. It reminded him of his parents, actually. Not that Jeff and Bruce were old enough for that, but just how they related to each other. "You two have been together a long time, haven't you?"

Jeff stopped and pretended to count on his fingers. Bruce tapped the side of his lover's head gently. "Fifteen years, three months, ten days, and eight hours," Jeff said proudly.

Gerald's jaw dropped a little. "Wow!"

"He's slipping, Bruce," Brett teased. "He couldn't tell us minutes or seconds tonight."

"He's giddy," Bruce said. "Give him time. He'll get over it."

"Never going to happen," Jeff said as he started dishing up food.

As dinner went on, Gerald mostly listened to the other three talk, though he joined in from time to time. His thoughts were focused on the big topic of the night, though. Marriage. He'd never thought about it before in relation to anyone but his mom and dad. It wasn't like he had been planning to get married, so he simply didn't consider it something he needed to think about. But this, this was a surprise, and it was sort of throwing him for a loop.

Brett noticed Gerald was a little quieter than usual, except it occurred to him that he didn't know what was usual for his lover in a crowd. They spent so much time at the farm that they hadn't been out with other people before. The bonfire hardly counted since they weren't together then and Brett had spent most of his time playing host. Brett thought he ought to remedy that, although he couldn't think of anywhere he'd rather go than his couch—or his bed—with Gerald beside him.

The evening progressed wonderfully, in Gerald's opinion; he couldn't remember the last time he'd had such a good time visiting with friends. But once they were outside waving at Jeff and Bruce standing arm in arm on their front porch, Gerald realized he was really tired.

"Did you have fun?" Brett asked as they walked back to the car.

"Yeah, I did. They're great," Gerald said.

"They're the closest friends I have," Brett said. "They're the standard I've always measured my relationships against. I've always wanted what they have."

Gerald watched Brett as he walked around the car and had to actually snap himself out of a daze to get into the passenger seat. "They're beautiful people."

"They are," Brett agreed. "The very best. I'm so thrilled they'll finally get to make their commitment legal. It won't make them love each other more than they already do, but it'll give them a standing in the eyes of the law they've never had before."

"And that's important to them?" Gerald asked curiously.

"Of course it is," Brett said. "It means nobody will question their right to be together if one of them is injured. It means they can claim each other on their insurance. Bruce's insurance policy is much better than Jeff's, but until now, he hasn't been able to put him on it. It gives them a kind of security that your parents or mine have always taken for granted, that they've never had."

Gerald smiled a little, his chest oddly warm. "I can see you feel strongly about it."

"It's never been an issue for me personally," Brett admitted, "but I've lived a lot of it vicariously through Bruce and Jeff. I don't think they can be any more committed to each other, but this affords them some guarantees they didn't have before. And that is important."

Something in Gerald deflated a little, and he told himself it didn't mean anything. Never been an issue, Brett said. But Gerald couldn't wish for what he didn't know he wanted, now could he? Still a little conflicted, he filed the idea away just in case he might need it someday. He turned his chin to look out the window, wondering when one plus one equals two had become so complex.

"Is that something you think you'd want someday?" Brett asked, fishing for information. He'd hoped meeting Bruce and Jeff would spur this conversation without prompting, but that didn't seem to be happening.

"Haven't ever thought about it," Gerald answered honestly.

The answer was as frustrating as everything else Gerald said these days. "Would you be willing to think about it?" Brett pressed.

Gerald raised one shoulder. "I don't know why not." He turned his attention to his lover. "I've never had reason to consider such a thing. I think I can understand why it would be important to Jeff and Bruce."

Brett sighed in frustration. "Would you be willing to think about it with me?" he asked finally, needing a straight answer. "I'm not asking for a commitment now. I just need to know if you could consider it."

Gerald leaned his head back against the seat as relief flooded through him, watching his lover with a gentle smile. "Who else would I consider it with, Brett?" he asked, his voice soft.

"I don't know," Brett replied. "I just didn't know whether you'd consider it with me."

Gerald still watched him. "Yes, Brett. I'll consider it with you."

Brett's smile lit his entire face. "Good."

BRETT frowned down at the books, the projections for the rest of the year and for next year, trying to decide what he could guarantee, what he could hope for, and what he could dream about. He'd need all that information to approach a bank or other investor about infusing some capital into the farm so he could make the improvements he wanted. The indoor ring needed a new heating system, and he wanted to upgrade the outdoor ring and create a cross-country jumping course. He was also looking into therapy riding, but that was an even bigger investment of time and money.

Gerald opened the door from the back porch and stepped inside. "Hey, what's up?" He was still cleaned up, which meant he'd had a lesson but came here before heading to the barn to work.

"Looking at numbers for next year," Brett said with a sigh. "Math makes my head hurt."

"What sort of numbers?" Gerald walked to stand next to Brett and looked down at all the papers. He'd been reviewing the farm's tax situation the past couple of weeks, but he hadn't seen actual financials.

"Projected expenses, income, that sort of thing," Brett answered. "I need it to convince the bank to give me a loan."

"The bank will want records from the past few years of both income and expenses, including physical and liquid assets, as well as a written statement about what you hope to accomplish and what you'll need to do it. It would be best to include a budgeted requests list, and it should be estimated high," Gerald rattled off helpfully.

Brett sighed. "This gets more and more complicated every time I work on it."

Gerald chuckled and slid into the chair next to him. "Yes, it's complicated, but certainly doable. No thicker than dealing with the farm's taxes. I'll help."

"Really?" Brett asked, absurdly grateful. "I have all the records, but I wasn't here until about a year ago, so I don't know what's in the older ones."

"Yes, really," Gerald teased. "Best thing to do will be to get it all out and organize it first; that way you don't have to keep going back later. It will also get you familiar with what's been done in the past and how prices have changed over time."

"It's all in the office upstairs," Brett said, relief obvious in his voice. "My parents kept meticulous records. I just haven't had time to go through them."

"When do you want to start? How about an early dinner first?" Gerald asked, propping his chin in his hand with his elbow on the table.

"Sure," Brett agreed. Anything to delay having to go through those records. "What're you in the mood for?"

"How about I take you out to the hibachi grill?" Gerald suggested.

Brett's eyes got wide. They never went out. "Hibachi?" he parroted. "What's the occasion?"

Gerald raised an eyebrow and shifted in the chair. "I can't take you out?" he asked with a smile. He'd wondered if Brett would be surprised. Looked like he was.

"Well, um," Brett stuttered. "I guess. It's just, we always…." He shook his head as if coming out of a trance. "I'd love to go to the hibachi grill," he declared. If Gerald wanted to go out, they'd go out! "Just let me change into something a little less ratty."

Gerald's smile got bigger the more Brett stuttered on. "Okay," he said agreeably. "I'll wait," he said, amused.

Brett hurried upstairs, shedding his shirt as he went. He toed off his socks and tugged off his jeans, standing in front of the closet in just his underwear. He frowned slightly at the sight that greeted him. Didn't he have anything besides old jeans? Finding a pair of dress slacks in the back, he pulled them out, hoping they still fit. They were a little loose—he'd apparently lost some weight since he'd been home—but a belt solved that problem. He found a button-down shirt and pulled it on as well, digging out his dress shoes. He started back toward the stairs when he caught sight of a rarely used bottle of cologne on the dresser. With a smile, he splashed a little on and went back to the kitchen whistling. "Ready when you are."

Gerald turned to look, and the appreciation was clear in his eyes. "Well, I'm underdressed now," he said, glancing down at his close-fitted blue jeans and chambray shirt, tucked in, all accentuating his trim form.

"You look good enough to eat," Brett insisted. "It's just all I have besides work clothes. I obviously need some new clothes if we're going to go out much."

"Maybe we'll go shopping then," Gerald said as he stood and headed for the door. "Have you got a suit for the wedding?" He pulled his keys out of his pocket as they walked out onto the front porch.

Brett snorted. "Yeah, right. It's hanging upstairs next to my tuxedo." He followed Gerald out to his car, settling next to him in the passenger seat.

"Luckily, you have me. We'll get you a suit for that and whatever else you think you need," Gerald said distractedly as he backed the car out of the parking spot.

Brett groaned. "You're going to make me go shopping."

"Oh, Brett, I can't make you do anything you don't want to do, lover," Gerald said with a laugh as he steered the car down the drive.

"Yeah, but baby, I hate shopping!"

Gerald shot him an indulgent smile. "How about I make it worth your while, hmm?"

"How?" Brett asked suspiciously.

"Hmm," Gerald's tongue stuck out just a bit as he thought. "I could give you a reward for good behavior."

"What reward?"

"Suspicious!" Gerald teased, reaching to squeeze Brett's thigh. "You pick the reward." He got the car onto the highway and set the cruise control.

"You and me and a long ride out into the mountains," Brett said immediately.

"Such a hardship," Gerald drawled. He turned his chin and winked at Brett.

"It might be by the time we're done," Brett retorted with a grin. "Seeing as how I intend to fuck you while we're out there. And then you'll have to ride back."

Gerald twitched in surprise and looked at Brett sideways as he laughed. "That sounds like a hell of a fuck!"

"Oh, it will be," Brett promised. "It will be."

Seven

FULL from the delicious hibachi dinner and pleasantly tired after the long day, Gerald walked alongside Brett with his hands in his pockets as they made their way back to the car. It was dark outside, but the lights from the large mall lot and signs kept it lit well. Gerald enjoyed the dinner; it had been funny watching Brett react to the chef's entertainment at the grill, and seeing his lover try to catch in his mouth a piece of shrimp that was lobbed at him still had him chuckling.

"How about a nightcap?" he asked.

"Sounds like a plan to me," Brett agreed. "I've got drinks at the house."

"How about my house?" Gerald suggested, wondering if Brett would be interested in seeing it. They were on the right side of town, and it wouldn't take long to get there.

"I'd love to, Gerry," Brett agreed with a huge smile. "We've never gone there."

Gerald smiled, glad he'd pleased him. "Good. It won't take long. And I've got beer." He frowned a little. "I think."

Brett laughed. "Even more importantly, do you have lube?"

Gerald glanced up, his face even more pinched. "We better stop at the Walgreens."

Brett threw his head back and laughed. "I'll run in. Anything else you need while we're there?"

"Probably a razor. And a toothbrush." Gerald paused. "And deodorant. Damn." He laughed a little. "I guess I keep everything at your place now."

"We can go back to the farm," Brett offered, though he really wanted to see Gerald's place.

Now that Gerald had the idea in his head, he wanted Brett to see his house. He wouldn't call it home anymore, but it was the idea behind it. It was the one part of his life he hadn't shared with Brett, such as it was. "No, let's go. It will take longer to go back to the farm, and I have plans."

"I like the sound of that," Brett replied with a grin.

"Good," Gerald said with a wink as they got in the car.

IT took a half-hour shopping trip at Walgreens, but soon enough Gerald pulled into the drive that led to his house in a newer subdivision. It was a ranch-style building with a vaulted roof, big windows, and nice landscaping, built in the past ten years.

Gerald shut off the car around the back where there was a porch off sliding glass doors and an access entrance next to the garage. "Here we are."

"Nice," Brett commented with a low whistle, looking around at the spacious house. It wasn't huge, but it was definitely more than a simple bachelor's pad. He'd known Gerald was comfortable given the money he was willing to spend on riding, but he'd have guessed—if he'd thought about it—that his lover lived in a small condo or townhouse somewhere.

"Come on in," Gerald invited as he unlocked the side door. They entered a wide open sitting area with two big overstuffed couches and a decent-sized TV on a wide shelf. The room was separated from the kitchen by a bar. The walls were painted a rich wine red with white trim; the floor was a warm maple hardwood that matched the kitchen cabinets. A hallway led toward the front of the house, and a set of stairs ran up the left side wall. "Do you want the nickel tour?"

"As long as it ends in the bedroom," Brett joked.

Gerald grinned. "The master suite is upstairs. We can start there, if you like." He toed out of his shoes and kicked them to the side of the couch.

"I think I can wait the ten minutes it'll take for you to show me the rest," Brett deadpanned, "although you might want to talk fast."

"This is the great room." Gerald waved his hand around. "The kitchen, of course," he beckoned for Brett to follow. There was a formal living room and dining room, one on each side of the front door, and two bedrooms on that floor as well. He stopped at the bottom of the stairs. "The upstairs is really a loft setup in the garret."

"Skylight?" Brett asked hopefully. "I'd love to make love to you by moonlight."

Gerald smiled. "Come on," he said, curling his fingers through Brett's and leading him up the stairs. At the top was a small sitting area with a computer desk, but the rest of the space was totally open under the slanted ceiling, besides a queen-size bed with its headboard against the side wall. The tall windows on the back of the house opened next to it, and the bed was indeed bathed in light from outside. "Not a skylight, but—"

"Close enough," Brett said softly, his eyes taking in the airy room and gentle light. "Definitely close enough." Taking Gerald's hand in his, he turned his lover into a tender embrace, resting their foreheads together so that their breaths mingled between them, each exhalation caressing the other's lips.

Gerald let his eyes flutter shut as he raised one hand to lightly touch Brett's cheek. They'd had sex many times, often energetically. They'd taken their time over slow pleasures. But this, this felt different, gentle and loving, and Gerald just wanted to sink into it and never climb out.

Lifting his hand to Gerald's cheek, Brett spread his fingers along the ridged cheekbone, his palm resting against his jaw. Words backed up on his lips, declarations he wanted to make, but he wasn't quite confident enough yet. Soon, he hoped. Gerald said he'd be willing to consider a long-term commitment. Brett would just have to find a way to persuade him, and making love to him—truly loving him with every ounce of his being—would be the first step. To that end, he waltzed Gerald backward toward the bed, lowering him onto it fully clothed, and stretched out beside the other man.

Gerald let himself be moved, and when he felt Brett settle beside him he shifted to watch his lover's graceful movements. He immediately reached out to touch, just to make that connection, to know they were both there together. The quiet around them in the loft was a tangible force as it cradled them.

For a long moment, Brett simply lay there, palm cupping Gerald's face, head tilted into Gerald's hand. Time stretched, and the moonlight settled around them until nothing existed outside this room, this bed. To stop the words he dared not say, Brett leaned forward and connected their lips tenderly.

Sighing into the kiss, Gerald felt himself so totally in the moment that the world seemed to recede, leaving nothing but his lover there to hold him. There was nothing for him to do but express everything he felt in those kisses.

Slowly, Brett unbuttoned Gerald's shirt, pressing open-mouthed kisses over the skin as he revealed it. He inhaled deeply, letting Gerald's spicy scent wash over him. Gerald hummed softly in approval, sliding his hands over Brett's shoulders and back, caressing, trying to gently pull him closer. Brett scooted at Gerald's encouragement, aligning their bodies completely, just resting together as he kissed and stroked Gerald's skin.

Gerald wanted to say something, but he didn't know what. His fingers slid into Brett's hair, and he rubbed lightly as he slid his hand slowly down his lover's leg and met Brett's mouth for a longer, deeper kiss, one meant more to enflame than calm.

The kiss had the desired reaction. Brett's fingers dug lightly into Gerald's arms as desire sparked along with the love and tenderness swamping him. He lifted his leg along Gerald's, encouraging his lover to touch as he pleased.

Gerald did, dragging out the caresses, but hitting all the right places. He knew just where to touch Brett to turn him on and just what to do to make him harder. But tonight, he wanted to extend it until they were both crying and begging for release.

Brett sensed Gerald holding back, just as he was, and so he started the happy task of driving his lover wild with desire. He kept his touch light, but began seeking the sensitive spots: the inside of Gerald's elbow, the line of his ribs, the furrow above his hip where his well-defined abs began to narrow.

The soft gasp was a tell-tale sign of Gerald's arousal. He stretched a little under Brett's hands and let out a shuddering breath as his face flushed with warmth. He breathed his lover's name and returned the attention, half-distracted.

"Lie back and let me love you," Brett suggested softly, feeling Gerald's caresses stumble. "You can return the favor when I'm done."

"As much as you want," Gerald murmured, settling his shoulders back onto the bedspread.

Pushing up onto his knees, Brett pulled off Gerald's shoes, letting them thunk softly to the ground, then stripped away his lover's pants and boxers, leaving him delightfully naked. He was tempted to go straight for the beautiful, ruddy cock saluting him, but that would be rushing, and he didn't want to do that tonight. Instead, he lowered his head to Gerald's feet, lifting one into his hand and brushing his lips across the sensitive arch.

Gerald moaned and lifted his head to watch. The care put into just that little gesture was enthralling. He took a moment to thank God that he'd found Brett, who felt as strongly about him as he did in return. It filled him with joy, just as he soon hoped to be filled with passion.

Slowly, carefully, Brett worked his way up Gerald's foot to his ankle, his fingers massaging firmly, wanting to please him in every way possible. He nipped gently at the tendon between heel and ankle, enjoying the way Gerald shivered.

Gerald was starting to wonder what the hell he'd done to deserve Brett, because he sure needed to know to keep doing it. He wanted Brett around as long as he could keep him.

Working his way higher, Brett urged Gerald to spread his legs so he could kneel between them as he licked his way up his lover's toned calf to the back of his knee, nipping and sucking at the hairless flesh.

Laughing breathlessly, Gerald clasped Brett's shoulders as he wiggled under the attention. "Oh God," he finally whispered.

"Do you want me to stop?" Brett purred, not letting up in the least.

"No. Never." Gerald sighed as he shivered.

Brett chuckled. "That might make the horses a little testy." He kissed his way slowly up Gerald's inner thigh, stopping when the top of his head brushed against his lover's balls. Gently setting down the leg he held, he reached for the other, beginning the process all over again on the other side.

Gerald whined softly, unable to keep still under the light kisses and warm tongue. "Right now I couldn't care less about horses. God, please don't stop."

Brett grinned. "Don't let Misfit hear you say that." Not waiting for Gerald's reply, he sank his teeth carefully into the sensitive tendon on the back of his lover's knee. Gerald wailed softly, and one hand strayed to grasp his thickened cock and hold it tight. He didn't want to come yet. Not for a long while, if he could manage it.

"Did you need something, baby?" Brett teased, lifting his head to wink at Gerald before soothing the bite with tender kisses.

"Need you," Gerald breathed. "Always need you." He moaned as Brett's hands coasted over his sensitized skin.

"You have me," Brett promised, kissing his way up Gerald's thigh to his groin. "Any way you want me, you have me. Tell me what you want, baby. What'll make you feel good tonight? Do you want me to suck you? Or maybe rim you? I could keep licking all over. What do you want?"

"You drive me fucking wild with that tongue," Gerald rasped, the desire overwhelming his normal reserve. "I want to feel it all over, inside and out."

"Your wish is my command," Brett teased, running his tongue from the base of Gerald's cock to the tip, then moving farther up to lick one peaked nipple, then the other. Gerald whimpered with every swipe and shivered as the wet trail left behind was exposed to air. One hand grasped desperately at the bedspread, the other at Brett's arm.

"Easy, baby," Brett soothed. "We're just getting started." To prove his point, he rubbed his still-clothed cock against Gerald's hip. "See. I'm still wearing clothes. Now, turn over for me so I can get at your luscious ass."

Gerald's eyes closed as heat tore through him, and he moaned as he turned over and pulled a pillow under his chest. There was no way he'd be able to stay on his knees for this. "Please."

Brett grinned and started at the nape of Gerald's neck, working his way down his spine, lingering over each vertebra before finally making his way to the upper curve of his lover's ass. The way Gerald spread his legs made it obvious what he wanted, but Brett didn't give it to him right away. Instead, he took his time licking the cheeks, paying attention to every millimeter. With every touch of Brett's tongue Gerald's hips moved slightly against the bed, pushing his cock teasingly into the fluffy spread, and Gerald gasped out a sound of disappointment. He couldn't get enough pressure to help relieve the building ache in his groin.

Grabbing Gerald's hips to hold them still and keep him from getting himself off too soon, Brett parted the muscular cheeks and licked along the sweaty crease. "Talk to me, baby," he urged. "Tell me how it feels."

"You're teasing me," Gerald moaned, pushing his ass up toward Brett. "Please... I need it! I'm empty without you."

Brett had been teasing, but the desperation in Gerald's voice caused a sudden spike in his own desire, and the slight contact no longer satisfied him. Hands spreading Gerald's ass more, Brett buried his face, his tongue spearing as deep as he could get it, lips working on the outer pucker.

"Oh God!" Gerald cried, rocking backward, trying to get more of that slick muscle in him so it fucked him and drove him wild. He chanted Brett's name as the tension in him spiraled higher. Ever since the first time Brett had done this to him, he'd been unable to resist, and it turned him on faster and harder than anything else. But Gerald still craved Brett's cock inside him.

Brett tongue-fucked his lover until he couldn't ignore the throbbing in his cock. Pulling away and ripping open his pants, he looked around for the Walgreens bag. Finding it on the floor next to the bed, he tore open the box of lube, grabbed the tube, and coated his fingers with the slippery gel. "Tell me you're ready for me," he pleaded.

"Way ahead of you," Gerald panted, clumsily climbing to his knees. "I'm hurting for it."

Determined not to hurt Gerald, Brett slid two fingers into the glistening hole.

"Please!" Gerald cried out. "No more! I need *you* inside me, *you!* Now!"

Brett's reserve shattered. He swiped his hand across his cock, lined up the tip, and pushed home hard, not giving Gerald a chance even to catch his breath before picking up a pounding rhythm. Gerald's thrilled scream echoed on the walls around them, and his cries were constant as he begged for more.

Brett gave him all he had, pummeling the upturned ass with every ounce of his strength, straining to join them one centimeter more, one bit closer to the complete match he already felt in his heart.

Absolutely sure he'd come apart at the seams if any more pleasure soaked through him, Gerald awkwardly reached for his bobbing cock. The barest touch set him off with a deep bellow of pained ecstasy. His hips jerked as he came; the come shot out to wet the bedspread below him.

Gerald's internal muscles massaged the full length of Brett's cock and triggered his climax, his hips stuttering in their rhythm, pulse after pulse of hot come filling Gerald's ass. The sudden laxity in the body beneath him startled Brett into pulling out. "Gerry?"

All that answered him was soft breaths and a shudder.

Rolling to the side, Brett stripped quickly and then did his best to juggle Gerald and the sheets so they could spoon together beneath the covers. With a sigh, he pressed a kiss to Gerald's cheek and fell asleep.

GERALD clucked a little to get Misfit's attention as the mare looked across the corral to where a bunch of kids were making noise. He smiled at their antics and patted Misfit's neck. "Good girl. Nothing to be excited about."

"They'll be gone in a few minutes," Brett assured both horse and rider. "And then it'll just be us."

"I don't know. I think Misfit might rather be with them than with me," Gerald said as the horse shied a little toward the kids.

"I doubt that," Brett replied. "She's skittish from the noise. There's a reason I don't use her with beginners. Tighten the reins a little and give her a nudge. Get her attention and make her listen to you."

Gerald did as instructed, and Misfit seemed to calm down. "C'mon, girl, we're doing fine," he said as they made their way toward the corral exit as Brett walked alongside.

Opening the gate, Brett stepped aside so Gerald and Misfit could go inside. He kept a close eye on the kids cleaning up from the last lesson of the day, making sure they didn't get too close to the high-strung mare while Gerald was still in the saddle. "You did great today," he praised as he shut the gate and followed Gerald into the barn. "Your first attempt at jumping an X. And you thought you wouldn't be any good."

"I don't think I've been that nervous in a long time," Gerald admitted. "I was afraid I'd do something wrong and Misfit would get hurt."

Brett laughed. "Which is why she's extra skittish tonight. You did fine. And I wouldn't have suggested we try it if I didn't think you were ready. Get her undressed, and we'll finish up the last of the chores. Then we can relax a little before bed."

"Relaxing wasn't exactly what I had in mind," Gerald teased as he dismounted and landed a little wobbly.

"I said before bed, not before going to sleep," Brett retorted with a grin. He'd wait a little longer before kissing Gerald the way he wanted to. He could still hear the last of the kids talking as their parents picked them up, and he didn't want anything to interrupt them.

Gerald grinned and began unfastening Misfit's tack, dodging her as she bobbed her head. "Misfit," he chided gently. "Let me get this stuff off, and you can fuss all you want in your stall."

Brett shook his head at their antics and went to get his work gloves. He turned Shah out and grabbed the manure cart. The staff cleaned the other stalls earlier in the day, but he didn't let his big brute out until all the kids were gone for the night, so Shah's stall still needed mucking. "Turn her out for the night rather than leaving her in her stall," Brett called out. "Let her stretch her legs."

Gerald got the saddle off, wiped Misfit down, and grabbed up her lead rope. He got to the field fence and led her inside. She kept bobbing her head, though, as he tried to unclip the lead. "Misfit," he said firmly. "Hold still."

And just as he got the lead off, Misfit shifted without warning and bumped into Gerald hard. Flailing, Gerald fell sideways and backward—right into the manure pile.

Misfit whinnied and galloped off, the sound drawing Brett's attention. "Gerry?" he called. "You all right?"

Gerald sat there on his ass in the mess, disgruntled, nose wrinkled. "Yeah," he answered, the tone of his voice obviously unhappy. He turned his chin to glare after Misfit.

Frowning, Brett tossed the pitchfork on the manure cart and went in search of his lover. He couldn't bite back the bark of laughter that escaped at the sight of the other man sitting in the pile of manure. "Did she knock you over?"

Gerald rolled his eyes. "You think?" He looked down at himself. "Great."

"Come on," Brett urged, extending his hand. "Let's get you hosed off."

With a sigh, Gerald took Brett's hand and got to his feet, only sliding a little. "You know, I've never complained about mucking out stalls, but this is a little much," he muttered.

"Don't worry; you'll wash," Brett teased. "Come on. There's a hose around back where we can get the worst off, and then you can take a shower when we go inside."

Gerald followed Brett around and stood looking at the hose as Brett bent over to pick it up. "That water's going to be cold," he predicted.

"Maybe a little, but I promise to warm you up afterward," Brett replied, turning it on and adjusting the spray so it wouldn't be too hard against Gerald's body. When he was satisfied, he turned the jet on his lover, watching with hungry interest as the thin T-shirt turned translucent and his lover's dark nipples peaked beneath the cloth.

Gasping, Gerald turned his back on the water. "Geez, Brett! That's cold! My balls are going to crawl up inside and not come out! Geez!"

Brett kept spraying, soaking the back of Gerald's T-shirt and the seat of his jeans. "I'll warm them up, baby. I'm sure I can get them to come back out for me."

Gerald gurgled a little and made himself turn around, though his teeth were gritted. "Now I know why the horses don't want a wash sometimes." He closed his arms around himself, his fingers sinking into the soaked cloth and pulling it taut against his chest. His jeans were soaked as well, sticking to every single curve and crease.

"God, you look good enough to eat." Brett groaned, ignoring the fact that Gerald's clothes still stank to high heaven. He didn't care. Clothes could be removed, and the skin underneath was always sweet.

Gerald shook himself, flinging water every which way. "I think the worst is off now. I'll have to strip down before going in the house, though. These clothes reek." He looked at Brett and waited for him to turn off the hose.

"Strip now," Brett suggested hoarsely, lowering the pressure on the water but not turning it off. "Let's get you completely clean, and then we'll warm you up."

Raising an eyebrow, Gerald tipped his head to one side and lowered his hands to his waist. He slowly unfastened his button fly, having to suck his belly in because the fabric clung so close.

Brett let the spray water the grass for a moment while Gerald's tawny skin came into view an inch at a time. When the jeans hit the ground along with the T-shirt, he raised the water again, dousing Gerald once more before dropping the hose and crossing to Gerald's side. "We can run for the house, or there's a nice, warm hayloft about ten steps from here. It's your choice," he offered, running his hands over Gerald's chilly skin.

Gerald answered that question by cupping Brett's face and kissing him, making it hot and wet as he rubbed himself against the other man's clothes.

Brett didn't need any more encouragement. Closing his arms around Gerald's waist, he staggered back into the barn, dragging his lover along, and kicked open the door to the hay loft. He pushed Gerald up the ladder in front of him, and then down on the blanket used to keep down the dust. Gerald immediately knelt up, working to get Brett's pants undone. Brett helped him by toeing off his boots and pulling his shirt over his head before falling back on his lover, biting ravenously at the column of his neck.

Gasping aloud and grasping Brett's shoulders, Gerald turned his chin to encourage the attention as he struggled to shove down his briefs.

Finally free of them, he wrapped his long legs around Brett's thighs and dug his cold fingers into his lover's warm skin.

"No lube," Brett groaned in frustration, though there was no way he could stop now. Spinning around, he straddled Gerald's shoulders, leaning down and sucking on the other man's chilly cock.

The heat of Brett's mouth sent a full-body shudder through Gerald, who parted his lips to try to catch his lover's erection as it bobbed before him. He teased at it with his tongue as warmth started to ripple through him.

Brett glanced back long enough to position himself to give Gerald easier and more comfortable access. He didn't want his lover feeling anything but pleasure. Returning his attention to the slowly awakening erection in front of him, he tongued it lovingly, working his way down its entire length to the usually heavy balls beneath. As Gerald had predicted, they were drawn up tightly. With a grin, he sucked on the cold flesh until it warmed and swelled against his mouth.

Sighing as wet heat chased the chill away, Gerald slowly sucked Brett's cock into his mouth, working it gently as he moaned quietly. He really liked a good sixty-nine; it let him draw out his arousal for a longer time, especially when he was slow to harden to start with. Although that wasn't a problem with Brett. With a throaty hum he lapped about the thick flesh between his lips.

Only the same intense concentration that had allowed Brett to compete at the highest levels of show riding allowed him to control the desire to thrust into the hot, wet heat around his cock. At this angle, he'd bet he could sink all the way down Gerald's throat with no trouble, but he wasn't about to impose. He'd wait for an invitation before doing that.

Groaning as the suction stiffened his cock and the pull of nerves in his gut, Gerald tried to return the favor just as firmly. He lifted his head from the hay in an attempt to get more of Brett's erection into his mouth, slurping around its length.

Taking Gerald's movement as an invitation, Brett rocked his hips carefully, not wanting to choke him, but needing to be deeper in the tempting warmth. As he did, he lowered his head until his lips brushed Gerald's groin, his cock all the way into Brett's throat.

Gerald gasped around the cock lodged in his mouth before tipping his head back to give as much room as he could to take it in. It was a thrill, feeling the circuit they completed as electric sensation zipped through them. He reached up to clutch at Brett's hips, urging him to move more.

Brett gasped as he sank deeper into Gerald's throat. God, nothing felt like Gerald's hands and mouth on his body! Slipping a finger into his mouth next to Gerald's cock, he wet it quickly, then returned to giving his lover the best blow job he could manage while lightly fingering his ass at the same time. He wanted Gerald delirious with sensation.

The press of Brett's fingers made Gerald gulp, taking in more of Brett's cock than he expected, but his lover pulled out just as quickly before pushing in again. Gerald moaned, the vibrations moving through his tongue and lips as he let his knees fall askew, trying to encourage his lover. Brett's mouth was driving him wild, and Gerald's erection was no question now. He wanted to move his hips, to push up and against that wicked tongue.

Gripping Gerald's hips with one hand, Brett continued to tantalize the tight pucker, pressing against it erratically, sometimes barely a brush, sometimes enough to slip in almost to the first knuckle. His head bobbed over the thick cock as he did, keeping Gerald on the edge with deliberate precision.

Gerald finally had to whine as he struggled to wiggle under Brett as the sensations started to build fast. He didn't want to come yet! It was so good….

Brett wouldn't be denied, though, his hands pinning Gerald in place as he sucked harder, determined to bring Gerald off quickly so they could go inside, take a shower—preferably together—and continue this in bed. With lube.

Gerald knew he'd lost the fight when Brett held him down, and so he opened his mouth to release Brett's cock and gasped for breath. "Brett... Brett...." He gasped as he began to shake and groan, the climax taking him over.

The desperate sound of his lover's moans nearly undid Brett's control, but he focused on the man beneath him and the flavor of hot come coating his tongue, barely managing to hold back as he sucked and sucked until Gerald began to twitch all over, unconsciously trying to squirm away from the sensation overload. The shaky moans under him degenerated into soft gasps for breath and then a long groan.

"Fuck," Gerald muttered.

"Did you know your language seriously degenerates when you come?" Brett teased, swinging around and pressing a kiss to the side of Gerald's mouth. "So, warmer now?"

"Fuck," Gerald breathed again before dragging his eyes open. "Warmer," he said hoarsely. "Yeah. You could say that."

"Then let's head inside and into the shower," Brett suggested. "I stink of horses still."

Gerald laughed breathlessly. "You're going to have to help me up," he said apologetically.

Brett laughed as well, pushing to his feet and grabbing Gerald's hand to pull him up as well. "Can you walk or do you expect me to carry you?" he teased.

"As much as that's an interesting idea, I think I'm done for the night." Gerald climbed to his feet and moved close to slide his arms around Brett's waist, nudging his groin against Brett's obvious erection. "But you aren't."

"So let's get cleaned up and we can see what you can do about that." Brett kissed him gently. "And who knows, maybe I'll persuade you back to life again."

Gerald grinned and grabbed his briefs from the hay, crumpling them up in one hand. "Who knows? If anyone could, it would be you." He looked out of the stable door. "I'm leaving those clothes, though." He looked down at his briefs and shrugged. "I guess if anyone's here they'll get a show."

"Everybody left before Misfit knocked you in the manure," Brett assured him, not bothering with his own clothes either. "We're perfectly safe heading back to the house as we are."

With a sigh, Gerald climbed down the ladder and started toward the house. "Today has been eventful," he said, picking his way across the gravel in his bare feet. "I'm glad I've got clothes to change into."

"You could always wear some of mine if you needed to," Brett offered, walking gingerly along behind Gerald, eyeing him as he did. "I don't know if my jeans would fit, but my sweats would, at least enough to keep you decently covered. I don't want anyone else ogling your ass."

Gerald looked over his shoulder. "I thought I was the one with the ass fetish."

"You may be, but I seem to be developing one," Brett replied. "Ever since the night we went swimming, I've wanted to get my hands on it. I just wasn't free at the time, and I had no idea if you were interested."

"Since we went swimming? You mean after the bonfire?" Gerald asked as he hopped up onto the steps, glad to be out of the gravel. His sated cock swung free against the toned muscles of his thighs.

"Yes," Brett admitted, riveted by the sight of his lover nude out in the open air. "I turned around as you were getting dressed, and I about grabbed you right then. My tongue was dragging the ground looking at you."

Gerald blinked, stopping in place. "I… I saw you," he confided. "With this impressive hard-on," he said, moving his hand to cup it. "But you were with Robbie." He shrugged. "Didn't even occur to me to think it might be for me."

"He was gone," Brett reminded Gerald. "Of course it was for you. I'm just sorry it took until he got his promotion for me to realize how ill-suited he and I really were."

Taking Brett's hand, Gerald drew him inside the house and shut the door. "He wasn't for you," Gerald told him. "He didn't love the horses or the farm."

"I can see that now," Brett agreed. "It just took me awhile to see what was right in front of my face." He pulled Gerald into his arms and kissed him gently. "I won't make the same mistake again. Not now that I have you."

Gerald smiled against Brett's lips and slid his arms around his lover's waist to complete the embrace. "Let's see what else you can see," he teased as he rubbed his thigh against Brett's still-hard cock. "I apparently still have your interest."

"Oh, yeah," Brett gasped. "Shower!"

"Shower," Gerald agreed. "And then you're going to fuck me," he said as he turned to start up the stairs, deliberately looking back over his shoulder.

"Oh, yeah!" Brett repeated, racing after Gerald's retreating ass.

Gerald laughed as he high-tailed it back into Brett's bathroom, grabbing the door frame to stop his forward motion before he hit the wall. He leaned over to turn on the water.

The sight of that upturned backside was just too tempting to resist. Brett slid both hands over the smooth, bare skin, squeezing tightly before he rubbed his cock down the crease. Gerald looked over his shoulder, bracing himself on one hand as he reached back to curl his arm around Brett's hip. "Sure you don't want to fuck me first?" he purred, rubbing his ass against the hard cock behind him.

"How about I fuck you during?" Brett suggested, grabbing a tube of silicone lube he'd bought against just such an eventuality. "You can brace yourself against the wall."

Gerald smiled slowly as he straightened. "You're on," he said, stepping over the lip of the tub and into the spray.

Brett crowded him close into the shower, rubbing against him eagerly. The hot water felt good on his skin. He squeezed a dollop of gel onto his fingers. "Spread 'em," he growled.

Gerald moved his legs apart so he could stand steady with his hands on the wall. Brett would be so close there wouldn't be anywhere for him to slide to anyway. An idea occurred as Brett's words echoed in his ears, and he reached behind himself to pull his cheeks apart. The hot water coursed down his back, over his fingers, and into his cleft.

"Like that?" Gerald asked after hearing Brett's comment. "C'mon, you know you want it," he teased as he pushed against Brett's finger.

"Oh fuck," Brett groaned when he saw how Gerald interpreted his order. It wasn't what he'd intended, but he was sure it had the effect Gerald desired as Brett's cock jumped eagerly, ready to be buried in his lover's hot ass. Smearing the gel, he poked gently at the tight pucker, enticing it to open for him. "I don't want to hurt you," Brett said, resisting the urge to shove inside and plunge deep.

Gerald grinned against his arm. "Use more gel," he instructed as he shimmied against Brett.

Brett groaned again, adding more lube and driving two fingers deep into Gerald's ass. "Tell me if it hurts," he requested. He wasn't averse to a little rough loving, but only if both parties were willing.

"Brett, you've been fucking me almost every day for weeks now," Gerald said breathlessly as he rubbed his thighs together. While he wasn't sporting an erection, it still felt really good to have Brett touch him. It would feel even better having Brett inside him. "It's not going to hurt."

Gerald was probably right, Brett acknowledged. He slicked his cock and pressed the tip against the loosening muscles. Gerald pushed back immediately, encouraging Brett to go deeper, until his groin brushed his lover's ass. "Oh yeah," Gerald groaned. "Feels so good."

"It's supposed to," Brett gasped, the hot water and hotter ass around his cock driving him wild.

Gerald started pushing back, driving the tempo, encouraging Brett to do more. He managed to brace himself on one forearm against the wall so he could wrap his free hand around his cock. He could tell he wouldn't be fucking Brett tonight, but there was no reason not to enjoy.

Brett wanted to hang on, to find a way to rouse Gerald again before he came, but that didn't seem likely, however much he wanted it. He'd settle for not embarrassing himself by coming after just a few strokes.

Laughing breathlessly, Gerald had to move both hands to the wall as Brett thrust into him. "Oh God...." He gasped as the cock sliding inside him pressed against his prostate, and he thunked his forehead gently against the wall.

That about summed it up as far as Brett was concerned, but finding the words to agree was beyond him. He thrust shallowly, keeping the pressure constant on Gerald's prostate in the hopes of making his lover feel as good as he felt.

Gerald was soon mewling and hanging on to the metal bar set into the shower wall as he quivered under Brett. "Oh please... please...." He struggled to breathe, unable to hold still as the stimulation went hot inside him. "Please touch me." He wanted to come again; it hurt so, so good.

Immediately, Brett reached around, grasping Gerald's cock with one hand, his chest with the other, finding his nipples and tweaking them, one, then the other, then back again, trying to give his lover everything he needed.

Low moans rippled from Gerald as his body went taut. "Oh fuck, you're gonna make me fucking come again...."

"That's what I want, baby," Brett whispered. "I want to feel you come apart around me. What do you need?" He shuttled his fist faster on Gerald's hardening cock as he waited for the answer.

"Fuck me—hard—harder," Gerald got out between pants as he shuddered. "Want to hear you when you come."

Despite his desire to feel Gerald come first, the words were all it took to shock a hoarse shout from Brett's lungs as his cock contracted and forced out the streamers of come. His hips stuttered through the aftershocks as he kept his hand moving, trying to get Gerald off.

Gerald actually whimpered as he shuddered into a burning orgasm; his cock twitched only a couple times to release a small spurt, but he didn't care. He was swamped and dizzy, barely hanging onto the rail as his head spun.

Panting, Brett leaned heavily against Gerald's back, the hot water now cool on his overheated skin. It took several seconds before he could straighten and reach for the soap to clean them off. He was so hypersensitive that even the nap of the soft cotton washcloth felt harsh against his skin.

"Fuck," Gerald breathed, still shaking, totally wiped out. "I'm not sure I can stand up much longer," he rasped, clinging to the bar.

"Me either," Brett agreed, dropping the rag to the splat in the water in the bottom of the tub. "We'll clean up tomorrow."

Gerald groaned and straightened up before shutting off the water. He turned to touch Brett's cheek and kiss him gently, his breathing still harsh as he mouthed his lover's lips and curled his arm around his waist.

Brett returned the kiss breathlessly, but his legs threatened to give out on him. "Let's get out of here before we both fall down. Did you not get enough?" he teased.

Gerald's arm tightened for a moment. "More than. For now," he murmured before kissing him again. He reluctantly let Brett loose and climbed out to dry off with a fluffy towel.

"As long as it's only for now," Brett said, following Gerald out of the shower and drying off as well.

Looking over his shoulder, Gerald spent a long moment gazing at his lover, wondering how he'd been so lucky so find him. He hung his towel on a hook by the sink. "Come to bed and let me hold you."

"For as long as you want," Brett promised, dropping the towel and following Gerald out of the room.

"BRETT. You cannot tell me you want to go to some mass retailer and pick a suit off a rack at random," Gerald said, throwing up his hands as they stood on the sidewalk in the downtown shopping district. "It's Bruce and Jeff's wedding! It's *special*!"

"A suit's a suit," Brett protested. "Why does it matter where we buy it? I hate shopping. I just want to find something as quickly as possible so we can go home. There are chores I need to be doing."

"A suit is not 'a suit', and I won't have you looking like a cookie-cutter office drone. Now come on," Gerald said, taking Brett's hand and starting down the street while mumbling to himself.

Brett followed along, shaking his head over this entire ridiculous situation. "I could rent one for the weekend," he suggested hesitantly.

Gerald didn't even look over his shoulder; he just squeezed Brett's hand tighter and kept walking until he stopped at the door to a classy men's store. "Now remember, I promised you a reward," he said, wagging a finger.

That was the only reason Brett was here. Well, that and the fact he couldn't refuse Gerald anything. Even so, he fully intended to take advantage of his reward just as soon as they finished this shopping expedition. "Let's get this over with."

Rolling his eyes, Gerald opened the door. "You like my suit, don't you?" He pulled Brett in after him.

"Yeah," Brett said warily, not sure what that had to do with anything. "So?"

"So this is where I got it, and you too can look that hot," Gerald said. He started winding through the store.

Brett raised an eyebrow in speculative interest. He wondered whether a suit would have the same effect on Gerald as it had on him or if his lover were so jaded by being around businessmen every day that the sight wouldn't do anything for him. This trip might have just gotten more interesting. "I always look hot," he retorted, not willing to let Gerald get in the last word.

"In your jeans, yes, I agree," Gerald said as he looked over several displays while a sales associate fluttered nearby. "But according to you, that has nothing on me in my glasses." He glanced up and winked. "Perhaps a well-fitted suit will re-create the phenomena in your favor."

He paused and looked thoughtful. "Maybe I should get my glasses out of the car...."

Brett groaned at the thought of having to restrain himself while Gerald was wearing his glasses. "Not playing fair," he protested.

Gerald whistled tunelessly and nodded to the salesman waiting, pointing out two different suits. "All right, handsome," he said to Brett. "Over to the fitting." He shooed Brett toward the raised stand in the back surrounded by mirrors.

Sulking, Brett moved as directed, feeling incredibly self-conscious as he stepped up onto the platform. Smiling, Gerald sat fluidly in an armchair placed where he could watch as Brett was measured.

"Relax, Brett. There's no one here to see but me," Gerald placated. "Soon you will have a gorgeous suit, and this will all be a bad dream."

Brett tried to relax as he moved this way and that, the salesman taking a variety of measurements to ensure the suit fit correctly.

"Now, would the gentleman like to try them on to see which cut hangs better?" the sales associate asked.

"No...."

"Yes," Gerald said firmly. "You can't buy it without trying it on, Brett. They may need to tailor it to your frame. You're pretty broad in the shoulders compared to that small waist."

"There is an unusually large difference between your shoulder and waist sizes," the salesman agreed. "A lot of coats won't hang right on you."

"Oh, all right," Brett groused. "Can I at least get down so I don't feel like a statue on display?"

Gerald hid his smile. "All right. Just stand by the mirror, okay? We have to be able to see you from all sides to make sure nothing hangs crooked."

Brett rolled his eyes but climbed down in relief, staying near the mirror as the salesman held out the first coat. He shrugged into it, twitching his shoulders to get it settled correctly.

Gerald watched as they went through several different jackets, the fitter occasionally looking his way and getting a nod or shake of his head. It was interesting to watch Brett; Gerald had been like him, once, when it came to clothes, anyway. He'd had to learn once he moved up in the executive world.

After half an hour, they were down to two suits that the salesman displayed for Brett's choice.

Brett looked back and forth between the two suits. He wished his mother was here. From an old family with deep roots, she had an ingrained sense for things like fashion. But Brett hadn't inherited it, nor had his life choices given him any reason to learn it on his own. "I don't know," he said finally. "You choose, Gerald."

Gerald stood up and walked to stand right behind him. First he held one suit up to his lover's chest, then the other. He smiled slowly and held one out for the salesman. "This one."

Just before he stepped away, he leaned to whisper in Brett's ear. "Matches your eyes."

"Will you be needing shirts, ties, cufflinks?" the salesman asked courteously.

Brett groaned. Gerald laughed lightly. "Yes. Pick something plain for the shirt—crisp white, I think—and an understated tie with that sheen that's fashionable now. I'll pick the cufflinks." He gestured for Brett to follow as the salesman bustled off to the storeroom.

Brett sighed and resigned himself to at least another half-hour before they could escape and get back to the safety of the farm. But Gerald was quick, choosing right away, and the salesman was efficient. They were out the door in less than fifteen minutes.

"There. That wasn't so bad, was it? Not even an hour," Gerald teased as he walked with Brett's suit hanging from his fingers over his shoulder.

"As long as I get my reward," Brett pouted, before smiling a little. "No, it wasn't awful, although I don't think I could stand to fill a wardrobe that way. How do you deal with it?"

"I learned, Brett. A little at a time. I still can't handle shopping every week or two. So I usually take a whole weekend and shop once a season," Gerald explained. "I wouldn't even go that often if I didn't have to be classy for work."

"That's a little better, I guess," Brett said. "My mother's family has all these really elegant people. They're always dressed in the latest fashion, even for situations when I'd consider old jeans and a T-shirt fine. I didn't grow up that way, obviously, but I always felt... second best next to my cousins, I guess. I don't want to go back to feeling that way."

Startled, Gerald stopped in place and turned to face his lover. "Brett, you will never be second best to me. That's not what this was about."

Brett shook his head. "I know that. You wanted to help me for Bruce and Jeff's sake, and you were right. I just look at myself in my grungy jeans and work boots most of the time and wonder what a classy accountant like you is doing with a guy like me."

"Don't you know I think of that too? What's this rugged, handsome cowboy want with an office geek like me?" Gerald said, feeling self-conscious. He didn't express things like this well at all. "That maybe I'm trying to tag along and be like you?"

Brett shook his head. "We're a real pair, aren't we, each worrying we aren't what the other wants." He leaned over and kissed Gerald gently. "You're exactly what I want, baby, and I'm thrilled that you're willing to learn about the farm, but either way, you're exactly what I want."

"Yes, we're a real pair, and we're drawing attention," Gerald pointed out through his light laugh. "Come on. Take me back to that farm, because if you're there, that's where I want to be."

"Come on then," Brett said with a grin. "The work's piling up as we speak."

"Literally," Gerald said drolly as they walked to the car.

BRETT tugged at the tie that came with his new suit. It fit perfectly, but that didn't make it less uncomfortable to someone totally unused to wearing such nice clothes. He couldn't remember the last time he'd worn a tie. He wouldn't dream of disgracing Bruce and Jeff by showing up in his work clothes, but he still wished there'd been some sort of middle ground. It was just for a short time, Brett reminded himself. Once the ceremony was over, he could lose the tie and coat for the huge party the two men had planned.

Gerald watched from where he sat in the second row of ten chairs set up in the formal living room of the gorgeous Victorian-style bed-and-breakfast. A few other of Jeff's and Bruce's close friends were scattered amongst the chairs, but there were only eight people present besides the officiant, who was doing the paperwork with the happy couple. But Gerald only had eyes for Brett, who looked stunning in his suit, just like Gerald knew he would. It would never compare to seeing him in jeans and flannel on horseback, but he was certainly a gorgeous sight all cleaned up.

Preparatory paperwork finished, the justice motioned for Bruce and Jeff to take their places with their witnesses, Brett and Sean, another longtime friend. "Dearly beloved," he began, "we are gathered together today to bear witness to the formal uniting of two lives already lived as one."

Brett listened to the words, resisting the urge to turn and look at Gerald as he spoke. Every word resonated in his heart, though, echoing his feelings for his lover who sat in the seats behind them. He reminded himself that Bruce and Jeff hadn't always been this happy, that they'd had to work through issues and questions before reaching this point. He and Gerald could still get there. Someday.

As soon as the ceremony was over and Bruce and Jeff had shared their first kiss as married men, Brett returned to Gerald's side with no intention of leaving that spot for the rest of the day. And for far longer, if he had his way. He just had to find a way to broach the subject with his wonderfully dense lover.

Adjusting his thinking had come pretty easily to Gerald once he'd gotten used to the concept of marriage being more than he'd always thought. Jeff and Bruce completed each other. It was a no-brainer. It was one plus one equals forever, just like his own parents and so many other happily married couples he'd known over the years. And as Gerald kept his eyes on his lover instead of the ceremony, he knew the equation fit his life too, now that he knew to apply it. That knowledge filled him with quiet happiness.

Greatly pleased when Brett returned to him, Gerald hooked their arms together, stepped close, and pressed a kiss to Brett's brow as they watched the others congratulate Bruce and Jeff. It was a beautiful moment.

"They're so happy," Brett whispered, leaning into Gerald's kiss. "I don't think I've ever seen them this happy."

Gerald just nodded, his lips shifting against Brett's hair. "They're glowing," he murmured.

"They'd learned to accept that this day might never come. I think they're entitled to glow a bit," Brett said. He knew he'd be glowing if Gerald ever agreed to marry him.

"Yeah." Gerald slid his arm around Brett's waist. "I'm glad to see them so happy. It's good for everyone."

Having received the congratulations of everyone present, Bruce and Jeff were eager to get to the party. "Come on, Brett. Bring that gorgeous stud of yours. I want to see you two dance together," Jeff announced to the room.

Gerald arched one brow in amusement. "Next thing he'll be setting me out in a field of mares," he murmured as he and Brett walked out into the hall.

Brett chuckled. "Not a chance. He's far too happy with the idea of you being gay."

"I hadn't noticed," Gerald said.

Brett snorted. "Then you're even more clueless than Bruce thinks you are."

Gerald stopped in place, blinking. "I'm not clueless."

"You didn't catch my attempts to see if you were gay the day we met," Brett reminded him. "And some of those lines were as obvious as the day is long."

"That doesn't make me clueless," Gerald continued to object. "I was… distracted."

"Distracted?"

"By the horses." Gerald cleared his throat. "And your ass," he muttered under his breath.

"What was that?" Brett teased. "My hat?"

Gerald's cheeks flushed. "Are we ready to go to the reception?" he asked, his voice a bit desperate.

"Sure," Brett replied with a grin, "just as soon as you tell me what else distracted you besides the horses. And no mumbling this time."

His cheeks darkening, Gerald glanced from side to side, checking who was around them. "Your. Ass."

"Oh, well in that case, I guess you're forgiven." Brett grinned. "After all, I have it on good authority that it's a spectacular ass."

"Move that spectacular ass. There's cake and champagne waiting," Gerald said, smiling and hoping his cheeks weren't as red as they felt.

Brett grabbed Gerald's hand and started toward the veranda where the food was laid out, grinning like a loon. "When you put it that way…."

Gerald laughed as Brett pulled him along. They were oblivious to the pleased smiles from Bruce and Jeff when they approached the cake-cutting; Gerald's attention was totally on his lover and didn't waver.

There were a lot more people who'd come to the reception; they toasted and cheered when Bruce and Jeff cut the cake, clinking their glasses to get the two men to kiss. Bruce grabbed Jeff in a bear hug, lifting him off his feet as he kissed him sloppily to the accompaniment of raucous catcalls.

The grin on Gerald's face was wide as they applauded and called for an encore, and his laugh spilled out as he watched the two men so obviously in love. He glanced to his side to see Brett smiling as well and knew it was a day to remember.

When they'd finished the cake and champagne, the music started and all the guests were invited to watch Bruce and Jeff's first dance as married men. They swayed together slowly through the strains of "As Time Goes By." The next song, though, was much more energetic, and the guests swarmed onto the dance floor to join the bump and grind. "Do you want to dance?" Brett asked with a grin.

Gerald's brows bounced up. "Uh. I don't know how to dance."

"Come on. It's easy," Brett urged. "Please?"

Letting Brett pull him onto the dance floor, Gerald sighed and grimaced wryly. "And you'll see what a klutz I really am."

"I've seen you ride," Brett contradicted. "I know you aren't a klutz." He pulled Gerald against him, hands settling on his hips and guiding him through the dance.

Gerald found that he didn't feel clumsy at all with Brett's hands on him, and he actually enjoyed the dance. But he liked it even more when the music shifted to the slow big band classic "Moonlight Serenade." "This is more my speed," he said, sliding one arm around Brett's waist and taking his hand.

"You won't hear me complaining about anything that gets us closer," Brett said, letting Gerald take the lead this time. His lover led them around the dance floor in a simple sway, occasionally turning them in a circle as other couples swirled around them to the romantic music.

"Mmm, closer. I love that idea," Gerald murmured as his arm around Brett's waist tightened.

"Just as soon as the reception is over," Brett promised. "I'm pretty sure Bruce and Jeff wouldn't appreciate it if I dragged you into the bathroom."

Gerald chuckled and set their foreheads together. "I suppose I can wait if you can."

Brett looked around at the crowd. "Do you think they'd notice if we disappeared for a bit?"

"Notice?" Gerald blinked and leaned back and looked around. "With all these people here?"

Brett cocked an eyebrow speculatively. "I'll bet there's a handicapped restroom with a door that locks," he murmured.

Gerald snorted. "It's a restored Victorian house. There's more likely a bathroom with a claw-foot tub upstairs."

"Let's go see what we can find," Brett purred.

Turned out they found a combination of both. A bathroom upstairs—with a claw-foot tub—had been enlarged by knocking out a closet. It was decorated in soothing blues, and being in the front of the house, it was away from the music and the crowd.

Brett snicked the lock shut. "Privacy," he said with a grin, advancing on Gerald and pinning him against the wall.

Gerald let Brett hold him in place and dipped his head to kiss him as his pulse sped. "Brett...." he breathed as he felt himself get hard when Brett's hand slid across the front of his suit pants and groped him.

"God, I want inside you," Brett groaned. "Please tell me you've got lube in your pocket."

"Jesus, Brett, it's a wedding! Of course I don't have lube in my pocket," Gerald said. He shifted his hips, trying to get some pressure on his cock.

"I guess I'll just have to suck you off then," Brett lamented, humping Gerald's thigh. "But when we get home, your ass is mine."

Gerald whined ever so slightly as the thought of Brett on his knees really made his gut clench. "I think I'm gonna come in my pants," he said shakily.

"And this is bad because?" Brett drawled, dropping to his knees and pulling open Gerald's pants.

"Because I have to walk through all those people to the car!" Gerald exclaimed as he dropped his chin to watch. "Awwww, fuck,

Brett, hurry! I didn't know I was so fucking turned on. I don't want to get caught." Gerald's voice was near desperate, very unlike him.

"We locked the door, baby. Nobody's going to come in and interrupt us," Brett soothed, though his movements were nearly as frantic, pulling Gerald's briefs down enough to get at his cock, sucking it deep.

Gerald quivered and let out a long, soft cry as he leaned back against the wall, his hips moving slightly in counterpoint to Brett's mouth. One hand threaded into Brett's hair, massaging gently despite how aroused he was.

Brett sucked harder, needing the flavor of Gerald's come on his tongue. One hand slid between his lover's legs to massage his tight balls while the other opened his own pants so he could get at his aching cock, jacking himself off in time to the suction of his mouth.

The first touch of Brett's fingers between his legs made Gerald jerk as a jolt struck through him, and as the attention dragged out a few minutes his breaths turned to gasps. "Oh fuck, that mouth," Gerald hissed as his hand moved to Brett's shoulder and curled tightly. "Fuck, lover, gonna… gonna…."

The smart comment Brett wanted to make about his ass being what turned Gerald on died in his throat as hot come splattered in his mouth. Gerald threw his head back on a silent, painful cry, and his body curled down over Brett, unable to stand the brain-melting sensation as he shook all over, barely able to hold himself up as Brett kept up the suction. After only a handful of seconds, Gerald mewled and tried to pull back as the stimulation threatened to turn him inside out while Brett swallowed over and over, sucking Gerald dry.

Jerking hard on his cock, Brett followed Gerald, keeping his mouth on his lover despite the whined protest. It only took a couple of pulls before he spilled over his hand and onto the floor, his moan muffled by Gerald's cock as he came.

Finally squirming free with a tortured gasp, Gerald collapsed onto the toilet and sprawled backward, legs spread, as he tried to get an even breath. His dazed eyes wouldn't focus on his lover, but it was all he could do to keep them open at this point. Sex with Brett of any kind had the side effect of tapping all his energy. Brett always seemed to take particular pleasure in exploiting that.

Gerald managed to crack an eye open and see Brett still on his knees, wet cock in hand, streams of come trailing from his fingers and puddling on the floor. Gerald twitched, hard. What a sight.

"I think we made a mess," Brett gasped, following Gerald's line of sight to the sticky mess he'd made.

Gerald laughed breathlessly. "At least we're in the bathroom. Makes it easier to clean up."

Brett chuckled. "Yeah. Hand me some paper towels since I'm already down here."

Gerald pulled some towels off the roll and handed them down before wetting another few and using them to clean himself up a little. Once he zipped up and tucked his shirt in, he wet another; Brett surely needed it more than he did. He looked down at Brett wiping up the floor and had to snicker. "We're terrible."

Brett shrugged. "We're at the wedding of two old queens. I think we fit right in."

Eyes bulging, Gerald slapped his hand over his hand, trying not to laugh. "Oh God" was muffled behind his palm as he half bent over.

Brett chuckled along with him. "Come on," he said, straightening up. "Let's get back to the reception."

Gerald sighed and tried to stop laughing as he walked to the door and opened it while looking back at Brett. "You know, only you would do something like—" As he turned around Gerald stopped dead in place and blushed furiously.

Outside the door, Bruce and Jeff stood, arms interlaced, huge grins on their faces. "If you're done, maybe you'd like to let the newlyweds inside?" Jeff teased.

Gerald's mouth opened, then snapped shut, and he bit his bottom lip. "Um…."

"Of course," Brett replied with a satisfied grin, pushing Gerald out the door ahead of him. "It's all yours."

As soon as Jeff and Bruce shut the door, Gerald turned around and looked at Brett with wide, wide eyes. He was so surprised; he had no idea what to do. "I hope I didn't get you in trouble."

Brett laughed. "With those two? Given that they're probably going to do exactly what we just did? We aren't in trouble."

Gerald relaxed, but then tensed again as his eyes flew to the door. He grabbed Brett's hand and started pulling him toward the stairs. "Time to go. Give them some privacy," he said as he hurried.

Brett laughed at the look on Gerald's face from hearing the sounds of pleasure in the bathroom all the way down the stairs.

Eight

GERALD moved easily with Misfit's walking gait, following Brett as the horses picked their way to the unknown destination. He contented himself with watching Brett sway in his saddle and anticipating the promised reward. Gerald wondered idly if Brett's plan would work—if he'd be able to ride home tomorrow or not. The idea of it just made him smile.

They cleared the forest line, coming out into a large, wide meadow. Brett looked back at Gerald. "Ready to pick up the pace a little?" he asked.

"I'm sure Misfit won't mind," Gerald answered, patting his mount's neck. "She's ready to run."

"Keep a tighter rein on her than usual," Brett warned. "She knows she's not in the ring, and she can just keep going if she can get away from you." Trusting Gerald to keep Misfit under control, Brett gave Shah his head, letting the stallion race across the field, tail high in his enthusiasm.

It didn't take any spurring for Misfit to go. She took off after Shah, drawing a laugh from Gerald at her exuberance. While they couldn't catch Shah, they certainly kept up at a short distance. Gerald was careful to follow Brett's directions, though. He didn't fancy falling on his ass when Brett had plans for it later.

Gerald pulled on the reins to slow Misfit down so he could ride safely without having to focus on it so much. His eyes followed Brett around the meadow, and he smiled when he heard Brett laugh. He shook his head, wondering how he had gotten so lucky.

Turning as they reached the other end, Brett guided Shah back across the meadow, letting him run himself out, soaring over a log in the middle of the field. He laughed aloud for the sheer joy of riding.

Feeling Shah slow finally of his own accord, Brett reined him back to a trot and rode to Gerald's side. "Ready to go on to our destination?"

"You haven't told me what that is yet, but I trust you not to leave me in a ravine somewhere," Gerald joked.

"I thought I'd surprise you," Brett said. "And I promise not to leave you in a ditch. Come on. It was my favorite place to go in the summers when I was a kid." He paused and considered. "Come to think of it, it still is."

Gerald urged Misfit to walk alongside Shah. "I'd love to see it," he said.

"It's just through the trees on the other side of the meadow. Come on; we can be there in ten minutes."

When Brett later pulled Shah to a halt, Misfit walked a little farther so Gerald could peer through the trees to see an old farmhouse sitting right on the water. "Is this the actual cove?" he asked.

Brett nodded. "And the original house. Added on to and improved, of course, but the original rooms are still there. My grandparents lived it in, but when my dad decided to add the stables and use lessons as a source of income instead of just breeding, they built the newer house by the arena. My grandparents lived here until they died."

"I think it's great that you've kept it up," Gerald said. "So many people would have just let it go altogether or bulldozed it." He kicked back slightly so Misfit would start walking toward the house. "And you stay out here sometimes? I guess that was before me, huh?" For the past four weeks Gerald had been at the farm exclusively. It felt like home now. It *was* home now.

"When I was a kid, I'd move out here for the summer," Brett explained. "My grandparents made sure I could swim and then they just let me run loose in the woods with the dogs and the horses for company. When they died, they left the farm to my dad, of course, but they left the house to me. It was home until my parents moved to Florida. All through college, that's where I had my stuff. I actually still have a lot of it there just because I haven't bothered to move it up to the big house. There's a shed in the back where we can leave our tack and a big field for the horses. Misfit isn't in heat, so we don't have to worry about leaving them together."

"So you're finally showing me *your* house," Gerald said.

"Yeah, I guess I am," Brett said, "although I wouldn't want to live there in the winter anymore. It's an old drafty farmhouse. The heating bill's astronomical. In the summer, though, it catches every breeze, and when that isn't enough, the porches are the perfect size for a mattress."

Gerald chuckled. "As long as there's no line of sight from the farm," he said.

"No, not at all," Brett promised. "The trees block it really well, and the lake's in the center of our property with no public access. There's no one around to see us for miles. You're all mine."

"Yeah," Gerald said in agreement. "So. Going to show me around before you jump me?"

"Nope, wasn't planning on it."

Gerald threw back his head and laughed, and Misfit pranced to the side and bobbed her head in an echo of her rider. "Well then," Gerald said. He dismounted, pulled the small bag he'd brought off the saddle, and laid Misfit's reins over the saddle.

"We should put the horses out at least," Brett said, trying as much to convince himself as to convince Gerald.

"We should," Gerald said agreeably, but he was fighting a grin. "Where? You said the field in the back?"

"Yes," Brett said, dismounting and leading Shah toward the back of the cabin. "We can stick the saddles in the shed there and put the horses out to graze."

They got things put away and turned the horses out in the back field, and soon they were walking along the edge of the water. "It's really gorgeous here," Gerald said as he skipped a rock out into the pond.

"I love it here," Brett said with a soft smile. "It's my retreat." He reached for Gerald's hand, squeezing tightly. "I've dreamed of having someone to share it with. Now I can't imagine sharing it with anyone but you."

Gerald returned the smile to his lover as they walked along. "I'm glad," he said truthfully. He couldn't imagine being anywhere else but with Brett anymore.

"Do you think you might… stay?" Brett asked softly.

Gerald stopped in place and frowned a little. "Stay? Why do you ask? I wasn't planning on going anywhere."

"Not just tonight," Brett pressed, "but always, like Bruce and Jeff."

Gerald's confusion deepened and was clear on his face. "Well, of course I'm staying, Brett. Where do you think I'm going to go?"

Brett sighed in frustration, pulling his hand away to run it through his short hair, sweaty from the riding helmet. "Back to your house? Off with someone else who catches your interest? I don't know. I just know I want you to stay, to marry me."

Equal parts thrilled happiness and soft affection echoed through Gerald. His face gentled, and he grabbed Brett's other hand, trying to calm his lover's agitation. "I'm not going anywhere," Gerald said reassuringly. "There's no one else that I would even consider marrying."

"Would you consider marrying me, Gerry?" The words were soft, pained almost. Brett looked up, met Gerald's eyes, his emotions painted vividly on his face. "Will you marry me?"

Gerald's eyes brightened, and he leaned to brush his lips across Brett's. "Yes," he said simply.

The sigh of relief that rushed passed Brett's lips was audible. "Why do you always make everything so difficult?" he murmured, pulling Gerald against him and kissing him until they both had to pull away to breathe.

The kiss consumed him, and Gerald couldn't even think for a long moment after their mouths separated. "Difficult?" he managed.

"You always answer my questions, but you answer only the exact question I ask. Everything is literal, in the moment," Brett explained. "It's a little hard when you're trying to put your heart on the line."

Gerald blinked at him, bemused. "I don't know. I just answer the question," he offered, shrugging slightly. "Why don't you ask the question you want the answer to?"

"I did."

Gerald chuckled. "Well then. I'm glad you asked. You don't need to worry about your heart. I'll take good care of it."

"I love you, Gerald Saunders," Brett declared slowly. "I just wanted to say that."

"I'm really happy to hear that," Gerald said, grinning before he leaned in to kiss Brett warmly. When he pulled back he frowned slightly. "You know I love you, right?" Gerald asked, eyes narrowed.

"Not until you just told me," Brett retorted, though after Gerald's agreement to his proposal, the words bore no heat. "I'd hoped, but you never said, never seemed to make plans beyond today or the next day. I wasn't sure you wanted anything more than that."

"Brett, I will *tell* you if there's something I don't want," Gerald said firmly. "Otherwise I'm more than happy to just be with you." He shrugged. "I guess it didn't occur to me to tell you I was here to stay once you let me start spending the night here."

Which was Brett's point exactly, but it didn't matter anymore. "Come on; let's go inside. I want to show you my real house, and then I want to make love with you. Really make love with nothing held back."

"I wish…." Gerald looked a little regretful. "I wish I'd understood to tell you more. I've never held anything back."

"I believe you," Brett said. "You just never seemed to volunteer anything either." He pulled Gerald toward the house, willing to put it all behind him now that he'd secured Gerald's heart and his agreement to wed.

Gerald followed along. "Um. I like the farm better than my house?" he tried.

"You're welcome here any time you want to be. You're *wanted* here *all* the time," Brett assured him. "You know that, right?"

"Yes," Gerald said confidently. A pause. "I like it when you suggest going places. It's thoughtful."

"You don't have to give me compliments just because you think I want to hear them," Brett said with a laugh. "Just tell me things as they come up instead of assuming I can read your mind."

"Oh. Okay," Gerald said, back in his amiable tone. Then he chuckled. "I just did it again."

Brett laughed. "Do we need to outlaw the word 'okay'? I had friends in college who promised each other not to say 'I don't care' because they were so bad at making up their minds about what to do. If they said it, they had to drink this awful raw-egg muck. It didn't take many times to break them of it."

Gerald stopped on the stairs, his face screwed up. "I'll try," he said. "Not sure how well I'll do, though. Honestly, I'm really happy to do what you like pretty much all the time."

"In that case," Brett drawled, "you won't mind going upstairs and getting naked with me, will you?"

"Oh no, not one single bit," Gerald said fervently. "I want to make love to my future husband."

Brett grinned and started pulling Gerald toward the house. "I love the sound of that!"

Gerald laughed and followed him through the front door. "I don't ever have to wonder if you like what I suggest, huh." It wasn't really a question.

"If you ever do wonder, just ask," Brett assured him, leading him down the hall to the stairs that led to the second and third floors. "My bedroom was always the one in the attic, although there's still a bed in the master suite if you'd be more comfortable there."

Gerald opened his mouth to say, "Oh-k… um. I'd rather be in your room." Then he grinned.

"There, see?" Brett teased, starting up the stairs. "That wasn't so hard, was it?"

"No," Gerald answered. "Just a different way of thinking, is all."

They bypassed the first landing and kept climbing up to the converted attic with its big bed and low ceiling. "Watch your head," Brett warned. "I wouldn't want to spoil the mood."

"It would have to be a hell of a bump, but yeah, I see your point," Gerald said, moving his free hand to rub Brett's ass.

Brett shimmied out of his jeans and briefs, looking over his shoulder provocatively. "Want to try that again?"

Gerald licked his bottom lip as he repeated his grope, this time with both hands. He hummed in approval as he wrapped one arm around Brett's waist and pulled him back against him so he could grind against him slowly.

Brett pressed back so the denim of Gerald's jeans rubbed against his bare skin. He reached back and cupped Gerald's ass. "Gonna take me to bed and show me a good time?"

"I'm going to spend some quality time with this ass," Gerald purred as he nipped at Brett's ear and groped.

"You won't hear me complaining," Brett groaned, leaning into Gerald's touch.

"Good," Gerald pushed him toward the bed. "Hands and knees, please," he drew out as he unbuttoned his shirt.

Brett pulled his shirt over his head without bothering with the buttons, moving swiftly into the indicated position, head turned back so he could watch Gerald undress.

It didn't take long, Gerald wasn't going to waste time on it when he wanted to touch Brett, and as soon as his clothes were on the floor he walked forward to rub his groin against Brett's ass. "Crawl forward a little," he requested as he slid a teasing finger through the cleft.

Brett moved as directed, scooting to the top of the bed and grasping the headboard. "Is that far enough?"

Gerald grinned and crawled up behind him. "That's just lovely." He draped himself over Brett to kiss his neck and shoulders, touching and caressing as he worked his way slowly down Brett's back with his lips, over his front with shifting fingertips.

Brett groaned with pleasure, beginning to move beneath Gerald's hands. His lover knew all his sensitive spots by now and had absolutely no qualms about exploiting them, leaving Brett gasping and desperate for more.

Knowing what he wanted to do, Gerald smoothed his palms over Brett's ass, kneading gently as he kissed the very base of Brett's spine and then each cheek as his fingers slid to spread them apart. Heart pounding—he hoped they both would enjoy this—he lightly lapped along the damp crack.

Brett's hoarse shout conveyed his shocked pleasure as he felt Gerald's tongue for the first time. "Oh God," he groaned in delight. "Feels… too good."

Taking that as approval, Gerald continued his careful licks along the cleft, getting himself used to the idea as he listened to Brett's moans. Listening helped. Then his tongue dragged across the twisting flesh that guarded Brett's dark hole.

"Oh fuck! Gerry!" Brett couldn't get anything more coherent out at that point. Gerald was rimming him. Gerald, who'd never rimmed anybody before in his life, was rimming him. The thought was nearly enough to make Brett come on the spot.

Since Brett didn't pull away, Gerald figured he must be doing something right. And it wasn't bad. Kind of hot, really, having Brett squirm because of his tongue. He continued to work his way down until he couldn't crane his neck further, so he returned to pulse his tongue against sensitive flesh.

"Please!" Brett begged, the teasing flicks of Gerald's tongue over his hole enough to have him trembling. "In me. God, need to feel you in me!"

"In you?" Gerald teased, lifting his mouth to gently bite the curve of Brett's ass. "In here?" he asked, sliding a finger across the clenching muscle.

"Gerry!" Brett wailed, pushing his ass back against the teasing finger.

With a smirk, Gerald leaned over and licked him sloppily before poking his tongue inside, startled and quickly pulling back after Brett's body tightened around him.

"No, please, more!" Brett flailed when Gerald pulled away suddenly.

Gerald laughed, taken aback, and he gently rubbed Brett's side before sliding his tongue back to work, hoping to draw more of those cries from him. Every noise got Gerald's body's attention.

Brett obliged, words failing him, but grunts and gasps and moans falling liberally from him as Gerald continued to tongue fuck him. His eyes closed beneath the storm of sensation, his body clamoring to come… but he wasn't ready yet! If he did, Gerald might stop!

Carefully pushing into Brett, Gerald wiggled his tongue slightly, hoping it didn't taste too awful. But he also knew how careful they both were when it came to cleaning up and cleaning up well. Yeah, it tasted dark and wet and smoky, sort of. Nothing he couldn't handle so far. And Brett's panting made him want to try more, so he thrust his tongue deeper.

Brett's head dropped between his shoulders, chest heaving as he panted in time with the tentative thrusts of Gerald's tongue into his ass. It felt so fucking good! "More," he begged breathlessly, his voice barely a whisper as he rocked back against his lover's mouth. Gerald pushed closer until his cheeks lay against Brett's spread-open ass, and he kept working his tongue in and out faster as Brett's breathing sped up.

Feeling his balls start to tingle, Brett grabbed his cock, squeezing the base hard to stave off his climax. "No," he begged, pulling away. "I want to feel you inside me when I come."

Gerald leaned back and wiped the saliva from his lips and cheeks. "I won't argue," he said roughly. He ached after listening to Brett gasp and beg. "Is there a bottle of stuff here?"

"In my jeans," Brett grunted. "I've never brought anyone here before you so I don't have any in the drawer, but I figured we'd end up in bed."

Snorting, Gerald shuffled off the bed and found the bottle. "Well, I can't say I would have bet against you," he admitted, climbing back up behind Brett and popping the top on the bottle. "I have a really hard time not paying attention to this," he said, groping Brett's ass.

"Have you heard me complaining?" Brett asked, pushing back against Gerald's strong hand. "I'm already loose and open from your tongue. Just slick up good and give me a long, hard ride."

Gerald groaned and slid two fingers slick with lube into him. Brett was right. He was ready. Another coating on his cock just to be sure, and Gerald rocked right in and moaned aloud as he was totally enveloped in one move.

Brett gasped and groaned as he was filled from behind. He reared back onto his knees, hands reaching behind him to find Gerald and hold him tight, his head turning as he searched blindly for a kiss.

Grunting as he slid his arms around Brett's waist, Gerald kept pumping his hips back and forth as he craned his neck to meet his lover's lips. The kiss was hot and wet and sloppy as they sought a way to be even closer together.

Frustrated, Brett pulled away and flopped onto his back, reaching out for Gerald and pulling his lover down on top of him. "This way," he grunted, legs spreading.

Gerald landed on his elbows so they were sealed together from chest to groin as he made love to Brett. It was easier to lick Brett's lips now, to kiss the corners of his eyes and nip at the side of his neck.

Brett's arms encircled Gerald's shoulders, holding him close, as if he feared this dream would suddenly fade as it had all the nights he'd lain awake trying to work up the nerve to say something to Gerald. The hard cock moving inside him was no dream, though, except maybe a dream come true.

Finally raising his eyes to his lover's face, Gerald watched Brett as he moved, their lips barely brushing, until a thought popped into his head. "Brett, I love you."

They were the words Brett had fantasized about hearing from the moment he'd realized how deeply he cared about Gerald. They were also all it took to send him over the edge, coming untouched like a green kid.

Watching Brett's face as he came made the moment all the more beautiful, and Gerald kept pushing toward his orgasm faster and harder until Brett shuddered under him and he couldn't deny it anymore. With a gasp, Gerald came slowly, shivering.

The power of the moment left Brett trembling. He nuzzled Gerald's neck, searching for a kiss. "Love you," he whispered against the Gerald's lips.

Gerald smiled as he kissed him. "Good," he murmured.

SOMETIME later, Brett stirred against Gerald, his stomach rumbling demandingly. "I think dinner might be in order," he murmured, nuzzling Gerald's neck. Truth be told, he didn't want to move any farther from his lover than they were at that very moment, but his body wanted food.

Gerald's arms tightened slightly around him. "I suppose," he murmured without opening his eyes. "But it's awfully comfortable here."

Brett chuckled. "Surely I can come up with something to tempt you." He paused and pretended to consider. "How about me in an apron?"

"And nothing else?" Gerald's mouth turned up at one corner.

"If it'll get you out of bed and into the kitchen."

Gerald chuckled and opened his eyes. "I'm hungry too," he admitted.

"Let's go then. We'll eat, and then we need to feed the horses. And then maybe you'd like to go swimming," Brett suggested.

Gerald opened his mouth to speak, but paused and then smiled. "I'd like that," he said, eyes sparkling.

"What?" Brett asked, catching the hesitation. "What are you thinking?"

"I almost said okay," Gerald said as he chuckled.

Brett laughed. "See, I told you we'd break you of that habit." He sat up, looking around for something to put on. Finding a pair of old shorts, he pulled them on and got up.

Gerald sat up with a sigh and grabbed his jeans to pull on. They'd be fine for around the house. "I think we left the bags on the porch."

Brett nodded and headed back downstairs. "If you'll bring them in, I'll get the stove started." Without waiting for Gerald's reply, he knelt down in front of the old stove, making sure the gas was on before trying to light it.

Pausing for a moment to watch and smile, Gerald slid his hands into his pockets before walking slowly to the porch. There he grabbed the bags and carried them in, setting them on the heavy wooden table scarred with age. "What did you pack to eat?" Everything was ready to go when he'd gotten home from work.

"Canned stew," Brett replied. "It's easy to transport and to cook. I don't get out here often enough to keep the fridge stocked anymore, so I just bring canned stuff."

"Stew is good," Gerald said as he unzipped a duffel and started digging in it.

After getting the temperamental stove started, Brett turned back to Gerald. "Did you find the cans? The can opener's in the top drawer by the fridge."

Gerald plunked a couple of cans on the table and went digging for the can opener. "Are there bowls? Or are we eating out of the cans?"

"I'm pretty sure there are bowls above the sink. You'll probably want to wash them out, though. I'd bet they're dusty," Brett said.

Whistling slightly off key, Gerald found the bowls, got them cleaned up, and had it all on the table. He turned around and watched Brett, smiling slightly as he realized how natural it all seemed. "Need a pot," he mentioned.

"Here," Brett said. He opened another cabinet, pulled out a heavy cast-iron pot, and handed it to Gerald. "Rinse it out too, but don't use soap on it. Otherwise, we'll have to oil it all over again before we can use it."

"Cast iron?" Gerald asked as he took the heavy pan to the sink. "I've not seen this in awhile. Mom got rid of hers when she discovered the wonders of nonstick T-Fal."

"Yeah," Brett said. "These were my grandmother's. I have newer ones at the other house, but I haven't bought new ones to bring out here. Like I said, I'm not here very often because of the distance to the stables. It's a twenty-minute ride I'd rather spend sleeping in the morning and evening."

Gerald chuckled. "Maybe someday you can hire more help to do the early morning chores, and then you can sleep in with me occasionally. Or stay out here sometimes."

Brett smiled. "I'd like that, although I have other things to spend money on first, like refitting the indoor arena."

Humming in agreement, Gerald started opening the cans and pouring the stew into the pan. "You mentioned that when we talked about the bank loan. Any other big dreams for the future?" He set the pot over the burner as Brett stood back.

"Oh, lots, but they all require money, which means dealing with them one at a time," Brett said. "I'd like to set up a permanent cross-country jump course, and I'd really like to find a physical therapist who'd be willing to work here a couple evenings a week with disabled kids. I worked for awhile at a farm in Houston that was doing amazing things with kids who suffered from MS and other neurological diseases. But that means paying someone or finding someone who'll volunteer their time."

Gerald sat down at the table, running his fingers over his lips. "Volunteering and donating to charitable programs is a big tax write-off," he mused.

"You're going to be so good for my business." Brett laughed. "I'll have my sales pitch down pat by the time you're done with me."

"Well, I want to help, you know," Gerald said. "Might as well use the skills I've got."

"Absolutely," Brett agreed, pulling Gerald into an embrace and kissing him lightly. "All of them," he added, rubbing against his lover lasciviously.

Gerald slid his arms around Brett's waist as he chased his lips to steal a deeper kiss. "Now feed me before you fuck me," Gerald instructed. "I need sustenance."

"Oh, fine, have it your way." Brett laughed, turning away to check on the stew. "It needs to simmer for fifteen minutes. I bet I can fuck you in less than that."

"Yeah, right," Gerald said, putting his hands on his hips. "I'm not a teenager who can shoot off three times a day!"

"That sounds like a challenge to me," Brett said, pushing Gerald back toward the sturdy table.

Gerald raised both brows and laughed self-consciously. "Ah… no, not really, not when you start touching me."

"So," Brett purred, pinning Gerald against the table, "shall we see if I can make you come before the stew's ready?"

Chuckling, Gerald pulled Brett close. "How about some kisses now and action later, maybe at the lake?" he proposed. "Then I'll have plenty of time to really drive you wild."

Brett pouted, his dancing eyes belying the expression. "Oh fine. Make me wait. You've already agreed to marry me, you know. You can put out now."

Gerald's laugh rang out, and he stole a hard kiss. "I'll make it worth your while." He pinched Brett's ass. "Now stir the stew before it boils over."

Brett yelped at the playful pinch, but he obediently went and stirred the stew. "It's hot," he said after a few minutes. "I must have set the stove higher than I realized."

"Maybe that means you should listen to me more often," Gerald said saucily.

Brett huffed as he spooned up the stew and offered a bowl to Gerald. Gerald chuckled and sat at the table after snagging a couple bottles of water out of the duffel. It was no time at all and they were done, with Gerald cleaning up the dishes.

"So you said something about the lake," Brett said when they were done. "I don't suppose you brought swim trunks."

"Uh, actually, no, I didn't," Gerald said with a soft laugh. "I didn't know where we were going, did I?"

"Good," Brett replied, grinning widely. "I'll be able to fulfill all those fantasies I've been having since we went swimming after the bonfire."

"Fantasies?" Gerald asked, one brow raised.

"Yeah, you in my lake, naked," Brett said succinctly.

Gerald's lips pulled into a smirk. "Oh, I think I can handle that one."

"Good." Brett started moving, dropping his shorts as he reached the door. "Last one to the lake has to top."

Gerald sighed, knowing without trying that he wasn't getting his jeans off quick enough to win. He was already too turned on to think about yanking the denim off. So he took off in pursuit, his long practice in running catching him up quickly.

Reaching the water, Brett splashed in, turning back to grin at Gerald. "I win."

"I think we both won," Gerald said as he stood at the edge of the water watching his lover.

Expression softening, Brett returned the smile. "I think you're right."

Gerald unfastened his jeans and eased down the zipper, having to slide a hand into the fabric to shield his half-hard cock and hair from the metal teeth. He pushed the jeans down and then stepped out of them and into the water, wading toward Brett.

A grin splitting his face, Brett relaxed in the water, anticipation lighting his eyes as Gerald walked toward him. As soon as the other man was within reach, he pulled him close, letting their skin brush, cocks bobbing in the water as their bodies met.

Curling his arms around his lover, Gerald smiled and tipped his head back to look up at the stars. "Looks a lot like that night," he murmured.

Brett smiled, hands running over water-slick skin. "I only see one difference," he said as he fondled Gerald's cock beneath the surface. "Tonight you're naked, and I have the right to touch."

Gerald chuckled and shifted his hips to press into Brett's hand. "Yes, you do," he confirmed before dipping his chin to slide his lips wetly against Brett's.

Brett slid into the kiss, letting the water buoy them as their bodies rubbed intimately. The contrast of hot skin, cool water, and cooler air swamped his senses, leaving him glutted with pleasure. He wrapped his arms around Gerald's waist, pulling him into a tighter embrace, reveling in the knowledge that this man was his.

"Will it always be like this?" Gerald murmured when their mouths finally parted.

"Will what always be like this?" Brett asked just as softly.

Gerald shook his head, unable to put the tight sensation in his chest into words. Instead his hands gripped Brett and held him closer as their cheeks touched gently.

"Gerry?" Brett asked, concerned by his lover's silence. "Are you all right?"

Gerald's breath caught, and he nodded immediately and firmly. "Yeah. More all right than ever." He pulled back to smile for Brett.

"Glad to hear it," Brett replied, returning the smile. "You had me worried there for a minute."

Gerald moved one hand to flatten it over Brett's heart. "Don't you feel it?" he whispered.

"I do," Brett said with a nod. "Like we were meant to be here, like everything in my life has led right up to this moment. Like the rest of my life—our lives—is waiting for us to take the first step down that road."

Gerald nodded slowly. "Yes," he murmured. "Yes, that's it." He kissed Brett longingly before walking backward. "Come on," he coaxed. "Any more of that, and we won't get any swim at all."

"Did you really think we were coming out here to swim?" Brett teased, but he followed Gerald into the deeper water, stretching out on his back and relaxing into long, easy strokes.

"Like you said," Gerald answered, cutting through the bath-water-warm cove, "We have the rest of our lives, right?"

"I suppose we do at that," Brett agreed, swimming after Gerald. Catching up with his lover, he snagged a foot, pulling hard and dunking him. "Tag, you're it."

Flailing about, Gerald surfaced with a gasp. "Hey!" He swiped at Brett and started chasing him.

Laughing, Brett flipped onto his stomach and swam off as quickly as he could. His mirth hampered his usually fluid strokes, though, and slowed him down.

Gerald caught him, gave him a moment to catch his breath, and then dunked him in return as he laughed. Once Brett bobbed back above the water, he kissed him firmly.

"Love you," Brett murmured through the kiss. "Love you, love you, love you!"

Gerald sighed happily and held him closer for a long moment before he lifted his head and looked around. "What's that sound?"

Brett paused to listen. "Cicadas," he said after a moment. "They're really loud this year. They say it goes in seventeen-year cycles, but I hear them every summer. Although they aren't always this loud."

Gerald shook his head. "No, it sounds like a shower running."

"Oh, that's the spring that feeds the lake. It's down beyond the house. We can swim that way if you want, or we can hike out to it tomorrow if you want to see it."

"Another time," Gerald murmured. "I've changed my mind. I want to make love to you under the moon." He slid his lips along the line of Brett's neck.

"We can go back to the house and make love on the porch," Brett replied huskily, head tipping back, "or we can swim down to the spring and make love in the pool there. Whichever you prefer."

"Mmm. The porch will be easier another time when I don't want to wait. Let's go see the spring," Gerald said as he nipped at Brett's throat.

"You gonna let go of me so we can swim?" Brett teased, his arms still firmly in place around Gerald's waist as he kicked in the general direction of the spring.

Gerald sighed aloud, exaggerating it. "I suppose." He huffed, but it was offset by his smile as he started swimming alongside Brett.

A five-minute swim later, Brett led Gerald out of the lake to the warm spring that bubbled in the darkness. The pool was only about waist-deep, the rocks lining it worn smooth by the water running over them. "Now, you said something about making love," he said, opening his arms in welcome.

Gerald slid against him as his hands moved along warm, wet skin. "Yes," he breathed. "Over and over and over." He kissed Brett's shoulder, neck, and cheek between each repetition.

Brett shivered despite the warm water. "Yes," he husked, head tipping back as he offered his body to his lover. His hands guided the dark head lower, to his peaked nipples.

His tongue slithering over taut skin, Gerald hummed as he gripped Brett's hip and curled one arm around Brett's back so he could tip his lover back against the rocks, leaving his body spread out in front of him.

Brett reclined back on his elbows, legs spread, body on display for Gerald to enjoy. He gasped as his lover licked and kissed his way down his torso and then back up again, random wanderings that stopped just short of tickling that left him floating on a sea of anticipation and arousal.

"Even this water can't cut the taste of your skin," Gerald said between suckling his nipples and biting at his hip bone. "And I want to taste more." He dragged his tongue along the hot, hard cock between Brett's thighs.

Brett's hips bucked up into the inflammatory touch. He pushed farther out of the water so only his calves were still submerged. "All you want," he husked. "Just tell me."

"You," Gerald growled. "You and only you." He covered Brett with his own body to make a ravenous attack on his mouth.

Brett returned the hungry kiss, their teeth clashing in their urgency. Gerald's skin was hot against the cool night air, sending shivers down Brett's spine as he pushed up against his lover. Hoping he could hold their combined weight with one hand, he wrapped the other arm around Gerald's shoulders, fingers digging into hard muscle.

Gerald ground himself against Brett's thigh, his thick cock slipping against damp skin. "Need you around me," he muttered as he licked and sucked at his lover's swollen lips.

Brett's legs parted wider as he gasped, his hips tilting up to give Gerald access to his body. "Want that," Brett agreed, lying flat so he could reach behind himself in search of his entrance. He was still loose from their earlier lovemaking, so he was sure it wouldn't be too difficult to take Gerald even without lube to ease the way.

Eyes intent on Brett's, Gerald slowly slid down his body until he was between his knees. First he teased Brett's erection with lips and tongue; then without warning he pulled his mouth away from the needy flesh and sank to drag his tongue under Brett's balls.

Brett cried out in delight when he realized where Gerald's tongue was heading. "Oh fuck," he groaned, spreading his ass cheeks wide and pulling his knees up to his chest so he was completely open to his lover's mouth. "Gerry," he groaned.

Gerald wasted no time, wanting to prepare Brett well. The desire cramped his gut, he wanted Brett so badly. He thrust his tongue deep without preamble, thrilled by Brett's unfettered reaction.

Trembling, Brett rocked against the questing tongue, crying out with each inward thrust, moaning in protest each time it withdrew. "Fuck me, fuck me, fuck me," he chanted, an impatient, desperate litany as Gerald ratcheted his passion higher and higher until Brett thought he would go out of his mind.

Reaching to encircle and pump Brett's cock, Gerald kept sucking and invading, his tongue spearing through the ring of spasming muscle, giving Brett no break to breathe.

Brett thrashed around as he tried to stave off his climax a little longer, but Gerald was too good at pushing all his buttons. "Gonna… come!"

Gerald's hand moved faster on Brett's cock, his fingers tightening in rhythm that matched his tongue, and unable to hold back anymore, Brett's balls pulled up. His entire body contracted as he spewed his release across Gerald's fingers and his own belly. He collapsed back against the rocks, panting harshly as the stimulation continued, extending the aftershocks of his orgasm until he was completely limp.

Moving above him, Gerald slid his fingers through the slick come and slicked his cock before nudging between Brett's legs and beginning to push inside. The stretching and licking he'd done had opened Brett even more, and he was able to push into the grasping heat without much resistance. He moaned and palmed Brett's thighs, spreading them farther as he started to move in and out.

Brett writhed on the smooth rock, body overstimulated by Gerald's loving. Between their earlier interlude at the house and his recent climax, he didn't expect to come again, but he wanted to make Gerald feel as good as he did, so he roused himself enough to consciously clench and release his muscles in time with Gerald's thrusts, sucking him in with his ass the way he would have with his mouth.

"Oh fuck," Gerald choked out, arching his back as he thrust hard into Brett again and again. "You...." He gasped and his eyes screwed shut as he tried as hard as he could not to come so quickly.

"I what?" Brett rasped, bucking up to meet each thrust, every movement they made creating splashes that splattered against their skin.

"You... feel incredible," Gerald said as he panted, opening his eyes with one last sharp snap against Brett's body and crying out, almost mournfully, as he climaxed. He shivered while his hips moved slightly, extending the feeling by moving his cock through the hot come inside Brett until he convulsed.

Brett thought Gerald was the one who felt pretty incredible, hot and hard inside him and flooding him with warmth as he climaxed. Then Gerald collapsed atop Brett, pinning him to the rocks. He stroked Gerald's dark hair gently, letting them both come down from the powerful high.

When Gerald dragged himself up, his hand gripping a rock and causing little splashes that sprinkled Brett's chest, he stared down at him, and his tongue darted out to wet his lips. "I love you."

"I love you too," Brett said with a soft smile.

Nine

"I'VE got a meeting with a realtor next Tuesday, so I'll be late getting home," Gerald said out of the blue as he drove them across town.

"A realtor?" Brett repeated. "What are you thinking about buying?"

"Not buying. Selling. Selling my house in town, I mean," Gerald said.

"Why are you selling your house?" Brett's face showed his confusion clearly.

Gerald got those furrows between his brows as he stopped the car at a red light and looked at Brett. "Why do I need the house?"

Brett shrugged. "I don't know. It just seems like a big decision, and you hadn't mentioned it, and well, I'm just a little surprised, I guess."

"But we did talk. I mean…." Gerald felt an odd apprehension fill him. "You… you don't want me to move in?" he asked, bordering on upset.

"Of course I want us to live together!" Brett exclaimed. "God, don't even think I don't want you with me, but it's your house, and I know how much time and money you've put into it. It's in town, so much more convenient for you than driving in from the farm every day. We could split our time between the two places, maybe at your house during the week and at the farm on the weekends, or rent it out, or—"

Relieved, Gerald listened to Brett ramble for a moment before just leaning over, touching his cheek, and kissing him gently. Brett returned the kiss eagerly, wanting to erase all thoughts of not being wanted from Gerald's mind. Gerald smiled and slowly eased out of the kiss. "Sorry," he murmured. "It was the 'not answering the question' thing again, I guess."

Brett shrugged. "We're getting better about that. Like I said, I was just surprised because we hadn't talked about it. I don't want you to feel like you have to give up your house just because I'm tied to the farm. We can look at other options besides selling it."

"I've thought about it quite a bit lately," Gerald said as he cleared his throat and started driving down the street again.

"You're the accountant," Brett pointed out. "I trust you to make the right financial decision. I just don't want you to feel pressured into it."

"I want to do this, because we're going to be together from now on. And I can help, so I will."

"Help?" Brett asked, perplexed. "Help with what?"

Gerald looked confused. "With everything. The house, the farm, the bills, vacations, anything like that."

"But you're already doing that. Well, not vacations yet, since we haven't planned one, but all the rest. What does selling your house have to do with any of that?"

Gerald chuckled. "I figure I'll get close to a half a million dollars out of that house, Brett. That's a lot of vacations and planning for the farm's future, don't you think? Not to mention retirement."

Brett blinked a couple of times as Gerald's words sank in. "Oh, you mean…." He paused. "But that's not why…." He took a deep breath and reminded himself that they weren't just occasional lovers, that this was a relationship like his parents had—or like Bruce and Jeff did—two people working together toward the same goal. "I think that's a hell of a lot of money," he agreed. "And I think you should invest it any way you see fit. If that's in the farm, I certainly won't say no. You know how much I've been agonizing over the best way to finance improvements."

Gerald turned into a driveway in front of a large sprawling ranch-style house with red shutters and lots of greenery and flowers. "Yes, and that's what gave me the idea. You've got plenty of money in the farm, Brett, if you really wanted to mortgage it to make those improvements. But there's no need to when we can use part of this and then invest some in the farm's name for future improvements," Gerald said. He turned off the car and pulled the keys from the ignition. "Besides." He glanced over at his lover. "It's my home too, now."

Brett gulped down the emotion that closed his throat, leaning over to kiss Gerald quickly. He wanted to linger, turn the car on, drive right back to the farm, and make love to Gerald all night long, but they'd accepted Gerald's parents' invitation for dinner. Standing them up was hardly the right way to make a good impression on his future in-laws. "You really shouldn't say things like that when I have to be around other people," he said hoarsely. "It's hell on my libido."

Gerald smiled innocently. "I like that effect," he murmured. "But come on. Food and family first. Then you can take me home and do all sorts of lovely, dirty things to me."

"I'm going to hold you to that," Brett threatened, climbing out of the car, keeping his back to the house as he adjusted himself discreetly. He couldn't very well meet Gerald's parents for the first time with his cock tenting his pants. He was just glad he'd worn relatively snug briefs. Hopefully they'd keep his body in line for the next few hours. Following Gerald up the sidewalk, he studiously kept his eyes on his lover's shoulders, tempted though he was to ogle his ass.

Gerald led the way up the walk, opened the screen door, and stepped inside. "Hello!" he called out, gesturing for Brett to follow.

"In the kitchen!"

An older woman came around the corner, drying her hands on a dish towel. "Hi, honey," she said to Gerald as he kissed her cheek.

"Hi, Mom. This is Brett," Gerald said.

"Please, Brett, come in," Mrs. Saunders invited.

"Thank you for having me," Brett replied politely, handing Gerald's mother a mixed bouquet of flowers he'd picked up at the local florist. "I'm glad to finally meet you."

"Oh, how nice," Mrs. Saunders said. "Please call me Edna."

"I'm glad you like them, ma'am," Brett said, not quite able to call Gerald's mother by her first name.

Gerald sniffed the air. "Lasagna?" he asked hopefully.

"Of course," Edna said. "It's your favorite, isn't it? Your father's in the kitchen. He's fixing the garlic bread." She turned to Brett. "Come in to the kitchen. We're not formal here."

Brett followed them back into the kitchen, seeing immediately where his lover got his warm, welcoming nature. "Can I do anything to help?" he offered.

"You can take this pan," the older man on the other side of the bar said, holding out a cookie sheet holding rows of golden-brown garlic toast.

Brett looked around for a hot pad to protect his hand. Finding one hanging near the stove, he took the pan from Mr. Saunders. "Do you have a bread basket for these?" he asked.

"In the drawer there, by the fridge," Edna said.

"Dad, you put him right to work?" Gerald asked as he walked in with his mom. "Brett's a guest!"

"He was here!" Mr. Saunders said with a shrug. "Now watch out, Gerald. Second tray going in."

"Brett, this is my dad, Frank Saunders," Gerald said.

"Nice to meet you, sir," Brett said.

"You came the right day, Brett," Frank said as he shut the oven. "Good food today. Not that it isn't good every day."

Edna bustled past with a harrumph, and Gerald spoke up. "Guess you're getting good use out of the double oven, Mom."

"Yes, Gerald. A very good choice of Christmas present," Edna said.

Gerald peeked in the other oven. "Two pans? Are Marjorie and Bill coming?"

Then a door smacked open, and two kids ran into the kitchen. "Gramma!"

"I'll take that as a yes," Brett murmured with a grin, watching the kids jump on their grandparents before running over to hug Uncle Gerald as well.

"Who's that?" the younger one asked after a moment, pointing to Brett.

"That's Brett, Emily," Gerald answered.

"Why is he in Gramma's kitchen?" Emily asked.

"It's dinnertime, isn't it?" Gerald said.

The little girl shrugged and took off, hollering after her big sister, who was carrying plates into the next room with Edna. Before Gerald could say anything, a man entered carrying a baby seat, followed by a woman who looked remarkably like Gerald.

"Hey, Gerald," the man greeted before looking at the man standing next to him.

"Hey, Bill. This is Brett," Gerald introduced.

"Hi, Bill," Brett said, setting down the bread basket to offer his hand. "Nice to meet you."

"And I'm Marjorie," the woman interjected, "Gerald's sister, since he forgets such relevant pieces of information sometimes. It's about time we finally met you. We've heard nothing but stories about you for months now."

"Only good ones, I hope," Brett joked to hide his discomfiture. Gerald had been talking about him for months?

"There are only good ones to tell," Gerald said mildly as Emily ran back in, ran around his legs and then Brett's before running right back out again.

"Flatterer," Brett retorted.

"Well, if there aren't any good ones, he's certainly keeping them secret," Bill said. "He can't sing your praises highly enough."

"Enough," Marjorie scolded, seeing the sudden flush of color on Brett's cheeks. "You're embarrassing our guest. Besides, it's dinnertime."

"Here, Gerald, take Abby into the living room and set her next to the couch," Bill said, holding out the baby seat.

Gerald amiably hefted the seat and moved to touch Brett lightly on the back so that he'd walk in front of him. "That way," Gerald nudged.

"Actually, no, I need his help since he's good with a cookie sheet," Frank said from where he was pulling a big, deep tray of bubbling lasagna out of the bottom oven.

Brett grabbed the second cookie sheet, dumped the bread into the bread basket, and followed Gerald and Frank into the dining room.

The girls were running circles around the large table as Edna and Marjorie gabbed over them; Bill was setting out silverware, easily dodging the kids. Gerald veered off to the right through to the living room beyond the dining room and set the baby seat in the floor out of the way before returning to the dining room.

"All right, girls. Time to eat," Marjorie said, and the two little ones took one more lap before climbing into what were obviously their chairs, both with strapped-on booster seats. Marjorie sat next to one of them. There were three seats to each side of the huge, groaning table, Bill at the foot on the other side of the kids, and Frank stood at the head.

"Sit, sit, Brett," he urged as Edna sat next to him, leaving two side seats between her and Bill.

"So nice to have a full table," Edna said with a smile.

"You think you made enough food, Mom?" Marjorie asked, surveying the feast.

"Well, the whole family visiting, you know," Gerald's mother said blithely.

Gerald chuckled and sat down next to his mom, pushing the seat back for Brett and looking up at him, eyes warm and affectionate.

Brett smiled and took the empty seat, a flush of warmth filling him at the thought that he might be one of the family too. He missed having his parents close enough to see regularly. From the looks of it, though, he'd gained a second set of parents, something he hadn't been sure he'd ever find. Until Gerald. Beneath the cover of the table, he found Gerald's knee and squeezed gently.

His lover's hand almost immediately covered his and squeezed in return.

"Hannah, not until we say grace," Marjorie scolded as the older of the two girls leaned to snitch a piece of garlic bread.

"All right then," Frank said, holding his hands out to each side, and the family began clasping hands.

Lifting Gerald's hand in his and joining hands with Bill, Brett bowed his head as the family blessed the food in unison. He committed the words to memory, hoping he'd have plenty of other occasions to say them along with Gerald's relatives.

"Now eat up!" Edna declared, and they started passing empty plates to her to get large, sauce-dripping slabs of meaty lasagna with plenty of cheese.

Gerald picked up the salad bowl in front of him and got some on his plate before passing it to Brett. Then he leaned to look around the table, and he snagged two bottles of salad dressing, setting them within easy reach. Brett looked at them and chose the vinaigrette.

"Hey, don't use all the vinaigrette," Bill warned. "Gerald will arm-wrestle you for it."

There was some laughing around the table as Gerald made a funny face at him and opened the bottle of ranch.

"You don't like vinaigrette?" Brett asked Gerald curiously as he poured a little on his salad.

"Uncle Gerald hates it," Hannah interrupted before Gerald could reply. "He teases Mom and Dad and Grandpa all the time because they eat so much of it."

Gerald's face screwed up. "I don't like anything vinegary."

"He won't even eat my homemade slaw," Edna said knowingly.

"I'll eat his share too," Brett offered, holding his plate out for a serving of the lasagna Frank was dishing up. "I love slaw."

"Wonderful, because I don't like slaw either," Bill murmured.

Gerald chuckled. "Mom loves her slaw. Not many other people do, but Mom does."

Edna bapped Gerald in the arm, only drawing a snicker from her son.

"Well, I'm looking forward to trying it," Brett insisted. "It's been a long time since I've had fresh slaw. Probably not since I moved away from home."

"I thought the farm was your home?" Marjorie asked.

"Farm! Horses!" Emily said, bouncing in her chair until Bill got her calmed down by handing her a carrot from the raw veggie tray.

"It is," Brett replied with a grin for Emily, "but I only moved back about a year ago. My parents ran the stable until they were ready to retire, and that's when I came home."

"Can we see the horses?" Hannah asked eagerly. Marjorie shrugged apologetically to Brett.

"Of course," Brett said with a smile. "You're welcome to come out anytime. I've even got a pony the perfect size for you and Emily if you'd like to ride sometime."

Gerald snorted. Brett was talking about Tiny, probably.

"That would be a lovely weekend trip. Maybe we'll all come along," Edna said.

"Haven't seen a horse up close before, I don't think," Frank said as he spooned up some green beans.

"Sure you did, when we went to the rodeo last year," Bill said.

"I don't have any broncs." Brett laughed. "But you're more than welcome to come out for the weekend. I've got plenty of space at the farmhouse for you to all stay."

"Speaking of space, Dad, can I borrow your truck?" Gerald asked. "I want to move some things out of the house before the realtor starts showing it."

"Realtor?" Frank asked.

Gerald just nodded since his mouth was full of lasagna.

"But you love your house!" Marjorie exclaimed. "Why are you putting it on the market?"

Gerald's brow furrowed as he chewed and looked at his sister.

"Yes, Gerald, it's a beautiful house," Edna added. "You spent so long looking for just the right one."

"Where are you taking the furniture?" Bill asked.

"To Brett's," Gerald said matter-of-factly after swallowing.

"But why?" Marjorie asked.

"We're getting married," Gerald said before taking another bite of lasagna and beginning to poke at his salad.

It wasn't exactly the way Brett would have chosen to tell Gerald's family, but then, this was Gerald's family, so he figured his lover knew best how to handle things.

"Oh, well then," Edna said with a bright smile and a shrug. "That makes sense."

"Married?" Marjorie repeated, staring at her brother.

Gerald raised an eyebrow at her. "Yes, married."

"But that's wonderful! You're getting married! Finally!" Marjorie exclaimed, practically bouncing in her chair.

"Great news, Gerald," Bill said.

"Well, Brett," Frank said. "You must be a special guy. We didn't think we'd ever find someone to put up with Gerald."

"He *is* special," Gerald defended.

"Oh, that's just so sweet," Marjorie said with a happy sigh.

"I'm thrilled Gerry will have me," Brett finally managed to get out. It was really difficult to hold back a laugh over the different responses.

And now he could see where Gerald got his easygoing nature; he was just like Edna.

"Gerry?" Marjorie echoed.

"You call him Gerry?" Edna asked, and then she laughed.

"You know he would never answer to that growing up?" Frank said as he leaned forward toward Brett, waving his fork.

"No, I didn't know that," Brett said, brow furrowing as he glanced to Gerald.

"Because *somebody*," Gerald said with a significant glare in his sister's direction, "always called me a pipsqueak mouse."

Brett grinned as Marjorie defended herself and the two siblings began squabbling.

"Now, kids, stop arguing and start eating," Frank scolded.

Gerald sighed and looked toward Brett, a smile hovering on his lips.

"I can't believe you just announce you're getting married over lasagna," Marjorie pouted.

"When else would he announce it?" Edna asked. "When he's walking out the door?"

And just like that, the conversation moved on, marriage announcement accepted, and Emily started talking about her new puppy while Marjorie bemoaned cleaning the carpets all the time.

"Why sell the house, Gerald?" Bill asked. "You could spend time there when you want a break from the farm."

"It's got a lot of equity in it," Gerald explained. "With the markets, it would be better spent in investments right now." He picked up the basket of bread. "Garlic bread?"

"Investments are good in auto stocks right now," Bill said knowledgeably, taking a piece without breaking the conversation. "The stock is so damn cheap, and you know it'll have to go up at least some."

"Bill works at Merrill Lynch," Marjorie explained as she added green beans to a protesting Hannah's plate.

"I'm going to diversify," Gerald assured him. "Brett has some great plans for the farm, so we'll invest some funds there too."

"Business investments, good plan," Bill said, nodding to Brett.

Brett just chuckled. Didn't seem like much fazed this family. He liked it. When Bill asked more about the business, Brett was happy to chat about it.

The friendly dinner went on through dessert until Gerald begged for mercy and led Brett into the living room where the baby was miraculously still sleeping. "I think I'm going to explode. I've not lived in this house for twenty years, and Mom still treats me like I never take care of myself."

Brett chuckled. "I think it's part of being a mother. My mom's the same way."

"Where are your parents now?" Edna asked, joining them in the living room. "You mentioned they'd retired from the farm, but not what they're doing now."

"They've moved to Florida," Brett replied. "Dad said he'd had enough of Connecticut winters to last a lifetime. And Mom says his arthritis is much better now that they're down there. The sun bakes it out of him."

"Now there's an idea, Edna," Frank said.

"We're not moving to Florida," Edna said forbiddingly. "Not as long as I have grandchildren around to spoil. And now I have a chance at more!"

Brett's brow flew up as Frank rolled his eyes and settled in the recliner, leaning back in it comfortably.

"Get comfy, Dad," Gerald joked, meaning both the chair and Connecticut.

Edna wrinkled her nose. "We've lived here more than fifty years. Another twenty, give or take, won't hurt those bones."

"Maybe you can vacation in Florida," Gerald suggested.

"I'm sure my parents can tell you all the good places to stay," Brett offered. "My mother's a bargain shopper extraordinaire."

"There you go, Edna," Frank said dryly. "Another bargain shopper."

"That sounds lovely, Brett. Thank you," Edna said.

Then the baby started crying.

"Wow, Mom, we've got to go. Horses to take care of, you know?" Gerald said swiftly. Edna actually snickered and stood up to walk them out.

Brett followed Gerald to the door, pausing to shake hands again with his lover's parents. "Thanks for having me, and let us know when you want to come out to the farm. You're welcome anytime."

Frank nodded. "And you're welcome here anytime, Brett. Gerald, you just call when you're ready for that truck, and Bill and I will come over to help."

"Thanks, Dad. Great food, Mom," Gerald said.

"Wait!" Marjorie called, hurrying in from the kitchen with two paper bags. "Food for the road!"

Gerald glanced at Brett and rolled his eyes. "Thanks, Marjorie," he said as he accepted the bags and a kiss.

"And I don't suppose I'll hear the end of the horses until we bring the girls out, so I'll call. Is that okay?" Marjorie asked Brett.

"It's fine," Brett assured her with a smile. "You really are welcome anytime."

"Great to meet you," Marjorie assured him. "We'll talk about the wedding soon! Lots of plans to make." And she bustled off in Abby's direction.

"C'mon, Brett," Gerald murmured, edging out the door.

"You two come back Sunday for lunch, all right?" Edna called after them.

Gerald waved at her awkwardly and continued to the car. "No way am I taking diaper duty," he murmured.

Brett laughed as he followed his lover out to the car. "Ah, the joys of having siblings. Makes me glad my sister isn't local anymore. I see her a couple of times a year, just long enough to get my fill. And then she's back to Virginia."

"Oh, I love Marjorie and Bill and the girls. It's just I don't love diapers, and apparently Uncle Gerald needs to have those *skills,* you know?" He carefully put a bag each in the back floorboards.

Brett laughed again. "Not really, but I can imagine," he sympathized. "I like your family. Your mom's great."

"A lot of people say I take after her," Gerald said as he started the car.

Brett chuckled. "I can think of worse people for you to take after."

"Yeah, I guess so," Gerald agreed. "We've always gotten along really well. Most all my family does."

Somehow, Brett was not surprised. "Take us home, baby."

SETTING down his toothbrush, Brett headed back into the bedroom, grinning when he saw Gerald curled up on the bed, reading a magazine. "You're just asking for it, aren't you?"

Gerald glanced up through his glasses with a glint in his eyes. "Who? Me?" he said.

"Don't give me that innocent look. You know exactly what your glasses do to me," Brett said, crossing the room to the bed.

Gerald smiled and let the magazine drop to the covers. "Oh yes, I most certainly do," he drawled.

Brett crawled up the bed over Gerald's reclining form until he could kiss the smile off his lover's lips. "Just make sure you keep on doing it."

"I plan to."

ARIEL TACHNA lives in southwestern Ohio with her husband, her daughter and son, and their cat. A native of the region, she has nonetheless lived all over the world, having fallen in love with both France, where she found her career and her husband, and India, where she dreams of retiring some day. She started writing when she was twelve and hasn't looked back since. A connoisseur of wine and horses, she's as comfortable on a farm as she is in the big cities of the world.

Visit Ariel's website at http://www.arieltachna.com/

MADELEINE URBAN is a down-home Kentucky girl who's been writing since she could hold a crayon. Although she has written and published on her own, she truly excels when writing with co-authors. She lives with her husband, who is very supportive of her work, and two canine kids who only allow her to hug them when she has food. She wants to live at Disney World, the home of fairy dust, because she believes that with hard work, a little luck, and beloved family and friends, dreams really can come true.

Visit Madeleine's website at http://www.madeleineurban.com/

Dreamspinner Press
For more of the best M/M romance, visit
Dreamspinner Press
www.dreamspinnerpress.com

Printed in the United States
142797LV00004B/20/P